## PRAISE FOR SARAH LEIPCIGER'S
# THE MOUNTAIN CAN WAIT

"*The Mountain Can Wait* is a taut, psychologically gripping novel populated by original characters constantly at battle with nature, family, society, and themselves. This is a book that kept me up at night. Leipciger has Margaret Atwood's rare flair for crafting an intelligent and suspenseful novel."

—Nickolas Butler, bestselling author of *Shotgun Lovesongs*

"In this assured debut novel Leipciger beautifully captures the tender and mercurial relationship between father and son, Tom and Curtis Berry. These are characters you care about, flawed and haunted by regret, existing in the harsh yet undeniably radiant world of the Canadian Rocky Mountains. Leipciger writes with great compassion and precision; her language is an exquisite mix of muscle and grace. *The Mountain Can Wait* resonates with wonderful imagery that will stay with me for a very long time."

—Michèle Forbes, author of *Ghost Moth*

"*The Mountain Can Wait* is as haunting, wild, and compelling as the landscape it describes."

—Claire Cameron, author of *The Bear*

"Written with painfully nuanced care that displays affection for nature and the laconic, working-class characters, the result is...genuinely moving." —*Kirkus Reviews*

"Teeming with the abiding sense of seclusion found only in deep, enveloping forests and on inaccessible islands, and redolent with the independence and eccentricity it takes to live in such an environment, Leipciger's stellar debut novel delicately parses a shattered family's chaotic journey to peace and recovery."
—Carol Haggas, *Booklist*

"In language that highlights natural beauty and the challenges of living in the bush, Leipciger explores what a sense of responsibility really entails, the finer points of family dynamics, and the strong hold a place can have on a person, from Whistler to the tiny isles around Vancouver Island."
—Julia Jenkins, *Shelf Awareness*

"An entire moral universe is at stake here, rotating between duty and self-reliance. When Tom helps a trapped goshawk escape, he thinks, 'To be fully equipped for life in body alone, autonomous, to move through this world needing nothing—that was beautiful.' Leipciger questions, punctures, and then partially reconstructs this ethic, one that's matched by the rigorous beauty of her own writing."
—Britt Peterson, *New York Times Book Review*

"The heart of this story is the love between father and son, and the backdrop is spectacular; Leipciger's descriptions of the scenery are splendid and intensely evocative."
—*The Times* (UK)

"A deft and beautiful novel about all that is untamable and wild, in both the landscape and in ourselves."
—Maggie O'Farrell, author of *Instructions for a Heatwave*

# THE MOUNTAIN CAN WAIT

### A Novel

## SARAH LEIPCIGER

BACK BAY BOOKS
Little, Brown and Company
*New York  Boston  London*

Copyright © 2015 by Sarah Leipciger
Questions and topics for discussion copyright © 2016 by Sarah Leipciger and Little, Brown and Company

Back Bay Books / Little, Brown and Company
Hachette Book Group
1290 Avenue of the Americas, New York, NY 10104
littlebrown.com

Originally published in hardcover by Little, Brown and Company, May 2015
First Back Bay trade paperback edition, April 2016

Back Bay Books is an imprint of Little, Brown and Company, a division of Hachette Book Group, Inc. The Back Bay Books name and logo are trademarks of Hachette Book Group, Inc.

The publisher is not responsible for websites (or their content) that are not owned by the publisher.

The Hachette Speakers Bureau provides a wide range of authors for speaking events. To find out more, go to hachettespeakersbureau.com or call (866) 376-6591.

ISBN 978-0-316-38067-6 (hc) / 978-0-316-38069-0 (pb)

*For James*

# THE MOUNTAIN CAN WAIT

# 1

**The night** was still black when Curtis pulled his Suburban away from the curb and turned toward the mountain highway, leaving his apartment, his sleeping street behind him. He would have preferred to ride his bike but the tire was flat and anyway it was too cold, and rain was coming. He would find some side road up the mountain where he could park and stay warm until the sun rose, and then he'd hike for as long as his legs could carry him. Ascend to a place where the view was different and things that towered and loomed down here would narrow to pin shadows and then to nothing.

With his windows rolled down, he tickled the curves slowly, and the high that had been fading in him came back up. Calm poured through his body and the wind was music. The cold, dewy air tasted like spring moss, like pine. The needle on the speedometer slipped across seventy kilometers and he slowed down to forty. But minutes later, when he glanced at the needle again, it was back up at seventy. The road began a long-curved descent and he pulsed the brakes.

He engaged the dashboard lighter and lifted his right thigh, and wedged his fingers into his back pocket, feeling for his small tin box. It wasn't there. He reached farther and excavated the gap in the back of the seat. The road was a tunnel. He glanced at the passenger-side footwell but saw only a badly folded road map and a refillable plastic coffee mug that he had stopped using because he'd lost the lid.

Her face in the headlights flashed like a coin, the features etched in silver blue. She was an instant, the sulfuric flare of a match, and though he had time to hit the brakes his foot found the accelerator instead. And there was a dull slap. Something white seemed to pause in the air. The sound of a broad, square nose of metal pummeling muscle and bone was flat and without ring. He stopped the truck with its nose pointing into the middle of the road and, confused, felt for his tin in the other pocket, as this somehow still seemed important. Looked for it in the footwell. In his bag. In his lap. The dashboard lighter sprang. He turned off his headlights and the ignition and listened to his own breathing and the ticking of the engine, and then peered out his window for many minutes into the dark. There was nobody there. He got out of the truck and walked slowly up the road; no one in the ditch, no one on the pavement. He looked back at the truck, askew in the road, the door hanging open like a crooked tooth. He continued along the opposite shoulder, low mist in the trees, the crunch of gravel. Up ahead in the ditch, two white, high-top sneakers, one pointing up, the other toward him. A pair of bare legs. He thought: It's too cold out here for that. The rest of her was hidden by the mountain pines.

Curtis stood very still in the road, shivering, then bent at the waist with his hands on his knees and tried to spit. He stood back up and turned around and pressed his feet deeply into each step so that the world might not hear his retreat. When he pulled the door shut on his truck, the hinge bit loudly into the night. The clunk of the cold metal latch. He drove home at a crawl, passing no one, the engine rattling his teeth in their sockets.

**2**

The dog had been sick for three months when Tom decided to end its life. It was January when they noticed something was wrong—the first time in fourteen years that Rocky rejected meat from the table. His portion of roast beef went untouched for twenty-four hours in his steel bowl before Tom gave up and scraped the woody slab of dry meat and coagulated gravy into the garbage.

The dog didn't eat for another three days, so Tom took him to the vet and the vet had a look at his teeth, smelled his breath, palpated his abdomen. He suspected it was kidney failure and took a sample of Rocky's blood and urine to be sure. He phoned Tom at home later that day with the results, something about the proteins in Rocky's blood being ten times what you would expect in a dog. Given Rocky's age and the advancement of the disease, the vet recommended against treatment and predicted that the end would come in weeks. It was clear that Rocky knew what was happening. Tom took the dog's soft, dry muzzle in his palm and looked deeply into his eyes and said, "What we'll do, dog, is we'll just wait this one out, eh? We'll just let you do this your way." Tom could wait.

But by April, Rocky was still alive. In the mornings when Tom went downstairs, he expected Rocky to be gone, through his flap in the back door, gone to die alone the way a dog should. But every morning he was there, crumpled like an old coat under the kitchen table. Erin wouldn't touch him anymore, said she could feel all his bones rolling under his skin. Tom heard her complaining to Curtis over the phone, saying that Dad was barbaric, and asking how she could convince him to take Rocky to the vet and put him out of his misery. But Tom wasn't going to do that. Rocky was a bush dog, a mountain dog. Wouldn't be right for him to end his days in some clean and clinical place.

But the dog wouldn't die. His loyalty got the better of him, Tom was sure, and the poor bastard couldn't leave. It was in the dog's eyes, his plea to be let go. Tom tried to move him along. He'd say things like "Go on, dog, take yourself off now. We'll get on without you" or "It's your time, old buddy. Go on an' git!" But Rocky left the dying too long, and in the end was too weak to muster up the energy for it.

So on a Wednesday morning, after Erin left for school, Tom went down into the basement with the key to the gun cupboard in his fist. He unlocked the metal door and stared hard at the big-game Remington and at the long rifle that he used for rabbits and raccoons and any other varmint that looked fat enough to eat. And though it was a little on the heavy side, he chose the Remington because it would have been a hell of a thing to have to shoot twice. From a trunk under the stairs he pulled out a box of soft points and slipped two rounds into his coat pocket.

Upstairs, Rocky lay curled up on top of the heating vent in the living room. Unable to look at him, Tom held the rifle close to his body, away from the dog's gaze, and took it out to his Ford, stopping in the kitchen to retrieve a half-empty mickey of Jack Daniel's. He came back in and wrapped up Rocky in a knitted blanket and carried the limp, forty-pound bundle out to his truck and laid him gently in the passenger seat. The hardest part, harder even than what was coming, was Rocky's total lack of interest in what was happening to him. The dog curled himself deeper into the blanket and his eyes closed slowly, but not completely, as if he didn't have the muscle power to keep them shut.

Tom drove to the north end of town, over the Nechako and past the hulking pulp and paper mill. It was a sunny morning and the last surviving islets of gritty snow shone hard and wet on the grassy roadside banks. He soon reached the Forest Road, a potholed dirt track that wound half a dozen kilometers northeast into the bush before ending in a teardrop-shaped lot. He rolled down his window a few inches and navigated the truck gently over bumps and ditches while Rocky dozed silently next to him. Tom made up a tune in his head and hummed it.

This was Tom's country, Rocky's country, and he could drive the Forest Road with his eyes closed. For years he came up here alone with his mountain bike, and later, when Curtis and Erin were small, after Elka left, he brought the dog with him on his rides. Rocky was almost fully grown when he was a year old, and by the time he was two, his black coat flowed over his hard muscles like oil and he weighed sixty pounds. When they went riding together, Rocky carried the water and repair kit in a pack tied to his back. He never tired. If he smelled big game up the trail, elk or bear or moose, he ran ahead, and by the time Tom caught up to him, the bush would be cracking and vibrating with the animal's retreat.

Once Rocky's antics with a bear nearly got them killed. Curtis, eleven by then, was riding with them. They were pedaling slowly, asses off their saddles and in granny gear, ascending a steep slope, when Rocky ran ahead. He crested the hill, and by the time they got close, they could hear him growling. Something big was huffing back at the dog. Tom told Curtis to wait while he rode on. He had to dismount and lift his bike over a log and then push it around a tight bend in the narrow trail. A large black bear stood full height on her hind legs several meters ahead. Her cub, glinty-eyed, clung to swaying branches midway up a pine just to the left of where Tom stood. Rocky was in an attack position, halfway between Tom and the long-nosed bear.

"Come on, Rocky," he whispered, patting the dog's haunch. The bear went back down on all fours and took a step closer, sniffing the air and showing her spotted pink gums, her strong teeth. She swung her head and scratched the dirt with paws big enough to take a man's scalp, preparing to charge. She lifted her nose and rolled her top lip, hissed. Rocky's growl crawled to an even deeper, more ancient place. Again Tom commanded him to come, angrily, from the back of his throat. "Get over here, dog."

"Dad?" Curtis had come around the bend and was there on his bike, splatters of mud on the soft, rosy skin of his cheeks. His skinny shins, under a pair of bony, square knees, were streaked with dried blood from an earlier crash.

Rocky faked a lunge at the bear and then backed away again. Fucking idiot dog.

"Curtis, go," Tom said. His throat had gone dry. Curtis

got off his bike to turn it on the narrow trail and pushed it, moving away clumsily. The bear huffed and, with her massive head swinging low, galloped a few steps toward them. Tom squared his shoulders, tried to make a wall out of his body with his son on the other side, and coughed out a loud bark. The bear stopped in midstride, dug her claws into dirt and dry leaves, and rolled her head away from him, pacing.

She would bluff a charge once, maybe twice, but they had to get out of there. Tom pushed his bike backward. The agitated bear puffed and grunted. Lifting his bike back over the log, he misjudged the height and caught the chain, popping it off the sprocket. He leaned over the bike and pushed the derailleur forward, creating slack so the chain could be maneuvered back into place. A drop of sweat prickled his nose and dropped coldly onto his arm, and he was suddenly aware that everything had become brighter. The dog and the bear made guttural sounds at each other, sounds that were getting closer to him. The cub bleated desperately in the tree. Tom waited for the wet thunk of a claw in his exposed neck, the back of his head, for the grate of tooth on skull. The derailleur slipped from his sweaty fingers and the chain fell back between the cog and the frame. One of the links jammed and he yanked it, jamming it further. He stopped. Reminded himself that the link got stuck with little force, so it would take little force to release it. He hoped that Curtis was well away. With greasy fingers, he gently pulsed the chain back and forth until it slipped free and then pushed the derailleur forward again until there was enough slack to loop the chain back onto the cog. He caught a whiff of bear, the musk in its fur and gamy piss. When he stood back up, Curtis was still there, one foot on the ground. "Go," Tom whispered fiercely. "Don't wait for me." Curtis hesitated, then clicked into his pedals and disappeared over the lip of the incline. Rocky yelped and ran past him at full pelt, and disappeared over the lip as well. Tom had no control over what might happen next. The bear would decide how this was going to finish, and to the sound of cracking branches, Tom mounted his bike and followed his son and dog down the hill.

He'd heard of bears stalking people; he didn't think a sow with a cub would, especially not one so well fed, but they rode without stopping until they got back to the truck. Rocky was acting strangely, running too close to their tires, his tail between his legs. He would run ahead of them, then behind, then ahead again. Dog didn't seem himself for days after that.

Now, in these last minutes, Tom parked his truck at the top end of the teardrop lot and settled down into his seat. Rocky raised his head half an inch, opened his eyes partway, and then sank back into himself. Tom reached into the backseat for the bottle of Jack Daniel's and poured a hot gulp down his throat. He leaned over and massaged Rocky's ears, the back of his head, and then got out of the truck and retrieved the rifle from the backseat. He moved away so Rocky wouldn't hear the *schuck* of the bolt being pulled back, or the clink of the rounds being loaded into the magazine. Or the slide of the bolt pushing a round into the chamber.

Around him, the bush waited patiently, all stillness and quiet in the water-blue morning, while Tom prepared, not for the first time in his life, to do something he didn't want to do.

# 3

**A few** weeks after Tom buried Rocky, Curtis came home. Tom was at the barbecue in front of the garage when Curtis pulled into the driveway in his Suburban. When he cut the engine it sputtered and whined. Surprised to see his son, Tom squinted at him through the cooking smoke.

"Shouldn't you be at work?"

"I asked for a few days off." Curtis peered around the lid of the barbecue at the grill.

"Why'd you do that?"

"Wanted to see you before you took off to the bush, and you know, Rocky. Sorry I couldn't make it earlier." He stretched his arms up behind his head and twisted his body side to side. "My back fucken hurts, though. I drove straight through."

Tom eyed the vehicle. "You take the Duffey Lake Road in that thing? There any snow left?"

"A bit on the switchbacks. No hassle, though." Curtis's face turned soft and sympathetic. "But how are you, Dad? That must have been pretty bad, doing it yourself."

One of the pieces of meat was stuck to the grill and Tom worked at it with a pair of tongs. He shrugged. The shot had been clean. "Had to be done."

"You could have taken him to the vet."

Tom pointed toward the Suburban with his tongs. "How long has your truck been making that noise?"

The three of them—Tom, Curtis, and Erin (the girl out of her room for the first time that day)—sat elbow to knee at the kitchen table. To make the food go around, Tom rustled up a pasta and cucumber salad and shared the meat between them. They ate in silence until Erin reached across the table for the ketchup, revealing a blackened thumbnail.

"What'd you do to your thumb?" Curtis asked.

"Unlucky with the hammer. I was trying to put a shelf up in my room."

"You what?" said Tom.

"Why didn't you get Dad to do it?" asked Curtis.

Tom got up with his plate and scraped the bones into the garbage, hiding a smile that Erin would mistake for sarcasm, spurring her to bolt like a deer to her room. In spite of the injury, he was glad that she had identified something she needed and hadn't asked for help. And when he thought about it, she hadn't asked him to do anything for her in a very long time. Even if it was only because she didn't want him around, he welcomed this hardening, this growing of teeth and claws.

Tom appreciated having Curtis home; it had been a rare thing in the few years since he'd gone. But his bag in the hallway, the emotional hang of his face—it was too much. His turning up unexpectedly brought a strangeness to the house, the feeling of something being different. After dinner, in search of a job that he could do with precision, with an empty head, Tom went into the basement and got his long rifle out of the gun cupboard so he could clean it.

Mixed with the hollow hum of television chatter, the comfortable rhythm of Curtis and Erin's conversation floated down to Tom through the vent under the ceiling.

He removed the bolt and clip, then secured the rifle to the table by tightening the barrel in a vise and supporting the buttstock on a rubber block. From a cabinet under the stairs he took out a neatly packed tackle box that contained cleaning instruments and cans of Kroil oil. He laid an old towel on the table next to the rifle and placed the instruments on it, one by one.

Erin and Curtis were laughing up there, hard. Maybe even at Tom's expense. They were so easy together, could hurl mean jokes at each other and not get hurt. Curtis could behave with her in a way that Tom would never dare—could pull her up when she was doing something stupid and she wouldn't hate him for it.

He laced a small patch of white flannelette with cleaning solvent, folded it over the pointed tip of a jag rod, and pushed the rod through the barrel. Now a grayish blue, the flannelette popped out of the muzzle and fell off the end of the jag. He repeated this with squares of clean flannel until the cloth came out white, unsoiled by residue.

He taught both of his kids to shoot when they were young. Curtis didn't have the grit to kill an animal, but even when she was twelve Erin could pick a marmot out of a tree without a trace of sentimentality. She hadn't gone hunting with him in a few years, but maybe this fall, when he was home from the bush, he would try to get her out for a weekend. Take her up to the cabin he had his eye on in Smithers, see what she thought of it. Both his kids knew he'd been thinking about it, but he hadn't told them yet how close he was to buying the place, and maybe the news would go down better if they could actually see it. Walk the land with him, sit on the porch, eat the pheasant they would shoot themselves, the fish they would catch.

With a brass brush, he pushed more solvent through the barrel to retrieve the last specks of fouling and then dried the barrel carefully with a flannelette. He dried the muzzle and, using a flashlight, inspected the bore for any traces of metal fouling. He lubricated the inside of the barrel with oil and rubbed down the metal components—inside the chamber, in and around the trigger mechanism, the rear and front sight apertures—with a clean rag doused in oil. Clean as a whistle.

What the hell were they laughing about? He leaned on the table with both hands and listened hard with his head cocked toward the vent. If he went up there, right now, would they let him in on the joke? This was the way it was, every time those two got back together, like lifting a folded corner from a page in a book. A loud thump vibrated through the ceiling, as if one of them laughed themselves right off the couch. He shook his head and looked down, dismayed, at his towel and cleaning instruments, now shining with a slick of Kroil oil glugging from a can that had been knocked on its side. He mopped up the mess with a rag.

The following night, home alone with Curtis, Tom cooked a pot of chili. Erin was out babysitting twins who lived at the end of the road. She'd been doing more of that lately and saved her cash in a small wooden box of Tom's that had once contained nails.

After Tom and Curtis ate, they went out to the driveway and Curtis smoked a joint.

"So you think you'll ever get another dog?" Curtis asked. He crossed his arms over his chest, dug one hand deep into his armpit, and dangled the joint in curled fingers by his chin.

Tom shrugged. "Haven't thought about it."

"I was trying to remember when we first got him. Wasn't Mom threatening to give him away?" He took another long pull from the joint. As he exhaled, he said, his voice pinched, "He kept pissing in the house?"

"We got Rocky just after your mom left, when we were staying with Grandma. She was the one who wanted to get rid of him."

"You sure it wasn't my mom?"

"She was gone."

Curtis squatted down and picked up a handful of small stones, and skipped them one by one down the length of the driveway. He had become so broad across the back. A strong, perfectly curved spine, defined lateral muscles in a Y shape that rolled and flexed and shifted with every stone he tossed. A man's back that would one day begin to tire, would soften and sink like land without trees. And his neck, with fine, golden hairs, rolled with the strong ligaments underneath his skin.

"Did you fix that thing at work?" Tom asked. "Those shifts they didn't pay you for? No one's going to do that for you."

"Yeah, it's fine," Curtis said, and scooped another handful of stones. He stood up and sifted them through his fingers, letting them drop to the ground.

"Have you thought any more about that carpentry thing?"

"Can't afford it."

"Not washing dishes, no. Find some work on a site."

Curtis ground out the joint on the stoop and put it in his pocket, rubbed his bare arms. "It's fucken cold."

Back inside, Tom made a pot of strong coffee and settled into the couch next to Curtis, put two mugs on the table at their knees. He reached down to the floor for a wool blanket that lay at his feet and threw it over Curtis's legs.

"I could lend you the money for the apprenticeship," Tom said.

Curtis shook his head, his nostrils slightly flared. He pulled the blanket off his legs and reached for the remote control. They watched half an hour of news.

"So, hey," Curtis eventually said. On the television, the weatherman stood with his hands clasped behind his back.

"So, hey what?"

"I've been sort of hanging out with this girl for a bit. For a few months."

"Oh yeah? Only one girl?"

Curtis looked at him with a partial smile. "What do you mean by that, old man?"

"Usually there's more than one."

"Bullshit."

A commercial came on and Curtis turned down the volume.

"So what's her name, then?" Tom asked, because it seemed that Curtis was waiting to be asked.

"Tonya."

"She your girlfriend?"

Curtis shrugged. "She's why I didn't make it up here before."

Tom shook his head. "Be careful with that."

"You still haven't seen my place. I was going to ask you to come down, maybe meet her."

Tom sat back and stretched deeper into the couch. "I'd come down to see you, check out your place."

"And her?"

"If she's still around."

Curtis turned the volume back up on the TV, his face flat.

# 4

**May came** and with it the earthy smell of new growth after long months of cold, sun warm on exposed skin. Tom's foremen started calling with problems and requests. They would be leaving for the Takla Lake camp in two weeks, and he still had to make arrangements with the rental place for the shower and outhouse facilities; the generator needed to be serviced, the crew vans hauled over.

He was about to begin the second phase of a three-year contract for the spring and summer tree-planting season, and if he delivered again, the name of his outfit would be held in high regard. It would be worth enough that when he sold it at season's end, with one year's solid work remaining on the contract, he could buy the land in Smithers, and there'd still be enough left over for Erin to go to the university. And there'd be a good chunk for Curtis too, maybe for a down payment on a place of his own, or for the apprenticeship.

The day before he left for Takla Lake, a Sunday, Tom mulled over all this again while bent under the hood of his truck, gently wire-brushing the contact points inside the distributor cap. After every few strokes, he took care to blow the corrosion dust off the cap before it fell back into the distributor. The kitchen CD player was outside as far as the cord would stretch; punk music jumped thinly from the speakers. Erin sat on the cement stoop outside the kitchen door, a pair of old jeans lying across her knees. She pulled roughly at a needle and thread, sewing a patch onto the seat of the jeans. Every now and then she stopped to watch him work.

Her legs were even longer than they had been the last time he looked. She was taller than most of the boys her age, and skinny as a rod, as Elka had been. Even before she was twelve, her little-girl roundness had begun to morph into awkward angles. Her nose grew a fraction too big for her face; her shoulder blades popped out like wings. When she was thirteen, her forehead and chin shone with oil. She knew everything there was to know about zit cream. She spoke to her friends on the phone and sounded like the TV, using words like "astringent" and "blemish." The cupboard under the bathroom sink became off-limits to Tom, stacked neatly with Tampax, absorbent pads, bottles of clear liquid. Tweezers and clippers and files. This knowledge, this under-the-sink arsenal (as esoteric as anything he possessed having to do with silviculture or mechanics), was collected secretly. While he never found out how she'd learned all this, or who from, because it sure as hell wasn't him, it was a load off his back to know that she could take care of herself. He had watched her closely, most of her life, for any signs of the dark thing that had afflicted her mother. He kept his vigil from a distance, as if through binoculars, so as not to scare her away. Had been wary of how long she kept her bedroom door closed, of what she ate, of what she stored in her closet. And now, at seventeen, she was strong and sleek as a boat, ready to pull anchor.

He asked her if she wanted to help him replace the fan belt or, because she had a knack for it, get her hands into the wiring loom and try to fix his heater.

She gripped a fistful of hair in one hand and inspected the tips so closely that her eyes crossed over the length of her nose. When she found a split end, she bit it off and spit it out. Without looking away from the tips of her hair, she shook her head no.

The day Curtis and Erin's mother left for good was the hottest day of the summer. That morning, Tom found her note propped against the bathroom mirror. He read it, folded it neatly into quarters, and tucked it into the back pocket of his jeans. He drove Curtis and a three-month-old Erin to his mother's house.

When they arrived, Curtis, five, was upset about something, the wrong t-shirt, and refused to get out of the truck. Tom ignored him and lifted Erin out of her car seat. Holding her in the crook of his arm, he touched her cheek with the edge of his calloused thumb, his skin so thick he couldn't feel hers.

His mother was at the far end of the backyard, pushing a lawn mower twice her size with her wiry arms. She finished the last two rows of lawn before greeting Tom where he stood by the back door. Wiping her forehead with the back of her hand and walking up the grass toward him, she said, "You need me to have the boy today?" She looked over Tom's shoulder, squinted into the darkness of the house. Then, with a sigh, her tone flat: "Where's Elka?"

He moved the baby to his other arm and dug the note out of his pocket. She read it with a grim smile as if this were something expected.

They took the sleeping baby inside and laid her on a blanket on the floor. Tom took his usual place at the kitchen table, with legs outstretched into the middle of the floor. Fruit flies were settled into a bowl of peaches on the table. He waved his hand over the bowl and the flies rose, scattered, then settled again.

"Curtis eat anything yet this morning?" Samantha said.

"I told him we'd camp out in the backyard tonight. He's too excited to eat."

She cracked eggs into a glass bowl. "She always comes back," she said, whipping the eggs with a fork.

"Not this time. I don't think so."

Curtis came in then, his t-shirt off and his hair sweaty from the time he spent sitting in the truck. He stood by the kitchen door waiting to be noticed.

Erin woke up and, after rolling her head and stretching, started to bleat.

"Will she take a bottle?" Samantha asked, picking Erin up. The baby was calm for a moment, bouncing her face off Samantha's chest, nuzzling, her mouth puckered for Elka's breast. When she realized there was nothing, she started hollering again.

"Can we set up the tent now?" asked Curtis.

After two circuits of the drugstore, Tom located the section for baby feeding. Faced with a wall of powders, plastic bottles, and rubber teats, he randomly grabbed several types of each. Better to figure out the process himself than to ask the girl behind the till. He'd gone to high school with her, and she knew Elka. A long line of people stood at the counter. Each one of them, he figured, accounted for another few minutes his baby would have to wait.

"How's it going, Tom?" the girl behind the till asked when it was finally his turn.

He nodded, licked his lips. His cheeks felt hot.

"Kids okay? Elka?"

"All fine," he said, spilling cartons and packages from the crooks of both arms onto the counter.

She inspected each item as she rang it through and stopped when she got to one of the egg-shaped packages containing two rubber teats. She looked at him. "You sure you want these? They're for twelve months plus, see?" She pointed out the numbers on the packaging.

He shrugged and tried to laugh. "Elka didn't tell me what to get. What about these other ones?" He fished through the items for another, similar package with a different label.

"Well now hold on a sec," she said. "Wait here." She squeezed through the gap in the counter and went down the aisle. A man directly behind him in line shuffled his feet, cleared his throat.

"Them ones there don't go with the bottle you've got," she said, squeezing back through the gap. "These are the ones you want. Right age, right bottle."

He scratched the stubble on his chin. "I'm clueless with this stuff," he said.

"Aw, sweet." She scrunched her nose, made eye contact cautiously. "Now, you know you have to sterilize these first, eh?"

As he rushed out, catching his plastic bag on the door, she called after him to say hello to Elka.

Erin refused it. Turned her head away from the bottle as if the formula were laced with skunk piss. Samantha and Tom passed her back and forth, each suggesting that they might try something that the other hadn't thought of yet, like two people trying to coax a truck out of a muddy ditch. They even tried to spoon the formula into her mouth. By the middle of the day, Erin's throat was so hoarse that her crying was more like a wheeze; her thin hair was plastered to her head. At one point Tom took her out back to walk under the trees. In calmer times this was something she seemed to like, to watch the leaves fluttering, and the soothing sway of branches. But she was too angry to be distracted, so he bounced her off his forearm and watched Curtis run naked through the sprinkler.

Around midnight, she stopped crying and became difficult to rouse, so Tom took her to the hospital. The triage nurse asked him how long it had been since the baby had eaten, or taken any fluids at all. He wasn't exactly sure. Elka had woken up with her that morning, maybe seven o'clock? She fed her in bed, like she usually did, then got up to have a shower. Then she was gone.

"Let's have a look at her fontanel," the nurse said, pulling the blanket away from Erin's head. The soft, vulnerable patch at the top of her head, the place that had scared Tom when he first explored the anatomy of his babies, was sunken in, a rounded triangle. It pulsed deeply and rapidly. "Okay, then," the nurse said casually. "So, not surprisingly, what with this heat, she's a little dehydrated. Let's just take you through and get some fluids into her."

Erin was taken from him and he watched while a young, tired doctor worked slowly and calmly, inserting a drip into a blue, tributary-like vein in the back of her small hand, a vein so faint it almost wasn't there. Blood clouded back up the tube and the doctor secured it to Erin's hand with white tape and a splint. He then filled three small vials with blood from the crook of her arm, her protests weak from a dry, round mouth.

Later, formula disappeared into her nose through a feeding tube, stimulating her lips to make little kisses in her sleep, now peaceful. Once Erin had been given what she needed, Tom became aware of his surroundings. They were alone in a tightly spaced, curtained cubicle. Erin lay in a crib and somewhere close by a machine beeped. There were no chairs, so he stood.

At six in the morning, a square-shouldered nurse with a cigarette-lined face came in through the curtain. "Is this baby Erin?" she said. She brushed Erin's cheek with the backs of her fingers, leaned over the cot, and smoothed Erin's thin, moist hair to the side of her head. Continuing in a deep, soothing voice, she looked at Tom and said, "Where's her mother?"

At first he thought he should lie, cover for Elka, but his mind was all twisted and tired. I don't know, he thought, and may or may not have said the words aloud.

The nurse's eyebrows raised slightly and she jangled a bright toy just out of Erin's reach. "Okay, so we're going to move you guys to the ward. We want to keep her here for twenty-four hours, make sure she starts feeding properly. She looks fine, though, don't you, baby? Don't you? I'm going to take this nasty tube out, and we're going to give you a lovely warm bottle." She turned to Tom. "She was just too upset yesterday. She's calm now. She'll take it without too much hassle."

On the ward, the nurse came back and coaxed and coaxed

until eventually, with all the tumult and loss she seemed to sense was now ahead of her, Erin stubbornly, abjectly, drank from the bottle.

He reported Elka missing to the police and wrote to her mother, who still lived on Aguanish, the island where Elka grew up, and spent the next months searching. Motels and dark bars in places like Quesnel, Vanderhoof, Fort St. James, 100 Mile House. He never expected to find her, but because it was the right thing for his kids, and because he was bound to her whether by love or by obligation, he looked.

Eighteen months after she left, a guy Tom had known at the mill called him from Toronto saying that he was pretty sure he'd seen her in a pool hall. She'd cut her long hair to the neck and was a lot skinnier than he remembered, but either it was her or a cousin at least. She was acting pretty drunk, he said, but it seemed an awful lot as if she was pretending. When he asked her if she knew anyone in Prince George, she got up from the stool she was sitting on and walked out.

And even though it was a long shot, Tom got on a plane. Like turning over the last stone. It was the first time he'd been east of the Rockies, and on the drive from the airport into Toronto, what he noticed was the flatness. The landscape was bone gray and leafless and cold enough to hold on to the thin flurry of snow that blew darkly out of the iron sky.

He checked into a hotel just east of downtown and the next morning he found the pool hall. It was closed until later in the afternoon, so with Elka's worn-edged photograph in his palm, he started up the block. A doughnut shop, corner grocery and florist, a video rental place. The morning was sunny and cold, the previous day's snow a dry powder that puffed out from under each boot step, leaving a cloudy set of tracks on the sidewalk. A shoe repair and key cutter, pizza by the slice, a barber's, bank. For lunch he ate soup with dumplings in a Chinese restaurant and then continued systematically up and down each street, fanning away from the pool hall. He showed Elka's picture to street cleaners and shopkeepers and a couple of women pushing their kids on swings; they eyed him pitifully and he moved on. By three o'clock, he went back to the pool hall and showed her picture to a guy who was lifting upturned chairs off the tables. He had never seen Elka but said it was worth hanging around for other staff members to come on shift. Tom ordered a soft drink and sat at a round table in the corner. A man and a woman played at one of the half-dozen pool tables, and the music was low enough that he could hear the soft clacking of their game. They shared one cigarette between them, passing it back and forth between shots.

If he had found her, she would have gone back with him. She'd told him enough times that for her, he was like some kind of shelter. If it could have been that easy, if someone in that pool hall had looked at her picture and said, "Course I know her. I'll show you," he would have dug her out of whatever hole she'd crawled into, brought her home, and settled her back in. And maybe she would have even been able to love their kids for a while without turning to mulch, like tissue paper in water.

He waited around until late into the night, when the tables filled up and smoke colored the room blue. He showed her picture to everyone.

He fell asleep on the flight home the following morning, waking just as the snow-covered Rockies unfolded silently under the plane. From thousands of feet up he could see how the mountains had been formed, could imagine the thrust of the earth's crust as it rose into the sky, creating these tidy ridges repeating and interconnected like the veins in a leaf. In his life and the lives of his kids, and in the lives of their kids, the mountains would mark no time. They were unflappable, a quiet comfort. They would always be there.

Erin was six when she fell through the ice one afternoon during those weeks between winter and spring. When the wind blew a certain way and there was a turn to the air that suggested new growth in a world where the ground was still frozen and the tree branches black and without bud. Curtis had wanted to go snowshoeing but Erin complained that it was too cold, and snowshoeing too hard, so Tom dressed her up and covered her face with a scarf and pulled her behind him on the wooden toboggan. The sky had been clear for days and the going was easy, the old snow glazed over with an icy crust. He was sweating under his coat. Under the trees, the snow was pocked with drip holes. They moved slowly through the bush, making their way to Black Pond, where they'd skate and drink the hot chocolate he carried in a thermos. They left after lunch and got to the pond at three, the forest shadows long and well-defined across the ice. Tom let go of the toboggan and stretched his tired shoulders. Curtis was lacing up his skates and Tom was taking off his coat to remove a sweater when Erin jumped onto the ice, running and skidding in her boots. She disappeared around a corner where the bank curved and the heavy boughs of a tall fir reached out over the pond, and there was no sound for a moment, just Curtis pulling at his laces and complaining about cold fingers, the whump of a load of snow falling from a tree branch to the ground. Then came the sharp crack. Tom went out onto the ice calling Erin's name, and when he came around the fir tree, he saw her floundering in a jagged hole of the blackest water. Water so black that it swallowed the arm of sunlight that crossed it. With the force of her panic, her head dunked under, and when she came up she was choking from the cold water she'd taken into her throat. Tom dropped onto his stomach and inched toward the hole, the ice wheezing and clicking under his weight. She waved her arms above the water. Her eyes rolled like a trapped animal's and she was panting.

"You have to breathe, Erin," he said. "Slow down and breathe." He called for Curtis to bring the toboggan. "I'm going to get you, but you have to breathe."

Her eyes were on him, black as the water. Her small mouth stretched back in a grimace as she raked and gulped for air. He moved closer but could feel the surface of the pond bowing under his weight. Freezing water seeped onto his chest and he knew he wouldn't be able to get any closer.

"Breathe slowly, Erin, calm down. Good girl. Get yourself to the edge where you fell in. That ice held you before; it'll hold now. Get your arms up over the edge."

Curtis was behind him with the toboggan. "You'll be okay, Erin," he yelled, the words scared, tight.

She dog-paddled to the far edge of the hole and grabbed at it. Jags of ice fell away and bobbed and slushed in the water and the hole grew bigger. She screamed and coughed and cried.

"No, Erin. Turn around and come to this edge. The ice is stronger here, towards me. Hurry."

She turned and paddled and got her arms up over the edge of the hole and it held her.

Tom pushed the curled end of the toboggan toward her. "Wrap your arms around it."

She was calmer now, blue-lipped. She wrapped her wet arms around the toboggan and he pulled. He moved her a few inches out of the water but then she let go, slipping back into the hole.

"I can't," she said, her voice slurred.

"You can."

"Too hard."

"It's not. You try harder, now. Get both arms right around it and hold your hands together."

"I can't."

"There's no time. Come on, now, both arms right around it."

She tried again and slipped once more, this time up to her neck. She got her arms back over the edge and laid her head on them.

Tom started to shiver, was wearing only his cotton shirt. He closed his eyes. Okay, he thought, okay. He breathed in deeply as if to make himself lighter and spread his legs to distribute his weight, and shuffled closer and closer until his face was inches from hers. The ice moaned under him. She'd been in the water for at least three minutes and now she had no strength; all her blood had rushed to the middle of her body, leaving her limbs heavy and numb.

"Get her out," Curtis yelled, his voice wet.

"Shut the hell up."

"I can't feel my body," Erin said, her voice small, the words without beginning or end, one long word.

Without thinking too much more about it, he plunged his

hands into the water and grabbed her under her arms, heaving her out and rolling away from the hole in one swift movement. Sliding in his boots, he carried her to the other end of the pond.

He took off her clothes and also his shirt, pulled her against his skin, and wrapped his coat over them both. He held her like that until her lips turned pink and then dressed her in his own and Curtis's dry clothes and bundled her onto the toboggan. They covered the distance back to the house in an hour, and while Curtis loaded the fireplace, Tom again undressed himself and Erin and wrapped their bodies together in blankets. He lay with her close to the fire, her cold skin pressed into his, and imagined his body heat radiating through her. She shivered for more than an hour, and when that subsided she was mostly still, shaking periodically as if her body, now warm, moved with nightmares of a remembered cold. Curtis was asleep on the couch and Erin slept too; Tom rocked with the rhythm of her breathing, unsure of how to move away. He wasn't in the habit of holding his children.

# 5

**Heading down** the road with his camp trailer hitched securely to his truck, Tom glanced out the window toward his mother's house. Samantha had waited in the driveway while he packed the last of his things into the truck, but after a loose-fingered wave, Erin had gone into the house. Now they were both gone and the front door was shut. Samantha would be offering Erin coffee, or something to eat, and then would help her unpack her clothes in his old bedroom, where she always stayed when he went north for the planting season.

He turned onto the Hart Highway and rolled down the window to let in the brisk spring air and the sweet-sour wood-chip smell of the lumberyards. He'd left two hours later than he'd told Carolina he would, had wasted the morning trying to speak to the right Nielson Logging guy on the phone. They'd made last-minute changes to some of the cutblocks he'd been contracted to plant, and he had to wait for them to fax him the new block maps before he could leave. He was heading up a day early, so he and Carolina could camp one night together.

After three hours of driving, he stopped in Hook Lake for a coffee, a sandwich, and a piss at the gas station—the last place that he could fill up with diesel for a hundred kilometers. He checked the connection of his trailer hitch and then carried on north. Gold flashes of the McLeod River ribboned through the pine trees to the west, and after another hour he came to his turn on the left, a winding dirt road to the campground. He parked next to Carolina's Honda in the small lot by the ranger's office and collected a lightweight backpack, his sleeping bag, and a wool coat from his truck. Three separate trails branched off the parking lot and he started on the one that led to Crossbow Creek, a three-kilometer hike to Carolina's favorite site. A cloud bank settled in front of the sun just as the trail took him into the trees and the temperature dropped. For the next few weeks up at the Takla camp, where he'd be heading the next day, the milk would be frozen in the mornings and the planters would have to hack through a layer of ice just to wet their cereal. The morning dew would be frosted until at least June. He went back to his truck to retrieve his quilted blanket and draped it over his shoulders. Carolina would laugh at him when she saw him coming and call him an old man.

Her light-blue, two-man tent stood alone at the campsite, pitched on a flat patch of rough grass close to the tumbling creek. A hearty fire burned a few meters away from the tent in a blackened, stone-lined pit. Tom dropped his stuff by the tent but kept the blanket and stood by the side of the creek. The water roiled deeply with spring runoff and there was the tumble of smooth stones passing over each other, like whispers.

A tussling, crackling racket echoed in the woods. Carolina came into the clearing dragging half of a dead tree and dropped it by the fire. Tom pulled his blanket tightly around his shoulders and watched her. Her round cheeks were flushed; a green wool toque covered most of her shaggy hair.

"Sounds like there's an elephant tramping around in them woods," he said, winking.

"Be a man and put the ax to that log."

"I'm sorry I'm so late."

She shrugged, made a noncommittal noise from the back of her throat. "I like it here, just me and this here creek and my book." When she got close he could smell the woodsmoke in her hat, her hair. Wrapping his blanket around them both, he put his face to her neck and smelled her.

She had brought two rump steaks, a bag of chips, chocolate, apples. Instant coffee and beers, which were cooling against a rock in the creek, and a twenty-six-ounce bottle of rum.

"What about breakfast?" he joked.

"I thought you were leaving at the crack of."

"But I'll still be hungry, woman. I expect you to be up and frying the bacon."

She elbowed him in the gut. "Then I hope you enjoy sleeping alone in your little blanket tonight."

He dug his hands under her layers of fleece and wool and warmed them against her skin.

At ten o'clock, the dusty purple of the northern sunset still hung low in the sky. She grilled the steaks over the fire and they ate them with chips and beer. She had cooked them perfectly, holding the meat over the flames just long enough to blacken the surface, leaving the bulk of it pretty much raw. He eyed her piece as she neatly tucked into it with a camping knife, hoping she'd leave some for him, but she ate it all. When they were finished, she sat between his legs and leaned her back against him, and they moved on to the chocolate and rum, passing the bottle back and forth.

Sniffing the bottle rim, he said, "It tastes like flowers."

She twisted around and licked the underside of his top lip.

They drank a quarter of the bottle and he stumbled into the bush to take a piss, shivering and feeling his way in the dark. This was how they were together, secret nights under darkness, enough food for one, maybe two meals. Always the necessity for blankets, bug spray, pocketknives, and candles. During the long winter months, when she wasn't teaching at the university, he sometimes took her to a cabin that belonged to a guy he knew from town, and she would read her books in a chair by the window.

They met because she popped a flat tire on her neglected bike, riding out of town along River Road. Through the window of his truck, he saw a woman in boots and a blue dress pushing a bike, with a deflated inner tube around her neck. She had a secondhand patch kit in her bag, one she had been given by an old boyfriend. She opened the grimy plastic box and handed the contents to Tom one by one. All it contained was a crumpled aluminum tube of rubber solution gone hard, a worn piece of chalk, a soft square of sandpaper, and a tire lever. But not a single patch.

"It's just too easy," she said to Tom, as he loaded her bike onto the bed of his truck.

He looked at her.

"No patches in the kit. You would understand if you'd met my ex."

She was fifteen years younger than him, and he was impressed, and always pleased, by her ability to point out stuff like that, the meaning of a small strip of rubber. She could see how things connected; she once told him she believed there was something on the other side of life that held it all together, like a river. And if you let yourself go along with it, you would never be afraid, or baffled, or alone. He wasn't sure what to make of all that, but as far as he could tell, she was never any of those things.

They ran into each other a few weeks after he first drove her and her flat tire home.

"Still taking your chances with that thing, eh?" he said, nodding at the same bike. He had come out of the drugstore, and she was there on the corner, straddling the bike with one foot on the road. A sun-shower had just fallen, freeing the smell of concrete from hot summer pavement.

"Indeed I am," she said, smiling as though she was happy to see him too. "Yep." She patted the handlebars.

He shifted his weight from left foot to right, stroked his chin, and puckered his lips, mock-serious. He hunched down on his knees and squinted at the bike's components. "Could use a new chain. Chain rings and sprockets need to go too. Your brake pads are shot to hell, the cables...Tires are bald. You could kill yourself riding this here cycle."

She shrugged. "Still here."

He looked at his watch. "Have you got some time today?"

He took her to Canadian Tire to buy new parts and then back to her place, the rented ground floor of a house near the university. She pulled at the grass and dandelions on the lawn and drank bottles of Kokanee while he stripped her bike frame and fit the new parts. She told him about her family back in Montreal, her work at the university. Told him—and at first he thought she was joking, but she wasn't—about how she'd been married at twenty, divorced at twenty-one.

He took his time, was meticulous, quiet, and replied to her questions and comments using only his eyebrows and a smile. After the sun went down, after he'd finished with the bike, he left dark smudges of bike grease on her skin.

Inside the tent, they made a nest out of blankets, thermal mats, and sleeping bags. They turned to each other, and like always, he wanted every part of her at once. She was much smaller than he was, and healthy and plump. Her skin was soft but her hands strong and articulate. When they first met, she used to joke that someone as old as he (forty!) couldn't be so well muscled, unwrinkled. His retaliation was to pinch the soft flesh at her hips, the mound of her belly.

Tonight, thickheaded from the rum, he lost his balance in her and in the shadowy confines of the tent. He slept without stirring and woke at the birdcall of dawn. And then he began to feel a familiar haunting, a pull from outside. She seemed to sense this, and before the morning poured itself into the sky completely, like milk into a glass bowl, she tried to abduct parts of him. Sucking his bottom lip into her mouth, walking her fingers, sentry-like, over the square frame of his hip, down the slope of his waist, and up and over his back. Locking his leg between her thighs. She nuzzled her face in his neck and they both fell back to sleep. When he woke up an hour later, the light coming through the blue tent gave him the illusion of being underwater in a swimming pool. He leaned over her and kissed the line of her collarbone. She swam up out of sleep, and he began to put his clothes on, shivering without the sleeping bag, away from her body. As he pulled on his wool socks, she placed her hand flat on his back.

He unzipped the tent flap and laced up his boots. They were cold and stiff and frosted with dew. First he went over to the trees and pissed, stretched and yawned. He collected the pot from where it sat next to the now ash-heaped fire pit and filled it at the creek.

He started up the fire again and boiled water for coffee. There was only one mug so he brought it to her in the tent, and then sat by the fire while she got dressed. In the daylight, the edges of things—trees, stones, the flames in the fire pit— that had been soft the night before were now hardened and better defined. He listened to the water and the distant crashes of the woods while she shuffled around in the tent. He calculated what time he would be in Takla Lake if he left within the hour. It was two hours from here up to Fort St. James, then at least another three hours to their camp at Takla. Most of this was on unpaved logging roads. His foremen were meeting him at camp before dark that night; they had two days to set up before the planters arrived.

She came out then and started packing her things into a large backpack.

"Can you get your stuff so I can take down this tent?" she asked. "You're carrying it back to my car, by the way."

"Come here," he said. "Sit down for a minute."

"No. Got stuff to do."

"Carolina, come and sit down for one minute."

"Here," she said, walking over to him with the mug in her grip, crunching the hard ground. "Is there any left in the pot?"

He grabbed her around the waist and pulled her into his lap. He stuck his hands under her sweater and pinched her.

"Fuck off, Tom!" She pushed at him to get away but he didn't let go.

"Just sit with me while I drink my coffee." He loosened his grip and she got up. She went back to the tent and his things came flying out of the opening. She started pulling pegs out of the ground, fed the poles out through the nylon. He watched with a lazy smile and heckled her for packing up the tent haphazardly. When she was done, she came over to him and straddled him at the waist, pushed him down so that he was lying on his back. She brought her face within an inch of his, her eyes a wet, blue blur. She pulled back and was in focus, her face distorted by all the things, he knew, that she was well within her rights to say.

"I have to look after myself," she said. She kissed his chin.

"I know."

"Because you're like a disease."

"Nothing deadly, I hope."

She punched him hard in the ribs and rolled off. Where her face had been a moment before there was now only pale, empty sky.

**6**

**Curtis loved** riding his bike when he was stoned. The smooth
and empty road stroked the contours of the mountain, the land
rising up to the right, sloping down to the left. It was beautiful
and inevitable the way the road was embedded in the rock, as
if it had always been there and would always be.

And he loved riding in the dark, in this dark, this mountain,
Whistler dark. No streetlights and, tonight, no moon. Just the
stars arching from one end of the sky to the other, rising up
from the mountain. He knew this stretch of road well enough
that he could ride it with his eyes closed. He tried this, hands-
free, and nearly swerved into the ditch. Laughing, he got hold
of the handlebars again and straightened himself out. Tonight
he could take a bite out of the wind.

And fuck, he loved Tonya. Really, really loved her. Back at
his place, after she'd called and he was pulling on his coat,
his roommates said he was a pussy. But what they didn't get
was that hanging out with her was just as easy as hanging
out with them. The first time they went riding together, she
picked him up at his place at five in the morning. She secured
his bike to the rack on top of her car with bungee cords while
he buttered four pieces of toast and filled a thermos with cof-

fee. She drove him down the mountain past Squamish, where the sky was just beginning to lighten above Paul Ridge and the sheer, gray rock face of the Chief was still draped in darkness, black striations like tears. They turned onto a dirt road and parked next to a culvert. When Curtis opened his door, he was hit with the sound of screaming—the throaty, circling calls of seagulls.

"Is there a creek nearby?" he asked Tonya.

She was standing on the frame of the open back door, untying her bike, the terraced muscles of her calves and thighs jumping. She peered at him from underneath her raised arm and smiled.

They rode their bikes a few hundred meters up a single-track trail to where the forest opened onto a gravel creek bed. Seagulls swooned and dove here, fat on hundreds of blood-pink salmon carcasses, all the glossy, openmouthed dead that had traveled upriver from the sea against current, waterfall, and bear claw. These were the ones that had made it, spawned, and then died in the same waters where they had hatched. Curtis and Tonya yelled to each other over the bird noise and the boiling white water. Holding her nose against the smell, she picked up a half-eaten salmon by its tail and flung it at him. They rode all that cold morning until the autumn sun heated their backs and they ate lunch on a rocky outcrop overlooking Howe Sound. Later, in the backseat of her car, he went down on her to the sound of screaming gulls.

When winter came, they skied together. She didn't get high very often but wasn't afraid to hotbox the gondola with him and his friends. She knew the backcountry better than any of them but didn't make a big deal of it, the way most guys he knew would.

And she never asked him to define what was going on between them. She'd rather talk about the white room, where the powder was so deep and so fine it sprayed up soft walls as you skied through it, tasting the crystals, breathing them, ice melting on your tongue. He just wanted to be with this girl all the time.

He pedaled slowly through the skateboard park near Tonya's house, the place where they first met. He, hungover and asleep, curled up like a baby in the smooth concrete halfpipe, his head on a pillow of autumn leaves. She, with her board under her arm, kicking him awake.

He now rode his bike to the lip of the big bowl in the center of the park, braked with his front wheel cushioning the edge, and crossed his forearms over his handlebars, peering down the slope. He considered dropping into the bowl. But the problem with eating hash—and he knew this when he ate it, what, an hour ago?—was that it was like going through a door at the back of a room and finding a smaller room, with another door. And then going through that door to another, even smaller room, thinking it was the last. But then there was always another door. Another room. Yada yada yada.

He was too baked. He got off and pushed his bike across the wet grass toward the woods at the far end of the park, looking for the gap that led to Tonya's street. But the darkness had swallowed the opening, or the trees had grown over it. He pushed his bike up and down the tree line, peering into the woods that were somehow darker than the whole of the night. He thought he found the place and pushed his bike blindly through the entwined arms of spiky pines, needles in his face, getting the bike no farther in than the saddle.

The air pressed coldly on his shoulders. Maybe he should

have stayed home. His head was full of sand. When she asked him to come over he should have said no, made her wait. Eight months before, he'd never even heard of her. And now he said her name to himself probably fifty times a day. Now he was being paranoid. No. Paranoia was just good defense against the truth. Groping around in the dark, like an idiot— that was the truth.

Her porch light was on and there she was on the front steps, one arm around her knees. She was smoking a cigarette, exhaling into the cold night. His pulse knocked against his throat.

"You're pie-eyed," she said.

"I couldn't find the fucken gap in the trees."

"The what?"

"The path, through the thing." He pointed over his shoulder.

"Okay."

She put on a movie and made him a cup of coffee, and sat curled in a blanket at the other end of the couch. In the dark, blue television light reeled across her night-black hair and her skin, which, in the daylight, was pale toffee. The colors of her Filipino mother. It hurt, how perfect she was. When the movie ended, she asked him if he wanted something to eat.

He yawned and stretched and looked at his watch: 2 a.m. "Nah." He rubbed his eyes and leaned his body across her legs and rested his chin on her shoulder, stroked her thigh. "You're still awake."

"Been waiting for you to snap out of it." She moved so that his head fell against the back of the couch.

He lay there, cheek pressed into the rough warmth where her body had been.

She pointed the remote at the TV and the screen went blank, and the room hummed. She felt along the wall for the light switch and flipped it, and the light in the room was ugly. Then she looked at him, and her eyes moved from his to the top of his head, and back again. "I had an abortion," she said.

"An abortion."

"In Vancouver, when you went up to your dad's. I wasn't going to say anything, but you have a right to know. For a few weeks, there was this thing, alive." Her face had the look of someone wading through some minor but essential job, like cleaning out a drain.

"How many weeks?" he asked.

"Are you fucking serious?"

She allowed him to sleep in her bed, and at first she responded when he reached across to her, kissing him deeply. When her breath quickened, he slid his hand under her shirt. Unhooked the clasp on her bra. She gripped the inside of his thigh but then pulled her mouth away and turned her back.

"I feel like we've lost the right," she said, her voice thick.

He lay awake until the grayness of morning picked out things in her room that he'd never noticed before: a trophy on top of the bookshelf, the closet door off its hinge, a small, aluminum garbage can. While she slept, he moved smoothly and quietly from the bed, pulled on his clothes in the hallway, and left.

**7**

**The paved** road ended on a seam where dirt began somewhere outside Fort St. James, and Tom adjusted to the bump and jar of the logging road, damp today from an early morning rain. The smell of water-pocked dust struck the back of his nose where it met his throat, and the taste was as good as home. The roads were cut up badly from the year's heavy winter and he swerved the truck to avoid the biggest potholes, thick with spring mud. In this place, the colors of the world were reduced to the deep green of the conifers and whatever shade of blue or white the sky happened to be, and the brown of these roads that cut their way, deeper and deeper every season, into the bush. Nothing changed here, the pines moving past kilometer after kilometer, the low-lying foliage closest to the road coated white brown with dust. Patches of dense natural forest, and then ordered, soldierlike spans of planted stock.

The uniformity of this place had a way of lulling a person into something like a dream. Once, when Tom was working as camp manager for another outfit, he lost a spare tire along one of these roads; it had bounced off the back of his flatbed during a fuel run and he hadn't noticed until he got back to camp. He could have lost it anywhere during the hundred-klick journey. He asked one of the planters to help him find it and they drove at a crawl, Tom looking out his window into the ditch and the other guy covering the passenger's side. After an hour they were losing the light and the guy Tom had brought with him had given up, dozed with his head against the window. They'd been working since five in the morning and it was now coming up to ten o'clock. After a full day's work, the road became hypnotic, nothing changing, no buildings or intersections to mark the distance. Nothing to watch out for. There was only the kilometer signage, small white signs dinged and battered, placed five kilometers apart, marking the distance from where the dirt road started so drivers could radio one another where they were on the narrow roads, heading deeper into the bush or returning with a load of timber back to the yards in town. Without this system, the only warning you'd get from an oncoming logging truck would be a rumble and a cloud of dust, and then it would be on top of you.

It was only a tire, and they could have taken the cost of it out of his paycheck. But he couldn't stand the waste and having made a careless mistake. The longer he drove, the harder it was to turn back, because maybe the tire would be around the next bend. Once or twice, he thought he saw a moose stepping out of the trees, but it was only his fatigue and the crawling shadow created by his headlights. The bush could play tricks like that, could easily fool you into seeing a thing that wasn't there.

He was getting closer to camp now, less than an hour away, and Carolina's smell was still on his skin, the smoke from their fire in his hair and on his jacket. Up ahead, the hump of a black bear on all fours marked a silhouette against the road. By the time Tom got to where the bear had been, all he saw of it was its round rump bounding into the bush, disappearing like a stone into water.

A voice he recognized called its position over the radio. "Two oh seven. Empty."

Tom picked up his handset. "Mr. Sweet," he said.

"Yes, boss," came the lisped reply, followed by laughter.

"See you in camp."

"Roger that, chief."

The approach to Takla Lake was a rough and winding trail just big enough for a vehicle to pass through, alder branches slapping the windows. Tom pulled into camp and saw that the cook van was already parked at the far end of the clearing, and there was Nix, back in camp for her second year, sitting on the tailgate, smoking. She watched him drive up and saluted with her cigarette when he rolled down his window.

"How long you been here?" he asked. "I thought you were coming up with Matt and Roland."

She shrugged. "They had to sort something out. Some mix-up with a water pipe?"

"You mean the shower pipe?" he asked.

"Dunno, chief. Something about a pipe." She wore sunglasses and had a red bandanna tied over her short, dark hair.

Tom looked across the calm, black surface of Takla Lake to the Skeena Mountains on its western shore. This crooked finger of water was connected to two other lakes, Stuart and Trembleur. Two hundred years before, the mountains would have seen the first Europeans canoe up from Simon Fraser's post on Stuart Lake to kill for pelts. Less than a hundred years would go by before they came looking for gold, and now it was timber. Generations of men had spilled sweat and blood into this land to feed their families and build their homes, but you wouldn't know it looking across the water to the mountains, with the three o'clock sun hovering above them.

Tom parked his trailer at the tree line at the back of the clearing, farthest from the lake. He put on his heavy jacket and joined Nix back at the cook van. He scanned the area. They'd set up the same as every year: mess tent by the cook van, and next to that a dry room so they could air their gear when it rained. Between the mess tent and the cook van they'd place the water tank and pump and an area for washing dishes.

The round, black ghosts of previous years' fire pits still marked the middle of the clearing, like small moon craters. The planters would set up their tents among the trees at the north end of the camp, close to the water but protected from the wind. By the entrance road Tom would put the shitters and showers, the showers fed by cold water pumped up from the lake.

"You ready for the new season, cook?" Tom asked, sitting next to Nix on the tailgate.

"I can't believe I'm back here cooking for these savages. You get out here and it's like you never left. I had another job lined up, you know, in a real kitchen. In the city. Cooking for people who eat with clean hands and don't go apeshit when you feed them lentils. I didn't plan on coming back to this."

"Nobody ever does."

"Except you."

He smiled. "Why didn't you take the restaurant job?"

"You pay better."

"You aren't going to cook anything funny this year, are you? None of that rabbit food?"

She leaned into him and drove her elbow into his ribs.

Tired of waiting for his foremen to arrive, Tom searched through Nix's food supply, balancing bread, cheese, and an apple in the crook of his arm. He heard the sound of wheels crunching over gravel and prepared himself for the circus of Daryl Sweet; it was like going into combat. Sweet parked his truck alongside the cook van and rolled down his window, draping his arm over the door, his swarm of blond curls tied back from his face. Two veteran planters, a guy and a girl, jumped out of the back of his truck—half the number that Sweet had promised to bring to help set up camp. They unloaded their bags and planting equipment and waved coolly at Tom. Made jokes to Nix about her vegetarian cooking. They wore the garb of the tree planter: army surplus pants, dirty sneakers, gray woolen shirts and fleece. Steel-toed boots hung from the backs of their bags. The girl—her name was Penny—had dipped her blond dreadlocks into pink dye so that her hair looked like candy floss.

This wasn't their first time in the bush, but after a year away, they came back with clothes that were soft and clean, and with fresh hair and unbitten skin. Almost all the planters were on their summer breaks from university, and planting trees was how they paid their tuition. The grime would settle back into their skin soon enough, though, and they'd be comparing the consistency of their bush shits within the week.

They collected their things and headed toward the trees at the north end of the clearing.

"Go forth, my children!" Sweet called to them, his palm flat against the outside of his door. "Grab the finest tent pitches for yourselves! Be rapacious! For in two days' time this place will be crawling with rats and rodents and other vermin of the vilest kind! And should you yield so much as one ounce of goodwill unto them, they will tear you from limb to limb, rip your tent pegs from the ground, and stick them so far up your asses you shall be eating them for breakfast!" He hopped out of his truck.

Nix rolled her eyes.

"Dudes," Sweet said, still with the hint of a childhood lisp. "What do you think of this fat bastard?" He pointed to a green Kona mountain bike strapped to the top of his truck and grinned at Nix. "Do you like it?"

"I have to wonder what dark and sickening deeds you get up to to be able to afford all the shit you have," she said, and stood up, brushing the dust off the backs of her thighs.

"What happened to the other two people you were meant to bring?" Tom asked.

"You know how hard it is, chief, to coerce these minions into doing extra work? We're lucky we got these two."

"But you offered what I said?"

"Of course I did."

"Hundred a day?"

Sweet put his palm on his chest and nodded.

Tom looked at his watch. "You know anything about this issue with the shower rig?"

"Not a problem, boss. I spoke to Roland and Matt before we left and they were smoothing it all out with the rental place. They gave them the wrong pump. I think Roland tried calling you at home last night."

Last night, swimming with Carolina in the deep blue of her tent. He was annoyed with himself now for missing the call.

"You know how far behind they are?"

"They had to wait for the rental place to open this morning. They're maybe two hours away? Double that if Matt's driving. But lose that look of discombobulation, chief! We take good care of you, don't we?" Suddenly Sweet's arm was around Tom's shoulders, squeezing, and then it was gone as quickly as it had come, a lizard's tongue. He was now unfastening his bike from the roof rack. "I trust you brought your ride this year, boss? And I don't mean your hot teacher," he said over his shoulder, heaving his bike down with one arm. He rolled the bike over to where Tom stood. "You want to take it for a spin?"

Tom shook his head. "You might as well grab your planters and dig holes for the latrine. We'll use this time while we wait."

"Boss? No. I don't do shit holes."

"They aren't shit holes until someone shits in them. Go and dig."

Later, under a cobalt sky rimmed with orange where it met the mountain ridge, the tired crew settled around the fire that Tom had built. It had been a good day.

Matt and Roland had turned up in good time with two truckloads of gear, and in spite of the shortage of hands, they'd all managed to raise the large mess tent and dry room, place the latrines, and run the wiring to the generator. Nix's cook van was set up, and tomorrow Tom would run the pipe for the water supply from the lake. The first reefer of trees had been dropped a few klicks down the road, and they'd go out there in the afternoon to rope silver tarps to the trees, building a large, cool cache to protect the hundreds of boxes of pine and spruce seedlings. Tom settled into the log he was leaning against and removed his boots. He stretched his stockinged feet toward the fire and opened his toes to the dry heat. Penny with the dreadlocks chewed sunflower seeds from a large plastic bag and spit the shells into the soft, rolling flame. She offered Tom the joint that had been going slowly around the circle, then pulled it back as Tom shook his head.

"I forgot, chief. You don't partake."

Matt, short and bullish, moved from the other side of the fire to sit with Tom. Smiling, he rubbed at the bristles of his beard. "How's that fine girl of yours?" he asked. His voice, as always, was like steam being released from high pressure. He swatted with his beefy hand at a cloud of mosquitoes that hung at his forehead.

"Erin?"

"No, no. Your woman. The professor." He kicked a log in the fire, pushed the coals with the heel of his boot.

Tom shook his head and smiled, watched the flames.

"What the hell do you and the professor talk about, anyway?" Sweet piped up from the other side of the fire pit. He sat up taller and raised his can of beer above his head as if he were about to make a toast. "Can't you guys just see the chief? Glass of Shiraz in one hand, discussing feminist avant-garde poets and how, like, powerfully they convey their feelings of inequality and oppression in a misogynistic society."

"Name us one femme poet, you fucking show pony," said Nix, pointing a burning stick at him.

Sweet took a long gulp from his beer can. "You keep messing with me, girl, and you'll wake up in your little kitchen van one morning to find bacon bits mixed in with the granola."

"So you can't name one, then," she said.

"Watch it."

**8**

**First morning** of the plant, Tom woke early and sat on the steps of his trailer, flicking off the small round slugs that had clung to his bootlaces in the night. The blue air cold enough for him to see his breath. He wore his heavy woolen sweater and wool-lined coat and a black toque. Wind gusted off the lake, buffeting and sucking the few tents that had been set up right on the beach. At the other end of the camp, Roland loaded tarps into the back of his crew van. Tom laced his boots and walked across the clearing to the serving window at the cook van and leaned on the frame. Nix's back was to him as she worked with strong arms to stir a large pot with a long wooden spoon. Steam and spitting oil and the smell of fried biscuits and cinnamon.

"Smells good," said Tom.

Her shoulders tensed and she turned around, her hand at her throat. "You scared the crap out of me." Her dark hair was plastered to her forehead.

He put his palms up.

"Help me get this stuff out," she said. She passed him a tray loaded with three jugs of milk, a bowl of butter, and a plastic container of sugar. He ferried more food out to the mess tent, breakfast and fixings for lunch: loaves of bread, plates of ham and salami and cheese, fruit, boxes of cereal. A jar of instant coffee and a hot-water urn.

He went back to the van. "Can I steal a bowl?"

With her back to him: "No."

"You going to make me go back to my trailer for it?"

"I give you a bowl, chief, I have to give everyone a bowl."

"Come on."

She shook her head and shuffled around some boxes and passed him a small stainless steel bowl.

"Spoon and a cup too," he said.

"Bring it all back clean," she said. She dropped a spoon into a chipped enamel cup and gave it to him.

He chose a box of cereal and made himself a cup of strong coffee. He sat at the end of one of the long, wooden tables and watched his planters drift into the mess tent, wrapped warmly against the cold. Some faces he recognized, some not. They filled their mugs with coffee and prepared stacks of sandwiches for the day, squares of cake wrapped in paper towel. The tent slowly filled with the din of morning voices, and then Roland and Matt sat on either side of him.

"Hey, I just heard about Rocky," said Roland.

Tom nodded, drank his coffee.

"You think you'll get another dog? You'll need one if you end up moving out to that shack."

Tom looked out the door of the tent. "True enough." He stood up and collected his dirty dishes and took them outside to the wash table. He rinsed them in a tub of hot water and left them on the table to dry.

The day had turned gray and fog skirted the mountains across the black chop of the lake. Sweet stood at the pump filling a large plastic barrel, and when he saw Tom he stopped and loped over to him, the color in his cheeks blooming as if he'd been slapped.

"I did a run out to my block last night, boss. Set my cache up."

"Okay."

Sweet waited.

"What?"

"Lots of draws. Slash everywhere. What are you trying to do to me?" He fingered a few fat curls behind his ears.

"You've got the most experienced crew."

"They'll quit when they see this. It's bullshit. What kind of land did Matt and Roland get?"

"Everybody gets their share," said Tom, making his way over to his truck.

Sweet followed him. "Have you even seen it?"

"Wouldn't've made a difference if I had." Tom opened his door and got in. "I know how bad it can get. So do you."

"You owe me. Another one."

"Only asking you to do your job."

Two hours later, Tom pulled into the landing where Sweet had left his crew van parked next to a white Nielson Logging truck, which meant that the company checker was already on the block somewhere. It was an aggressive move, for the checker to arrive on the first day. Other outfits had been sniffing around this contract, and Tom felt a little like he was in the scope. There could be no fuckups this year. He pulled his old vinyl bags, soft and worn, out of the back of the truck. This was the third or fourth set he'd had over the past fifteen years, and he thought he'd burn them at the end of the season, his last. He laced his arms through the shoulder straps of the harness, then tightened and clasped the belt. The three bags, dirty and scuffed at the seams, hung empty around his hips.

Mist settled into his hair and his wool collar as he stood at the edge of the road and took in the land. A small dirt track sloped down into a steep-banked draw, which was crisscrossed with fallen logs. Slash piles of sticks and branches, left behind after the trees had been felled, delimbed and bucked, and taken away by skidder, marked the land like pencil scribbles breaking through paper. It was slow-going land, frustrating as hell to work. He pulled his collar up around his neck and headed down into the draw, following the muddy chunks of track left by Sweet's quad bike. He balanced his shovel across his shoulders with both arms slung over it and hopped the puddles, frozen at their edges. Soon he came to the first planter's cache, a white and silver tarp fastened with rope to a stump and to sticks jammed in the dirt. He checked under the tarp: two boxes of seedlings and a jug of water, a muddy backpack. From here he left the track and headed straight up the slope of the draw, climbing over logs and dead branches, thistles hooking his pants and bootlaces. He slipped in the mud and ground the heel of his hand into a jagged stump. When he reached the ridge at the top of the draw, he could see the planter, Amy, moving fluidly toward the tree line, bending every few steps to put another seedling in the ground. She looked up and saw Tom but continued to plant, stopping only when he reached her. She put one foot up on a stump, balanced her shovel across her knee, and hung her arms over it.

"You welcomed us back with some beautiful land here." She smiled, her eyes narrow.

Tom rubbed the back of his neck and nodded. "Sorry about that. It's only because you guys are so good." He winked and reached into Amy's side bag, grabbed three bundles of seedlings, and unwrapped the cellophane that bound the root plugs together. He put them in his own bags and began to plant a meter off the line of seedlings that Amy had already put in the ground. Amy, short and muscled, was fast. She went ahead and Tom had to hustle to keep up. She planted her trees in good sites, in the crooks of stumps that would help keep the seedlings warm through the winter, or in the mulchy red crumbs of rotting wood. She hopped back and forth planting two lines of trees to Tom's one, and when Tom ran out of seedlings he reached into Amy's bag for more, and in this way they worked together in silence.

"This land is angry," Amy eventually said. She stopped and leaned against a waist-high log. She dug an orange from a deep pocket at her thigh and peeled it with dirty fingers wrapped in silver duct tape. "It wants to eat me."

Tom wiped the sweat from his forehead with the back of his hand and smiled. How many times had he listened to his planters theorize about clear-cut land, about the spirit of the land? All the cutting and dragging, they said, and all that loud, heavy machinery had to leave something vengeful behind. They'd all felt it, in the slaps from sticks unsprung, the snare of the thistle, the suck of their boots in the mud and the mosquitoes and blackflies that rose from stagnant water (like the living dead, they said, because no matter how many you killed, they mindlessly kept coming back). They'd all felt the downward pull, the earth angry with each one of them for studding across her great big wounds with their cork boots. Even though their job was to replace what had been so brutally taken, they said, she was pissed off at them, too.

Tom agreed that the land had spirit. But what got him was the injury they felt, the incredulity. Sure, the spirit was there where rock met sky, or in the fall of a needle to the ground, or the smell of sap on your knuckles. And it was there in a dried-up creek bed, a mudslide, a rotting carcass. But it was indifferent. It was indiscriminate.

"Sweet's already pissed off and it's only week one," Amy said, peeling the pith off a wedge of orange and flicking it to the ground. "I love the guy, but you know. He's a piece of work. You mind if I ask why you bring him back every year?"

"You guys are a great crew. He's your crew boss."

"You're afraid if he went somewhere else we'd go with him."

A few hundred meters away, the tree line was hazy with mist and drizzle. He looked at Amy. "He's never liked being told what to do. You learn to put up with these things."

"But if you don't like it, dump it."

Tom put out his hand for a wedge of orange. Amy passed him one, grazed with dirt, and he popped it in his mouth, sweet juice and grit. "Have you seen the checker?" he asked. "Her truck's on the landing. She'll be prowling around here somewhere."

"On day one?"

"She's new."

Amy wiped her fingers on the front of her shirt and stood up. "If you find her, tell her fifteen cents is a shit price for this shit land." She ducked under the log and started planting again on the other side.

Tom hiked back along the ridge until he found other

planters from Sweet's crew, LJ and Beautiful T, who told him that their fingers were frozen and they were considering slicing each other's tits off for agreeing to come back to the bush this year. He planted with them for a while, following their slow, steady pace. They sang Patsy Cline songs, to keep from going crazy, they said. As Tom was leaving, they told him to tell Sweet that if it didn't stop raining, they were going to spend the afternoon in the crew van smoking his cigarettes.

He worked alongside other planters, lightening their bags, helping them put their seedlings into the harsh ground. Being paid by the tree, they were grateful. Tom walked the length of the block, piece by piece, and returned to the landing nearly four hours after he'd left it, dirty and wet to the bone. The checker was sitting in the front of her truck. Tom approached the window and she rolled it down and he felt dry heat on his face, took in the smell of cigarettes and coffee. He leaned in and rested his forearms on the window frame.

"You want to hop in?" she asked. "It's warm." She wore a plain white baseball cap that looked too clean for the bush, and too big for her face. In the hollows of her cheeks, the pebbled shadows of old acne scars.

"Don't want to get too comfortable."

"Your foreman, Daryl, tells me this is the most experienced crew in the outfit."

Tom nodded.

"Because I found two planters without damp sponges in their bags. None of them were carrying plot cords, so I don't know how they expect to get their density right. I dug up about fifty seedlings and found three J roots." She sipped coffee from a small thermos cup and caught a drip on her bottom lip with her teeth. "I don't know what your standards are, but

I'd call that pretty sloppy. Blueberries aren't even out yet and they're fucking the dog already."

The buzz of a quad bike sounded in the distance.

"Maybe you should have a meeting with your foremen. Make sure everybody is clear on the quality we're expecting," she said, watching the rearview mirror.

Tom nodded and looked down at his boots, then looked up at her. "First day today. They need a little time to settle."

She put her thermos in the cup holder and rubbed her hands together, started the ignition.

Sweet pulled into the landing on his quad bike and sat idle, the engine sputtering.

"I'll follow you to the next block," she said. "I'd like to see all three of them today."

"We'll make Matt's, but Roland's is a good hour and a half drive out. It'll be getting dark."

"We'll fit it in."

Tom drummed his hands against the window frame and stood back and watched her pull the truck around. He walked to the edge of the landing where Sweet sat on his bike, his arms hung loosely over the handlebars.

"That one's going to be trouble," Tom said.

"Who, Camel Toes?"

"What?"

"Have you seen her camel toes?" Sweet smiled, rolling his tongue against his cheek.

"Don't let your guys get lazy."

The planters had all left the block and were back in camp while Tom followed a few meters behind the checker, watching her dig up seedlings, testing to see whether the root plugs had been bent into J shapes when they were planted. She was tall and had legs like a newborn calf but somehow moved with efficiency over the terrain, as if she'd already studied the placement of every log and rock.

They were on high ground and the land dropped away to the northeast, where the clear-cut ended in swamp. Beyond that, mountains. The sky was clearing up now and the clouds that remained were low, ragged swipes of pink across the white. It was cold and he was chilled, and hoped this would be over soon. She had already told him that she would be coming every week, which in his experience was a lot. Her shovel was very clean.

"You the sole owner of this company?" she asked him, batting at the pall of dusk mosquitoes that hovered around her head.

"I've got a shareholder."

"Who's that, then?"

"My mother."

"You from Prince George?"

"Yup."

"You ever do any logging?" She stopped and leaned against a tall stump. Every second it grew darker.

"I did one season."

"Good. Loggers are pigs."

"I don't know about that."

"Well, then why only one season?"

"You ask a lot of questions."

She pulled a pack of cigarettes from her coat pocket and lit one, and jiggled the pack in front of his face. "I'm from a small town," she said.

"Well."

She held up the pack a moment longer and then put it back in her pocket. She blew smoke out the side of her mouth.

"You think you're about done with this block?" he said. "I don't want to roll into camp too late."

"You should smoke," she said. "It helps keep the critters away."

"You about ready to go back?"

She inhaled deeply and flicked the ash onto the toe of her own boot and looked at him as if she were considering something. "Maybe another hour," she said.

Curtis was four years old when Tom started his first and only season as a logger. After the thing that happened in the bathtub, when Curt was a baby, Elka had seemed okay. There were doctors who talked sense, and some who didn't, and different combinations of pills. Then, a few years of relative peace and normality. Five years of working indoors at the mill was about as much as Tom could take, so he signed on for a season up near Smithers. Not too far from home if Elka needed him.

Two months into the job, the beginning of June, and the lower half of Tom's face was padded by a thick beard. He was in the canteen, eating a plate of meatballs, when one of the other loggers tapped him on the shoulder and said his mother was on the radio. Something was wrong at home.

Outside, the sun had dropped behind the mountain and the warmth of the day was receding. Two guys tossed a football in the clearing behind the bunk trailers, and as he walked past, the ball seemed to wobble and spiral through the air in slow motion.

The radio was kept in a small, veneer-paneled room at the

back of the foreman's trailer. Samantha's voice crackled over the line so that it sounded as though she was laughing. Tom's landlord, who lived above his basement apartment, had been kept up half the night by the TV on full volume. It was still blaring in the morning, so he let himself in and found Curtis asleep on the floor in front of the box. The boy was with Samantha now, but they still couldn't find Elka.

Tom borrowed a truck and was home within hours, kissing his son on the top of his head as he slept in Tom's own childhood bedroom. When he went to check out the apartment in the morning, he opened the door and Elka was there, sweeping up the crushed, candy-colored cereal that Curtis had spread all over the floor. She stood in the middle of the room, leaned with the broom handle against her cheek, and looked at him, her eyes like magnets. She told him she was pregnant again and that his new beard suited him fine.

# 9

**After a** week of working straight through cold, early mornings that turned into damp and windy days, Tom wanted to give his planters a day off. He announced this at dinner and was given a rough hug by the person sitting next to him. Someone else got up from the table and slapped him on the back. Two planters from Matt's crew were elected to drive the two-hour round trip, south along the lake, to the Takla Landing outpost to buy beer.

After he finished eating, Tom headed to the showers with his tool kit. People had been complaining about water pressure. Even in the bush, they said, they expected more than this sad trickle. He checked the connections at the pump and the cables to the nozzles. He was in one of the cubicles when Nix approached him. She lifted the canvas flap, kicked the toe of his boot.

"Do you ever stop working?" she asked.

"Eh?"

"All we ever see of you is the bottom half. Your top bits are always hidden under a hood or behind a tire or something."

Tom shrugged, turned his wrench against the nozzle fitting.

"Will you join the party tonight?"

He lowered his wrench from the nozzle and looked at her. She had her towel over her shoulder and gripped a plastic soap container in one hand, toothbrush and toothpaste in the other.

"If I get this done," he said.

Two fires burned on the beach as the sky above the Skeenas softened to pink and orange, the clouds breaking for the first time in a week. Three people floated in a canoe in the middle of the lake, and from the beach their silhouettes grew darker and darker until they and the canoe were one perfect black form, drifting on the water. Depending on the direction of the wind, every now and then their voices and their laughter echoed through the air, like birds. Tom sat on a flat rock at one of the fires next to Penny with the pink hair. She spit sunflower seeds into the flames and said to no one in particular that after this week, her cold bones ached and she felt like an old woman. Someone else complained that the blisters on his heels were the size of apples. Amy announced that her chafing was already so bad that halfway through the day she'd ripped off her underwear in the middle of the block and wasn't going to wear any for the rest of the season. They all agreed, though, that for tonight, things were looking up. They had beer and dope and a good fire; the weather was turning and maybe the sun would come out for their day off. Three guys deftly kicked a hacky sack, tossing the dusty bag from the toes of their shoes, the sides of their shoes, their knees, chests. A red Frisbee cruised a smooth and lazy arc against the backdrop of the lake.

Sweet's voice carried over from the other fire. He was hold-ing court, telling a story he'd recounted so many times that it was now becoming mythical. And even though pretty much everyone in the circle had heard it before, they sat with their firelit faces toward him. The year before, there had been a heat wave that persisted for close to a month. The dust hung heavy those long weeks and everyone's throats and noses were full of it, and the land was as dry and brittle as the fur of a long-dead animal. The company was working fire hours, from two in the morning until nine, to avoid the hottest, most hazardous part of the day. One morning, as everyone was packing up to go back to camp, Tom got a call on the ra-dio about a brush fire on Sweet's land. No one knew or was willing to admit knowing how it started—it could have been a cigarette butt flicked to the ground or it could have been a spark from a shovel hitting rock—but by the time Tom reached the site of the fire, there was nothing more than a sky full of smoke and a carpet of wet, black brush. Sweet had been quick with the fire box, pumping water from a nearby creek and arming each of his crew with a shovel big enough to dig a trench. If there had been any wind that day, the story would have been different.

"I saved the chief's ass," Sweet said now. "Isn't that right, boss?" he called across to Tom. "Everything you see here would have gone up in flames if I weren't the fastest-acting motherfucker this side of the Rockies."

Though they had put out the fire, they still had to call in the ministry guys to make sure there was nothing smolder-ing deep in the brush. Fires in the bush could last for months underground if they weren't extinguished right, living off dry roots and buried stumps. The sleeping, subterranean burn could one day creep up the inside of a hollow tree and rage into the forest.

Now the smoke from the fire shifted direction and settled over Tom, in his eyes. He squeezed them shut against the sting, dug his knuckles into his eye sockets, and waited for the smoke to shift again.

" 'I hate white rabbits,' chief! Say it!" This came from either Amy or Penny.

"Folklore," said Tom. "Does nothing." He waved the smoke from his face and coughed, his eyes still shut.

"You've got to have a little faith." This came from a voice closer to him, almost in his ear. He opened his eyes and there was Nix, sitting next to him, just clear of the smoke. He was about to get up to move but the smoke shifted again, rising up the center of the circle, and he could breathe.

"See?" she said. "The magic words work."

"But I didn't say them." He wiped his wet eyes.

She swayed into him, pressing her shoulder against his. "I said them for you."

Guitars came out, and drums. Somebody produced a flute. Tom got up from the fire and walked across the cold clearing, drawn to the punk music coming from an old ambulance painted midnight blue. The ambulance belonged to Luis, who was skinny and long-limbed, wore thick glasses, and was never without a wool toque. Tom didn't know a lot about him—only that he was a fast planter and hoarded a supply of Coca-Cola, which he shared with no one, in the depths of his ambulance.

Luis sat at the back of the ambulance, dangling his legs

over the tailgate. The two swinging doors were open, and inside was a dark nest of blankets and clothes. He held up the oily joint he'd been smoking in a half wave, offering it to Tom.

"I grew it myself," he said, his eyelids waxy. His face was red and swollen, as if he'd been punched. "I've got a whole closet full of mother plants, a water table. You can smoke this without any repercussions." He chuckled, held out his pinched fingers: "Here."

"What happened to your face?" Tom asked, refusing the joint.

"Fucking allergic to blackflies." Luis twisted back into his ambulance and shuffled through a pile of clothes. He sat back up holding a paper bag, soft with wrinkles. Pulled out a string of black licorice and dangled it.

"I'll take one of those, though," said Tom.

"You mind if I give you a red one? Black is my favorite."

Tom took the candy and chewed on the end as if it were a piece of grass, and looked out toward the lake. A few stars had come out, people danced, and the fires bent in the wind. Nix walked across the clearing toward her cook van with Sweet just behind her. He stopped her, said something, and she laughed, put her hand on his chest, and shoved him away.

"Why buy red if you prefer black?" Tom asked Luis.

"Hm?"

"Never mind." Tom grinned at him and moved on.

He decided to pack it in just the other side of midnight. Everyone was still up, either at the fires or the vestibules of their tents, drinking beer or red wine or mugs of tea. They would stay up all night and sleep, unburdened, all the next day. They deserved it. He would get up early in the morning, take advantage of the peace, and get on with his work. When he got to the door of his trailer he felt a light touch on his back, between his shoulder blades.

"You okay?" It was Nix, with a wool blanket over her shoulders.

"Going to bed," he said. He could barely see her face in the dark, only the hint of her features; when she turned her head, her profile was backlit from the fires.

"No, I know. Me too. I just wanted to say good night."

He pulled open the door and put one foot on the step and looked back at her. "Good night, then."

"Can I come in for a bit?" She said this as she shook the blanket from her shoulders and unfolded it and wrapped it around her body, so that her head was down and her words difficult to hear.

"Sorry?"

"Are you going to make me say it again?" She hopped a few times and hugged the blanket tightly around herself. "I want to come in with you. Can I?"

He looked at her dark shape, considering. He did want to bring her inside; there was something about this time of night that made him feel as though he could. Somehow the lateness of the hour and the dark meant that it wouldn't count— he couldn't even see her face. And he had thought about her, about touching her. Over the past week he'd thought about it plenty of times.

Somebody dumped a big log onto the fire, and a clap of sparks rose into the night and hung there spiraling, and then extinguished. And he had enough sense to think beyond this hour, this dark, and to how this would all look to him when the sun rose.

He wanted to be kind, but he was no good at flirting. He smiled, hoped that she could see it in the dark. "No. You can't come in."

"But you thought about it," she said.

**10**

**Elka died** four years after she left. News reached Tom via a brief letter from Bobbie, who still lived on Aguanish, in the same run-down cottage where Elka had grown up. By that time, Tom and Curtis and Erin were doing pretty good. House was clean; they ate the food he cooked. Curtis was starting to win trail races on his bike, and Erin could climb the neighbor's maple tree to the top. At the bottom of Bobbie's letter was a plea for him to come to the island, and if there was no other option, he could bring the children.

So he packed a small bag and left Curtis and Erin with Samantha. Crawling in first gear behind a laboring truck on the switchbacks before Pemberton, a black Lab panting out the truck's back window, Tom thought about the only other time he'd been to Aguanish Island. That first trip down, he had bruised the heel of his hand from hitting the wheel. On the narrow road that cut into the side of the mountain just north of Horseshoe Bay, he'd wanted to launch over the sea to the west; he couldn't get there fast enough. This time, at least, it didn't matter how long it took.

He slept on the ferry from Horseshoe Bay to Vancouver Island and then drove unimpeded the short distance to

Nanoose, where he could catch a smaller, foot-passenger ferry to Aguanish. The last scheduled crossing of the day was canceled due to high winds, and he was obliged to stay the night in a motel. The weather hadn't improved much by the next morning, so he sat down to a late breakfast in the marina pub and watched the cruisers swing on their moorings and waited for the wind to die down, as the man at the ferry terminal said it would.

It was just after 3 p.m. when he stood on the wet ferry deck, the flat-nosed boat plowing through the chop of the Georgia Strait. The clouds were low and heavy and scraped across the rocky hills of Aguanish. All the letter had said was that Elka had been found dead in Alberta. It wasn't news that he was surprised to get, but listening to Bobbie tell it was going to be hard, like lifting a bandage to see a wound.

From Owl Bay, Tom caught a ride to Bobbie's place with an elf-like woman in a yellow van. A trinket of beads swung from the rearview mirror as she turned south onto the main island road.

"You visiting someone?" she asked.

"My mother-in-law."

The road moved gently through dense Douglas fir flossed with hairy grandfather's-beard and mist. Something heavy rolled in the back of the van. Up ahead, two men in raincoats walked by the side of the road, and when she was level with them she slowed the van and leaned out the window. She asked if they needed a lift. Smiling, they waved her off, and she told them she'd see them later.

Elka had asked him once or twice if he would consider moving there. Some aspects of the place would have suited him—subsistence farming, producing his own energy, and wasting nothing. But what he couldn't fathom was the familiarity. All the people on the island knew each other. And the basket weaving, the spirituality, the self-centeredness. So much of Elka's upbringing had been about seeking some kind of inner peace, and he sometimes thought that maybe after looking so hard at herself, she'd bored a hole right through her middle.

"So who's your mother-in-law, then?"

"Roberta Sirota."

"Bobbie?" She looked at him, her eyes wide. "No kidding." She cupped the wheel loosely with the fingertips of her right hand and draped her left arm out the window. She cocked her head to the side. "You staying long?"

"Just down for the day."

"You know, a bunch of us built her a cob hut last year, a place to make her brews and creams and stuff."

He nodded. She turned onto a smaller, dirt road that cut into a seam of island bedrock. Patches of gray sea could be seen through the trees, and soon the road swung to the left and followed a cliff. There were glimpses of the coastline dipping in and out of rocky coves before the road turned in again. Tough pines and junipers accustomed to strong wind and saltwater spray. This was Bobbie's island.

The woman stopped the van in front of a familiar wall of blackberry. She leaned over to turn off the ignition, and the edge of her ear poked through the straight fall of her hair, like a kitten's tongue. "Tell Bobbie to come over and see me sometime," she said.

*　*　*

It had been nine years since he'd been to Bobbie's place, and nothing much had changed. There was the poorly built drift-wood gate that needed to be coaxed open with a knee, which led to a path through salal and blackberry into the yard. The brick cottage, surrounded by fruit trees and overgrowth, hunched stubbornly at the top of a slope. Where the ground leveled out along the side of the house there was the pond, half hidden by the skirt of a large willow. This, Elka once told him, was where she used to hunt tadpoles. And beyond that, the vegetable garden.

Dirty smoke curled from the chimney into the overcast sky, and from somewhere behind the house came the rumble and chuck of a generator in need of a new exhaust. He looked up at the front of the house, preparing to go in.

Bobbie must have been watching for him from the window, because she opened the door before he made it to the porch steps. She stood in the doorway, as if she were unsure whether or not to let him past. Her hair was now more white than gray, and she wore it in a long, thick braid thrown over her shoulder. Her eyes, dark and heavy-lidded, had sunk a little farther into her face, the skin tanned and tagged and deeply lined.

"Letter said you'd be here yesterday."

"Couldn't be helped. They stopped the ferry because of the weather."

"Bah." She swatted the air.

He put one boot on the bottom step and crossed his arms casually over his knee. "Can I come in?"

"I didn't think you were going to show up. I'm in the middle of something now." She wiped her nose with the back of her finger and went into the house, leaving the door open.

Inside, the smell of something waxy—lanolin. And woodsmoke. A tepee of burning logs in the fireplace, pockmarks on the rug in front of the hearth. Watching her move about in her kitchen, setting a blackened copper kettle on the stove, spooning loose leaves into a mug, he'd forgotten how tall and broad she was. How she could fill a room entirely.

"It is good to see you, Tom."

"Is it?"

"Let's not start things off this way, eh?" She lifted the kettle with a rag and filled the mug. She handed it to him as she passed and headed for the stairs. After a few steps up, she stopped. "You coming?"

Elka's old room. The walls were bare, the brown carpet grimy. Her bed was covered with clothes and cardboard boxes. More clothes, and dolls, and puzzle boxes split at the corners spilled out of the closet onto the floor. Bobbie sat heavily on the edge of the bed and exhaled what seemed to be her frustration with Tom, and with the whole world that stood against her. Tom, his hands firmly in the pockets of his jeans, leaned one shoulder against the wall by the window. In the backyard, one of the island's wild sheep grazed, and where the shed used to be there was some fool-looking mud hut in the shape of a mushroom. There were the salal and blackberry bushes that bordered the edge of the land, and beyond that the bedrock and Douglas fir that rolled away down to the strait, nothing more than a misty gray band between this place and the dark coastal mountains on the mainland. Bobbie selected something from the pile on the bed and held it up. A child's t-shirt. Other clothes were shaken out for inspection. Denim overalls, a raincoat, leotards. "Why didn't you bring the children?"

"Implication was I shouldn't."

"Well." She flipped through a shoe box of cassette tapes, her mouth turned down rigidly.

"Come on, Bobbie. I'm sorry I was late. Nothing I could do about it."

"There never is." She held up a green dress by its sleeves. "You want to take some of this stuff home for your girl? How old is she?"

"Four."

"Of course she is."

"Bobbie, I've come all this way."

"You've come all this way."

"And I'd really like to know what happened."

She sighed and looked up at the ceiling, and puffed out her cheeks.

"Did you know she was in Alberta?" he asked.

"She left me as she left you."

"I guess I just thought in all this time she might have contacted you."

"Don't you think I would have told you if she had?"

He watched her fold and unfold a wool sweater. She tossed it aside and knelt on the floor, and pulled a wooden tray out from under the bed. It was full of shoes: one yellow rain boot, scuffed runners, leather sandals furry with dust.

He lowered himself onto the floor and drew up his knees, and rested his arms across them, to allow her this power to stall. A twelve-year-old calendar was still pinned to the wall above the bed.

"It's amazing, really, that they were able to track me down at all, to let me know," Bobbie began. "But there was a postcard. They found it in her bag, already stamped and addressed. It was evident from its condition that she'd been carrying it around for some time."

"She happen to mention my kids in that postcard?"

"Well, no. It was meant for me. A message from a daughter to her mother."

"She had a daughter too."

Bobbie clasped her hands together and smiled sadly, as if all this had been ordained. As if no one need be sorry for the fact that his kids were growing up without their mother.

"She was found in a place called Wetaskiwin. Just south of Edmonton. Wetaskiwin. Word comes from the Cree, something about the hills where they made peace." She looked at him, as if she wanted some kind of confirmation. "Maybe she could have found happiness there."

"Maybe."

"They found her in a snowbank, right in the middle of town. Apparently it looked like she had just gone to sleep; they've ruled out foul play." She said this stonily, jutting her long chin at the floor.

"What do you think?" he asked.

"Somebody did something to her. Obviously. There was vomit in the snow where she lay, and her blood-alcohol level was very high."

He held his head in his hands and imagined Elka in the snow. "So you think someone forced the booze down her throat and then left her out there in the cold. She didn't do this to herself."

"No she did not."

He stood again and looked out the window, at the sheet of rain slanting across the coastal mountains, the strait all but obliterated. "She's never been well," he said.

"You just didn't understand her. You always thought I was a crackpot, and when I told you she'd get better if she stayed here, you completely disregarded me."

"Maybe there's a thing or two you didn't understand either."

She shrugged.

"Where's she buried?"

"She was cremated. A good friend of mine collected her ashes from a funeral home in Vancouver. I kayaked out to Stoney Island the evening I received them. Full moon, water like glass. I made a bonfire and cooked a kelp and carrot stew. Things got pretty intense with half a bottle of whiskey and some chanting, and then I fell asleep on the beach. Froze my ass off. But it was worth it. I gave her back to the sea at dawn, spread her ashes over the kelp bed." Bobbie looked at him with one squinty eye, as if she were considering something. "Good for the thyroid, kelp. It's packed with iodine, iron, potassium. I cook it down with essential oils and vitamins to make a salve that can kick the ass out of any burn from here to kingdom come. Would you like to take a bottle home?"

"You didn't think we'd want to be a part of her funeral?"

She looked at him, her dark eyes shining. "No one on this earth could ever come close to guessing what a man like you wants, Tom."

Later, Tom stood at the back door, the toes of his boots getting wet from the rain spitting through the screen. It was getting dark and he knew the last ferry would be leaving soon and he would be there for the night. Tomorrow when he got home he would tell his kids that the mother they didn't know was dead, and he wasn't sure how he felt about that, or how they would react. Right now, all he was was worn out.

Bobbie fed him a soup of lentils and potatoes and poured him a rough clay mug of huckleberry wine. They ate without speaking. He wiped the last of the soup from his bowl with a hunk of bread and sat back in his chair and looked at her across the table. "Bobbie. Why did you ask me to come here?"

She carefully put her spoon down and pulled her braid from one shoulder to the other. "You're the husband."

"You could have told me everything in that letter."

She went to pour more wine into his mug, saw that it was full and frowned. "Don't you like the wine?"

He laid both of his palms on the table and watched her.

"In the end, she came to me."

Tom pushed back his chair. "You brought me here so you could gloat?"

"No, you fool. She came to me, and I wanted you to have some real part of it. Telling you in a letter would have been cruel." Her lip curled. "Goodness, I forgot what an idiot you could be."

Bloated from the soup, wound up, he tried a few hours later to sleep on her couch, the last of the fire pulsing quietly in the grill. He woke at 5 a.m. when Bobbie clambered through the room in high rubber boots and a swishing nylon jacket. She carried a basket and walking stick, and when he woke properly at eight, she fried him the blue chanterelles and jelly ears she'd picked on the low eastern slope of the hill at dawn.

# 11

**That night** when Curtis pulled into the drive and saw his dad flipping meat on the barbecue, he felt guilty for living so far away. It could have been that he was being sentimental over the dog, or Tonya, or it could have been the way his dad looked at that moment: tired, thinner across the shoulders. With enough years in the bag, even a guy as tough and cold and capable as his dad could dull at the edges. He wore the same plaid coat he'd been wearing for years. Even the same barbecue, more than twenty years old, looked after so attentively it was as good and clean as new. His dad had always been great at looking after things that were inanimate. Curtis wanted to put his arms around him and smell what was always there, motor oil and cheap drugstore soap. But his dad was not a guy you put your arms around, or who put his arms around you.

His second night home, after dinner with his dad, Curtis met up with Sean in a bar and they sat at the Pac-Man table in the back and ordered a pitcher. Sean wore the Canucks hat that he'd been wearing since his recovery from the accident in his uncle's truck, the black peak curved and tattered at the edges. His hair curled up over the hem, like weeds claiming something abandoned. He poured the beer and pulled two cigarettes out of his pack and lit one, then lit the other with the first.

"I joined the IWA," he said, passing a cigarette to Curtis. He pushed a quarter into the slot by his knee and began to play Pac-Man. "Move your glass."

Curtis nodded. "A union man, eh? What about all that talk of moving down with me?"

Sean's lip curled, his eyes on the screen. "It's all ski bunnies and boarder dudes down there. I don't want to waste my paycheck on resort rent." His shoulder jerked with the control stick.

"You sound like my dad."

"There's worse people to sound like than him."

Curtis looked across the room to a pair of old boys drinking together at the bar. Looked as though they'd worked in forestry their whole lives, felling or processing or just heavy-load trucking. He watched Sean's game. "That pink ghost is right on your ass," he said.

After finishing two pitchers, they drove into the center of town for something to eat. They parked on Caribou and walked toward Tenth, past the bars and clubs letting out for the night. Packs roamed the sidewalk, some people his age, most younger. He recognized a few, a girl his sister knew, her face hardened by the cigarette between her lips.

Sean must have seen some kind of look on his face because he said, "You fucken asshole. How many hours you spend getting pissed out of your head in these bars?" He pushed Curtis off the curb.

Around the corner, a crowd in the street. Whooping and jeering. In the center, two boys wrestled, one with his shirt torn, his chest and neck flushed red. He took a dull-knuckled punch to the jaw.

"Aw, shit," Sean said. "I know that kid."

"The one getting his ass kicked or the other one?"

"I'll break it up."

"Leave it. It'll burn out in a minute."

"I'll break it up." Sean elbowed through the crowd and people booed. The two boys were locked together on the ground and Sean got his hands under the arms of the one on top and pried him loose. The boy spun around and took a drunken swing at Sean, knocking his hat off. Someone else jumped in and he and Sean each held a boy in a bear hug around the shoulders, the boys lunging and spitting. A girl was crying; others mewed. Eventually, the crowd dissolved.

Sean grinned at Curtis, shaking his head. Without his hat, there was his scar, tracking from his right ear and diagonally across his forehead, parting his hair. Curtis retrieved Sean's hat, dusted it off, and handed it to him. Sean flipped it onto his head by the peak, hiding the scar, a flipped truck, wheels spinning in the stars.

Later, they ate pizza on the swings in their old schoolyard under the hazy purple and white shift of northern lights, which had materialized sometime in the night without their noticing.

May had started out rainy, but by the end of the month, when he returned to Whistler from his dad's, relieved to be back, the weather dried and the sun was out all the time, the mountains clear against the sky. Curtis didn't think life could get any better, and then Tonya delivered her fucken great big news, and soon after that she cut him off completely. In the days that followed, he rode by her house a few times and saw her on her bike in the village once. She had seen him too—he was sure of it. The curve of her cheek was turned toward him just a little as she passed.

He called his dad at the camp, his dad's voice through the radiophone distant and his words hard to understand. Asked him if maybe he could come up to the bush for a few weeks to work.

"What's going on?" his dad asked.

"Just need to get out of here."

"That girl dumped you?"

Curtis clicked his tongue against the back of his teeth, unable to answer.

"You can't just leave your job."

"I found out she was pregnant. Got rid of it without telling me."

There was nothing but static, and Curtis imagined his dad chewing on his thumb, trying to think of something to say.

"Be glad she made the right choice, then," he said, the last word distorted by crackle.

Curtis put down the phone and sat on the edge of his bed and rolled a joint. He licked the paper and smoothed it with his thumb, shaking. Too many folds at the seal, a shit job. His dad had a real knack for reminding him what a mistake he was.

And then one night in June his friends filled his apartment, drinking beer, passing joints, playing video games. He settled into the couch and the smoke and pinched a deep drag from the joint that came his way, and he looked around the room at the people who surrounded him, people he knew only because he had made the decision to come to this place. Good people, all gathered in the apartment he worked and paid for, in the warmth that came from the oil he paid for. He could have gone anywhere but chose to come here. He bought the jeans he was wearing, and the bike that hung in the hallway, and the food in the fridge.

They all hitched rides to a party that was hot and dark and pumping. Curtis swallowed two ecstasy pills walking up to the front door and pushed his way through to the back deck, where people talked over the noise, where it looked as if the mountain held up the sky. He recognized a few guys who worked the lift and broke into their conversation, waiting, his stomach fluttering, for the drug to rise in him. He checked his back pocket for the battered mint tin he carried. It held another pill and two well-rolled joints.

In the kitchen, someone yelled for shots, and someone else produced a ski with six full shot glasses cemented to it. Curtis stood in line with five others and they drank in unison, and he coughed the hard taste of tequila off the back of his tongue.

Down in a basement bedroom, he found his roommate, Pete, sitting on the floor with a few English girls they knew. Pete was halfway through one of his self-deprecating stories and they were laughing into their laps as if it were the first time they'd heard it. Curtis sat among them and his legs turned to velvet. He rubbed his thighs. One of the girls gripped his shoulder and massaged it. He smiled at her and closed his eyes and listened to the music in Pete's voice. When he grew restless, he climbed the soft-carpeted stairs and placed himself close in the corner of the main room to dance. A DJ stood behind a table, her hands hovering over two spinning records, and behind her lights projected onto the wall, morphing with the music. He danced with his eyes closed, sometimes pressing his palms on the two cool walls at his shoulders. This was exactly where he wanted to be. Smiles shining and bouncing off smiles, okay for lips to touch strange lips. It was a false love, but who the fuck cared? Euphoria came up in him like carbonation and he pushed harder against the walls and stopped dancing just so he could feel the oxygen rushing cleanly down his throat and into his lungs. He opened his eyes and fingered the tin in his back pocket and there was Pete, kissing someone. No, he wasn't kissing her at all, just talking into her ear. His hand was on her back, between her shoulder blades, and he stood still while she continued to dance. Curtis closed his eyes again and danced and imagined that Pete and the girl were kissing, rubbing, licking. In fact, the whole room was in on it. He convinced himself of this, but when he opened his eyes, Pete was gone. No one was kissing. The girl was still there. Her hair was long and brown and tied back neatly with an elastic, a cord of hair looped and plastered wetly to the nape of her neck.

He forgot about the other people in the room and danced for hours, sometimes under the weight of a friend holding him tightly, but mostly alone. Depending on which way the music flowed, Tonya would come into his head, and he pressed against the walls and cast her off. But then one track weaved into another and her voice was sewn up in its layers, repeating, *There was this thing, alive.* In those days after she told him, he was like—it was so clear to him now—he was like a heap of junk jammed in the back of her closet. He knew how these things went; he'd lost interest in other girls enough times. The flick of a switch to something a lot like revulsion.

He knew what was happening, but he stuck to her, like dirt. Because there was that time in the park one night when they'd held on to each other for what seemed like hours. Of course there were stars. Billions of the tricksy fuckers. And there was the open-faced moon shining on the mountains. It was bone cold but still they stood there wrapped together, no words. So he held on like scum, like mold. Eventually she told him he was too much. They'd broken it anyway and she couldn't give him what he needed.

He reached into his back pocket for his tin and swallowed the third pill, bitter on his tongue, and went looking for beer in the kitchen. Found one floating in ice water in the sink. The dancing girl Pete had been talking to was next to him and asked him for a sip of his beer. She had eyes like a husky dog, one frozen blue and the other brown, and wore a silky t-shirt, and a skirt, and white high-top sneakers. The fronts of her calves were bruised like a little kid's.

She passed his beer back to him. "It's too cold."

"How can beer be too cold?"

"It hurts my teeth."

The third pill brought him back up, but not to the place he'd been before. He went looking for his friends and found some, like night ships, in a bedroom fogged with smoke. He sat cross-legged on the floor and dropped his arms loosely in his lap and listened to the resonance of familiar voices, a wheezy laugh. He asked for the time and was told it was 2 a.m. Pete passed him a plastic bottle of water and he drank, his lips trembling against the rim, hardly connecting with it, the plastic crackling under the pads of his fingers. A hair was caught deep in his throat. He passed back the bottle.

"No, have some more."

"It's got hair in it."

"It hasn't, you fuckwit."

"I don't want it."

So then a mug half filled with something black was put in his hands. It tasted woody and too sweet and coated his teeth like powder. This wasn't the place he wanted to be anymore. He wandered from room to room, up to a closed door at the very top level of the house. On the other side of the door there was deep, slow-pulse music and unrecognizable faces that rotated toward him like moons. All along he had been looking for Tonya.

He left the party without telling anyone and walked home under gathering clouds. In his room, he emptied his backpack onto his bed, then folded his blanket into it, a woolly hat, gloves, and a raincoat. A bottle of water. His movements were whispered, fluid, the drug still pulsing gently against him from within, against the backs of his eyes, against his inner ear. He pulled his bike down off its hook on the wall and found the front tire flat, and reached for the pump that should have been stowed in a bracket on the frame. It wasn't there, so he went back to look where he'd emptied his bag onto his bed. He couldn't find the pump in Pete's room, or the hall closet, or anywhere else, so he sat on the couch and swayed to music in his head. Pictured the road rushing under his front tire, the lines of the road like the grooves of a record spinning under the needle. Fuck it: he needed to be on the move. If he couldn't ride his bike he would drive.

When he returned home that night, he moved through the house with actions that were articulate and careful, as if he were balancing a plate on his head. He checked to see if Pete was home and was relieved to find that he was not. He went into the bathroom, careful not to turn on the light, and pissed for a long time. He stood by the sink and drank a glass of water and dried the glass with a hand towel, and when he put the glass on the edge of the basin it clattered into the sink but didn't break. He left it there. He lay in bed with his shoes on and could feel the ecstasy in his blood, still. If he closed his eyes, they popped open as if attached to strings. He listened to the rain, relaxed his face, and realized only then that he had been grinding his teeth. By the time morning came, blue, bright, and torturous, he had not moved a muscle.

## 12

**It was** the last hunting trip Curtis had been asked to go on. It was just the three of them: Curtis, his sister, and his dad. He was seventeen at the time; she was twelve and twice the shot. They stayed at a cabin somewhere high in the mountains east of Mackenzie and the weather stayed cold the whole week. Cold enough that as they started out each morning the dry leaves on the ground were frost white and his fingers ached in his gloves. There were flurries of light snow that, in the shade, stuck to the ground. The cabin was nothing more than a log shack with a corrugated tin lean-to at the side for storing wood. On the peak above the door hung the bleached skull of a moose, antlers spread open like palms. Inside, a couple of hard bunks and a wood-burning stove, a table, a countertop for preparing food, and an aluminum sink with cold running water from a nearby creek.

His dad woke them up before dawn each morning and they drank sweet, milky coffee around the table, the cabin smelling of gas from the camp stove. Then they headed out on quad bikes, breaking frost over rough trails to a navy-blue lake on a high plateau between several mountain peaks. They held binoculars to their eyes, scanning the rocky cliffs and pale scree faces for billies. On the first day they saw a bunch of deer and scrabbling marmots and at least one fox, but no goats. Erin was disappointed and their dad was impossible to read as usual, but Curtis was relieved. He didn't like killing things. In his life he had shot a few pheasants and squirrels, which was no big deal, and one deer, which he'd fucked up. He hit it broadside and the poor bastard staggered off into the trees, squawking. His dad ran after it and took aim and put it down. Came back shaking his head. "Never take the shot until it's right," he said. "You should know that."

They didn't see any goats the second day, or the third, and Erin started to complain. She wanted to shoot something. His dad put his arm around her shoulders and gave her a shake.

"Half the fun is getting so cold and tired your bones hurt. You've got to earn your kill. You think the goats are going to advertise themselves?"

"No."

"Have a little patience."

"But I'm excited."

"Glad to hear it."

Curtis watched them, his sister's head on their dad's shoulder, hunters in arms. They walked together to the lake's edge and skipped stones. Curtis decided that if he had to, he would kill a goat.

It wasn't until the end of the week that they spotted goats on the mountain. There were four or five of them. A few does, a kid, and a billy. Erin saw them first and passed the binoculars to their dad for approval. He slapped her shoulder, told her she had eagle eyes. They tightened their packs over their shoulders and started to hike up the mountain. Only a few hundred meters up his dad found one of the trails that the goats had broken to the lake, so the going was relatively easy. Steep but clear. They climbed in dense trees for the first two hours and then came out onto scrub and rock, squat pines that grew only to their shoulders. Out of the trees, the wind blew cold and hard. Snow started to fall and then turned to rain. The trail followed rock face and cliff, at some points so narrow and close to the edge that his toes ached with the anticipation of falling. Here, he would have liked to trade the rifle that hung from his shoulder for a bag of weed and his bike. He fell behind the other two, then found them sitting under a rocky outcrop, eating sandwiches and drinking hot chocolate from a steaming thermos. It seemed to him that they stopped talking as soon as he arrived.

From the outcrop, they left the trail and headed diagonally up a steep slope, crashing through old silvered timber and wind-toughened thistle. His dad seemed to know exactly where he was going—how that was possible Curtis didn't know. They couldn't see shit, only the slopes ahead, or back across the valley toward the lake. Eventually they came around a bend in the land, and up above, on a rocky, bushy cliff face, were the goats. About three hundred meters up the cliff, one of the does stood eating, and fifty meters above her, the billy was sitting on a rock, possibly asleep. Massive. Big as a bear. Curtis had no idea they could get that big.

"Should we give Erin a pop at him?" his dad whispered, winking at Curtis.

"I guess." Of course the first shot would be hers.

Erin was bristling. She took off her bag and squinted up at the billy, hands on her hips. Curtis slid the rifle off his shoulder and handed it to his dad. He raised the scope to his eye and pointed the gun up the mountain and stood there not moving. He lowered the gun and looked at Erin.

"It's too steep to get a good angle. We'll traverse to higher ground." He handed her the rifle and she proudly slung it over her shoulder. "Be quiet as you go," he said, and tossed her bag to Curtis as he turned to follow her up the mountain. The throw was short, and the bag landed at Curtis's feet. He picked it up and attached it to his own, and then caught up to them as they climbed through crags and shrubs. The wind blew painfully. They stopped at a table of rock where the land leveled out, and again his dad took the rifle and scoped their position.

"This is good," he said, passing the rifle back to Erin. "Now where are you aiming for?"

"Just at the top of the shoulder, sort of behind it. The heart."

"Yep. You can't get him while he's bedded down like that. Wait for him to stand up and turn a quarter. We've got the unfair advantage and we owe it to him to kill him right. No distress or pain."

"What if I miss?"

"Don't think that way. Look." He pointed. "He's less than a hundred meters away. Imagine it in your head first, and believe it's going to happen the way you want it to. You're a hell of a shot."

"I could still miss."

"You won't. But if you do, then we haul ass up there and finish it." He nodded at Curtis.

Erin got down on her knees and held out her arms for the rifle. Their dad stood a little behind her, watched as she flipped off the safety, brought the gun up to her face. It looked bulky in her arms, almost funny, and Curtis wanted to laugh but didn't dare. And she held it with confidence; she held it steady. Curtis watched his dad watching Erin, Erin watching the goat. Nobody said anything. The wind blew against his neck, sweaty from the hike, and he shivered. When the billy finally stood, Erin rose up taller and lifted the rifle, secured it in her arms, and then settled into a solid squat. Curtis's dad watched her go through each step, nodding.

"Bring the scope to your eye," he whispered. "Don't lean into it."

She did this and pointed the barrel up the cliff, her other eye squeezed tight. Curtis stood back, looking from the goat to his sister and back to the goat.

The shot popped cleanly through the air, and almost at the same time a cloud of white dust burst from the rock under the goat's feet. The billy took off and so did the doe, and another doe came bounding from behind an outcrop, and before Erin had the safety back on, they were all gone.

"That sucked," she said. A crescent of blood was welling on the inside curve of her right brow.

Curtis pointed at her eye, a smile tripping across his face.

"What?" She touched the cut and then looked at the blood on her fingers.

"You scoped yourself," he said.

Two days later, their last day on the mountain, they still hadn't shot anything. They were on the same cliff, at a higher elevation, stalking the same billy. This time Curtis held the scope to his eye and watched the goat through it. The billy stood on a rock two hundred meters above Curtis's position, the bulk of his body turned stubbornly away.

Curtis would kill this animal. He would. Would cut its heart out and eat it, if that's what it took to belong. The billy stood motionless. Today the sky was blue and there was little wind, and they'd hiked with their shirtsleeves rolled up. The billy turned to the side and Curtis pictured the trajectory of the bullet and he squeezed the trigger, and for a moment after the rifle recoiled into his shoulder he heard nothing. There was a puff of fur and the billy fell onto his back and rolled from the rock, all four legs in the air. He teetered on the precipice of the next outcrop down and then dropped and landed on the shelf below, and fell again from that one and gained momentum as his limp body flopped mercilessly down the cliff, dropping farther and farther until it looked as though he was going to fall off the edge of the world. He seemed to come to rest at last but then rolled and fell again, the blood patch from the gunshot wound growing bigger across his fur as his beaten body tumbled. Curtis looked away.

"Great shot," their dad said, suddenly close and slapping him on the back. "Perfect shot."

"Lucky shot," said Erin.

"Come on," said their dad. He picked up the bags and the rifle. "Let's go get him. Did you pack your knife?"

Curtis shook his head. "I can't."

"You can't what?"

"Rip his skin off and cut him all up. I don't want to see it." Blank eyes like holes, tongue hanging out between worn yellow teeth.

His dad looked confused. "You've done this before."

"Didn't you see the way he fell?"

"He was already dead. You shot him right."

"I don't want to hack at him and rip his guts out. You guys go."

Now his dad was angry. "That's not the deal here, Curt. Kill the animal, quarter it in the field, carry the meat home, and eat it. You don't leave it on the side of the mountain to rot."

"I wouldn't want to take the pleasure away from you."

"We're going to make sausages," Erin said.

"Shut up," said Curtis. He sat down and folded his arms over his bag.

His dad stood over him. "You really going to just sit there?" he said. He waited for an answer, and when none came, he looked out across the valley, chewing on his top lip. "You don't start something like this unless you're prepared to finish it."

"I guess I wasn't thinking that far ahead."

"I guess you weren't."

**13**

**A fickle** wind off Takla Lake blew Tom's trailer most of the night, and in the early morning he climbed out of sleep on the contrail of a familiar dream: Erin, mother to her own kids. They follow her like ducklings and she waits for them to catch up with her, scrabbling one by one out of shallow green water. And when one of them turns its head, the smallest one at the back of the line, it is Erin, her duck feet webbed and pink and unstable. She slips back into the water and when she emerges she is nubile, a princess. Her period has started and he can't help her. He turns his face away because he knows she's bleeding and naked and shows the first small buds of new breasts, and she needs someone to teach her how to manage the blood. He wraps her in a towel and she molds perfectly in his arms. She is weightless, awkward, fragile as an egg. He holds her in the palm of his hand and she is the size of a mango, a plum, a peanut. Shrinking until she falls through his fingers to the floor.

He sat up wearily in his bunk and pulled on his t-shirt, and over that a fleece sweater. He slipped his feet into his jeans, pulled the cold, stiff denim up over his knees. If he had had this dream at home, he would have gone to her room now and listened at the door for the sounds of her sleeping.

Outside the day was bright, and the trill of herons blew across the water like wind through a train trestle. The previous night's fire smoked weakly from a pile of white ash. Beer bottles lay scattered like teeth around the fire pit, chip bags fluttered low to the ground. At his feet: an empty vodka bottle, half a sandwich, orange peels. Tom stood very still, taking stock of each piece of garbage. Leaving food out was a stupid thing to do; it was negligent. He swore, kicked at the ash, crushing the black embers that still pulsed weakly under its blanket. He picked up the sandwich and stuffed it in one of the chip bags, collected a bottle with each finger. He put all this in one of the secure, bearproof garbage bins at the back of the cook van, letting its heavy lid fall with a boom. He'd had a good time with these people the night before, but he should have said something when he turned in. People needed reminding of details that out in the world amounted to not a lot but here in the bush meant everything.

He wiped his hands on his jeans and stood silently, regarding the camp. A gray wool sweater, heavy and dark with dew, lay curled in the dirt. By the water, the planters' brightly colored tents dotted the trees at the edge of the clearing, like a handful of dropped candies. For extra protection from the rain they had suspended bright blue tarpaulins over their tents by tying them to the trees. The light wind lifted the tarpaulins quietly, in a rhythm not dissimilar to that of footsteps, or the deep breath of sleep. Because of their day off, most of them wouldn't wake for hours. But Tom had a long list of things he needed to do. Matt's crew van was already falling apart, and

Tom had to readjust the ground pipe that supplied the show-ers and fix the pressure. If he managed his day right, there would also be enough time to make the trip to the outpost for a supply of cooking oil and bog paper. He looked across the lake at the mountains, tempted by their peaks. Only two or three hours of good, hard climbing to get to the top.

There was movement in the mess tent, a dry shuffle of card-board. The flap was open. Maybe it was Nix, setting up for breakfast. But the door to the cook van was closed, the hatch battened down. "Someone in there?" he called.

Something brushed against the inside of the tent. Tom walked slowly to the open flap, his arms testing the way ahead as if he were making his way in the dark. If it was a cornered bear, he would have to go for his rifle. And wouldn't that, he thought, be a hell of a way for his planters to wake up. A cry—*Kak-kak! Kak-kak!*—hammered dully against the heavy canvas walls of the tent. A hawk.

Inside the tent, the light through the canvas a yellow haze, Tom moved slowly across the beaten grass. There was a deck of cards on one of the long wooden tables, candles wedged in wine bottles, a few abandoned coffee mugs. More food left out thoughtlessly—an apple core on the ground, a bag of salted nuts sliced open. The animal was injured. A light stroke of blood was feathered across one wall of the tent. A swish and a flap by a stack of boxes at the back. One box fell over and the bird flew up to the tent's apex and hovered for two flaps of wing, and then glided back down and rested on top of the boxes. It was a goshawk and, judg-ing by its size, a female. Blue gray along her back and the top of her wings, underbelly striped black and white. Her stark, white brow a warning over deep, sunset-orange eyes.

Her long tail feathers were bent at wrong angles, as if she had been in a fight.

Tom pulled out a chair and sat, looking up at the bird thoughtfully. The hawk regarded him with superiority, her chest heaving. Her sharp black talons clicked against the cardboard.

"What am I going to do with you, bird?"

He went to the tent flap and opened it wider, called for the bird to come, but it didn't. He was going to have to catch her, and he needed some kind of protection.

The door to the cook van was locked and Nix had the only key. Tom didn't know which tent was hers so he picked his way through the blue tarpaulins calling her name softly, tripping and cursing over tree roots and taut ropes. He was only a few meters into the trees when mosquitoes found him. First one, then like rain, countless, indivisible. In his eyes, his nose. Finally he stood in one place and called angrily, "Nix, which tent are you?"

Someone called out, "Fuck off." Sleeping bags shifted. A snore sputtered and then died midstroke.

A zipper zipped farther into the bush. Nix's voice croaked echoey through the trees. "Who is that?"

"I need you to open the van. It's Tom."

He waited for her by the van door, watching the open flap of the mess tent, hoping the hawk would find its own way out. Nix was wearing the clothes she had been wearing hours before, when he had turned her away at his trailer. Her eyes were sleep-swollen; her short hair was flattened to her head on one side, and he was, unexpectedly, embarrassed to see her.

"What the fuck, Tom? It's seven thirty in the morning. Day off?"

"I need towels and gloves. The gloves you use for the oven. Have you got stuff like that?"

She glared at him and put her key in the door. When she came back out she handed him quilted gloves and a handful of rags. "What's it for?" she asked. She stretched her arms up behind her head and yawned. Her black sweatshirt lifted to reveal a crescent of pale skin at the top of her jeans.

"There's a hawk in the mess tent. You want to help me get her out?"

"Won't it just find its own way out?"

"She's injured."

"So?"

It was quiet in the tent now, and he thought maybe she had gone until he heard a sucking sound and a whip of air. The bird flew from behind the boxes to a stack of chairs at the far corner, where she seemed to fight with herself. A downy white feather rose up and was carried by a current of air.

"What are you going to do?" Nix asked. She stood by the open flap. She pulled the hood of her sweatshirt over her head and hugged her arms stubbornly around her small frame.

"I need you to help me corner her."

"What kind of bird is it again?"

"A hawk. Big one too. Looks like about five pounds."

"Do they bite?"

"Yup."

"People?"

"She's a hunter. She preys on little guys like squirrels and rabbits. Other birds. I've heard wolverines too. If she takes a nip at you it'll hurt, but you'll live." He offered her back the gloves.

She came toward him, scowling, and put on the gloves. She

feebly kicked her leg at him, catching him on the rear. "I was having a good dream," she said. "You ruined it."

"Listen, just come forward with me, really slowly. When we get close, you go that way, make your body as big as you can. I'll try and grab her."

As they approached, the hawk seemed to transform herself into stone under the stack of chairs, her body pulsing. Her head was cocked down and at an angle away from them, reminiscent of Curtis when he was a kid, averting his eyes from the attention of some new adult, because, he seemed to believe, if he refused to acknowledge that the person was standing there, that person would no longer exist. Tom crouched low and motioned to Nix to move toward the left side of the stack, blocking the hawk's exit. Swiftly, the bird opened her body and flew out from under the chairs. A wing whomped past Tom's face and a talon scraped his right cheekbone. He pressed the thin wet cut. The bird flew erratically above their heads, screaming. She charged at Nix, stopping just above her head, before landing back on the boxes.

"Screw it, Tom. Stupid bird nearly took my eye out." She pulled her hood more tightly around her face.

"Not even close."

The hawk wasn't scared anymore. She puffed up her chest and *kak*ed.

"I don't want to do this, chief."

"Didn't your mother ever tell you that sometimes you have to do things you don't want to do?"

"Fuck off."

"All you need to do is stand there. Be present."

"You're going to have to think of something pretty special to make this up to me," she muttered. She pulled the ties of her hood so tightly that only her eyes and nose were exposed.

"Make yourself big," Tom said.

He moved closer to where the bird was perched on the boxes, watching him with one orange eye. When he was about three feet away, he stopped. Kept his hands at his sides. There was no point trying to catch the animal; he would wait until she charged him again. She was a beautiful bird, the eye flat and geometric and uncomplicated in its singular purpose. Her weatherproof wings were folded elegantly and efficiently at the side of her body. To be fully equipped for life in body alone, autonomous, to move through this world needing nothing—that was beautiful. He regarded her and she regarded him and when at last she swooped, Tom was ready. He gripped her around her chest and by the back of her head and neck. She was knotted with strength and pressed her body against the force of his hands. Tom's left grip was full of hot, angry heartbeat; his right hand contained the skull, hard and knobbled like a walnut. Up close, her black, hooked beak appeared fiercely, flawlessly sharp. She nearly fought free a couple of times before Tom made it through the tent flap. He knelt on the ground and, before letting go, imprinted the sensation of this feather and flesh, this pulsing, fighting, wild thing, in his memory. He let her go. At first she hobbled in a stunned kind of way, taking slow, ginger steps. Tom stayed hunched to the ground. She cocked her head and wiggled, shuddered as if in disgust, and then took off in a wide, muscle-flexing arc over the mess tent and the surrounding treetops, her true wingspan now evident in a striped, fluted spread. Tom watched her until she cleared the tall pines and disappeared back to where she belonged, and in the quiet he could hear his own heart drumming behind his ears, trying to break out.

"Okeydokey, David Suzuki. I'm going back to bed," Nix said. She had pulled back her hood and was rubbing her hair up off her forehead. She bit her lower lip and stared at him for a long time, and he knew, if he wanted to, he could go with her.

He thought about what that might be like, his mouth on that bit of skin between the bottom of her top and the waist-line of her jeans. Her fingers on the back of his neck. "Thanks for your help," he said, and watched her go.

He would deal with Matt's truck first. It was at least a three-, four-hour job. Walking back to his trailer for his tools, though, he found that the urgency of the day's work leaked away with every step. He looked again across the lake to the mountains. The light had moved and sharpened since he had woken up; the peaks shone starkly in the sun, closer. A few pieces of food and a bottle of water in his pack, a paddle across the lake. He could be back by four o'clock and still have enough daylight to do the truck. The shower pipe would have to wait. So would the trip to the outpost for toilet paper. They would have to ration their shit tickets. Served them right.

Matt's cedarwood canoe rested upside down at the end of the beach, beaded with dew. Rivulets of water sweat across the glossy surface when Tom pulled it up on its side. He flipped the canoe over his head and walked it down to the water, breathing the sappy smell of varnished cedar. A minuscule red spider oscillated on a single silk thread hanging from the bow thwart, just at Tom's eye level.

As he paddled away from the shore, the boat cleaved neatly through the water as if he were the first person ever to canoe here.

Nix was something else. She had given him a hard-on just by rubbing the hair from her face. But he wouldn't do that to Carolina. Even out here, where distance and the scarcity of hot water and electricity separated this life from that. Because if he did, he would bring it back to Carolina and she would be left with it on her skin, like oil. Even if she never knew it. He dipped the blade into the water silently, and on the recovery of each stroke, drops landed on his legs, soaking coolly into his jeans. White-blue morning sky and black water that smelled like rain, and this small cedar canoe nodding, nodding. The paddle ran smoothly along the gunnel, and he turned his thoughts to the *shuuk, shuuk* of the paddle shaft drawing against the canoe with each stroke, and the pull of the blade through deep water, and the silky, rhythmic lapping of the canoe. In the middle of the lake he stopped paddling and watched the black water breathing. The breeze, stronger here, pushed him northward. To the left of his bow, a trout broke the lake's surface with arched spine.

Tom reached the far shore and cruised the bow up onto a small, stony beach just big enough for the canoe. He pulled the canoe out of the water so that it was beached nearly to the stern, and dug his compass out of the top compartment of his pack to take a reading of where camp was across the lake in relation to where he now stood. When he made his descent, he would need to come down roughly at this spot; he didn't want to go scrambling up and down the shore looking for the canoe. He tied the painter with a bowline knot to a slender alder and hung the compass around his neck. Carolina had given it to him; it was a good, solid compass. Waterproof, smashproof. He tightened the straps on his pack so that the bag fit snugly against his body. The trees grew densely down the mountain and ended here like a wall; he pushed through a web of bushy young pines and stiff alder branches and clambered in tentatively, unsure whether or not this mountain would let him in today. The ascent began almost immediately and was so steep in some places that Tom was pulling himself upward by root and rock. The pace he set was fast, and though it hurt, and though he was tired, his breathing and the movement of his limbs arranged themselves into a solid, working rhythm that propelled him forward. This was the place.

The slope flattened and he followed the undulation to a lichen-covered boulder, where he stopped to rest. He took off his fleece, rolled it into a ball, and stuffed it into his pack. Mosquitoes bounced off him languidly—so many more now because he wasn't moving—and he puffed them away from his face, swished his hand above his head like the tail of a horse. Mosquitoes drove some people to tear at their own hair, run in circles swearing, taking it personally—but it was no use getting worked up about it. They were a fixture in all this and it was only blood they wanted, and it would always be this way. He watched one of them deftly work its probe under the skin of his forearm, its abdomen swelling a deep burgundy as it drank.

Fragments of thought lit up and then were gone, like fireflies: The Erin dream. Curtis telling him about this new girl. Beer bottles in the dirt. The last time he saw Carolina, disappointed, her face surrounded by sky. Nix stretching her arms above her head.

He ate half an apple and moved farther up the mountain. Sweat dampened his hair, salted his skin, and the effort of the climb bit chunks out of the things that were bothering him. The breeze off the lake blew softly through the pines, the fir, the gentle sound brushing, muffling everything. Far off, the hollow echo of the woodpecker's knock; in Tom's ear, his own breath and the constant hum of mosquito. There were signs of animals that kept well hidden: bear scat, fox prints, the *chit chit chit* of some tree-dwelling vermin. He concentrated on the terrain under his feet, anticipated the peak. He stopped and turned to see if there was a view of the lake, if he could gauge how far he had gone in—what was it, an hour? Two hours? The bush—mainly pine but dotted with mountain hemlock and spruce—was too dense to see anything other than the far-off glint of sunshine on water. He leaned against pitted stone and opened his water bottle, took a long swig, and screwed the cap back on. He snorted at mosquitoes, pincered a fat one, and rolled its sticky carcass into a ball, his own blood left on his fingers. The alpine couldn't be too far off now. The trees were sparse there and he would be able to see right across the water to camp. But the going was rough. His boots often got caught in the scrub. Branches and irksome thornbushes hooked his bootlaces and his jeans. He hadn't worked his body this hard in a long time and he welcomed the burning tug along the muscles of his arms and legs.

A vein of moisture—slimy rock and moss—cut across his path and he followed it until he came to water trickling over a deep stone groove. He followed the trickle until it widened to a brook running fast and white, the last of the spring runoff. He drank, splashing the ice-cold water over his neck and face.

This mountain water was like blood in the body, nourishing the body, flushing it out. This was something he would mention to Carolina. She might really dig that. Or not: she might think he was trying too hard.

Soon enough the trees began to thin and the ground became clear of low-lying plants and shrubs. The pitch leveled off and eventually Tom was scrambling across a plateau of dry, thin dirt and lichen and rock. Patches of purple and pink, yellow and white alpine flowers grew in hardy little clumps between the seams of silvery-green rock. Whitebark pine and larch trees clung to life here too, tenacious on the rocky slopes, with tough, withered roots bent like fingers gripping a ledge. He looked out across the lake and could see his camp, the cream-white mess tent.

From here the peak was less than an hour's climb. He drank some of the water from his bottle and stood facing the wind. His skin was soon dry and his wet t-shirt cold; he pulled his fleece back on and scrambled the rest of the way to the top.

The peak was a bald, rocky flat that sloped down to bowl toward the west side of the mountain. To the north the ridge dipped and flattened to form a carpeted valley with the next peak, and to the south it dropped dramatically into a series of steep draws. There were blackflies and noseeums, but other than that, there was only the wind. Because this was just the right kind of place to run into a grizzly—good roaming territory and few bloodsuckers—he whooped and whistled to announce his presence, avoid a surprise meeting. He sat down and relaxed his arms across his knees, threw back his head, and closed his eyes. He tried to think of nothing but the

wind, and of the air filling his lungs, and of the blood keeping him warm. He ached a little, felt a little bit old. The skin
on his knuckles and at the base of his fingernails had been
scraped back by rocks. His fingernails were full of earth. He
inspected the deep lines of his palms and the tanned, roughened, marked backs of his hands, and considered how he had
come to *this* place. Powered here under his own engine, with
his own fuel. The people he had allowed to enter him. And
his children. His children? Like letting his heart and his lungs
go walking off without him. Couldn't quit them, even if he
wanted to. And sometimes he wanted to. More than anything. He looked out across the lake to the camp and the old
mountains rolling away like a song beyond it. It's good to be
here, he thought.

His knees objected with cautious, wobbly jolts on the descent.
When clear spots opened up in the trees, giving sight to land-
marks across the water, he took compass readings and kept
himself generally on a course that would lead back to the canoe. The descent took an hour, and when the lake came into
view at level ground, he was not at the little beach where he'd
left the canoe. He edged through a tightly packed clump of
alders, ferns, and huckleberry onto a thin band of dark mud
at the water's edge. Leaning out, he looked to the north and
south but couldn't see the boat. He shrugged his bag off his
shoulders and hung it from a branch, and then stripped down
entirely and walked out until the water reached his knees. His
feet sank into mud; he thought briefly of leeches. He did a
shallow dive into the dark, lapping water, and the cold took
his breath away. A burn tingled across his collarbone, licked
down his arms and legs. When he surfaced he called out a

loud whoop that echoed in the forest. With his head up, he took several hard strokes into deeper water so he could get a wider view of the shore. He dove deeply and opened his eyes to a reddish murk, pulled hard breaststrokes, spun around, and surfaced again to face the shore. From here he could see that the little beach with the canoe was only a few hundred meters to the north. He coasted out deeper into the lake, taking mouthfuls of the mineral-rich water and spraying it out again. It tasted like pine, like iron, a little like blood. Relishing the silky freedom of being naked, he spun and did somersaults and shot down as deep as he could to where it was darker and colder and the pressure on his ears made them tick. He spun and spun and his stomach flopped so much that it brought a laugh from his belly to his lips.

That night, Roland and Matt and Sweet built a bonfire next to the lake and fed it until it raged, and all the planters gathered around and watched as the smoke billowed and blacked out the stars. Tom held a mug of black coffee and watched the flames from the steps of his trailer, and he watched Nix walk across the clearing toward him. Without a word, she sat next to him and passed him a plastic container full of berries she'd gathered from the side of the road. Soft, red-capped thimbleberries, blueberries, sweet strawberries no bigger than a thumbnail. Sweet threw strips of wax-coated cardboard from the seedling boxes into the fire, which would ignite with white flame, then send shreds of black drift into the air, landing like fallout. Tom thought about Nix's leg next to his, the bounce of firelight in her face.

And later on, while he hunched toward the mirror in his trailer, working a strawberry seed out of his back teeth with his tongue, someone knocked lightly at his door. He knew it was her. He opened the door and looked past her to the fire that by this time had died down, the silhouettes of a dozen bodies around it still. A banjo sounded, and faraway laughter. Nix put her hand on his chest and pushed him back, ducked into the trailer, and slid onto the long seat. She brought with her the smell of the fire, and drummed her fingers on the table, the tips pink from picking berries.

He leaned against the counter and crossed his arms over his chest.

"Look at this," she said, holding both wrists out to him, belly white and marked with burns. "Oven scars. It's that tiny hovel you make me work in."

"You should be more careful."

She looked around the small space, picked up a short spirit level from the table, and turned it in her hands. "What do you need this for out here?" She held the small green window of liquid up to her eye.

"I don't."

"So why do you have it?"

"It was in my toolbox."

She lined the spirit level against the wall. "Your trailer is uneven."

"There something you needed?" he asked.

"What is it with you, chief? This whole wolf thing you do."

He shook his head and laughed.

"You just...disappear, and then you show up, and then, poof, gone again. You're always alone."

"I'm hardly ever alone."

"But you'd like to be."

He shrugged, fiddled with the stub of a pencil in his pocket, a box of matches on the counter. He strung together some other words but his voice sounded as if it were coming out of someone else's mouth.

She awkwardly pushed herself up from the table, struggling to swing her knees out, and came around to where he was and kissed him. She was a good shot. With one hand she cupped his jaw; the other was on the back of his head. Physically, she was different from Carolina in every way. Where Carolina was soft, Nix was hard. Where Carolina's body swooped or gave, Nix's angled, pushed. He stopped thinking about Carolina and moved to the weight of Nix's small tits in his mouth, the strength in her arms, her legs, the mechanics of her ribs rolling under her skin, her clit like a thimbleberry. He thought about the heat coming off her, even after it was over and he was wondering how he was going to get her to leave.

# 14

**The old,** boxy diesel train, comprised of one small coach and two flatbeds loaded with seedling boxes, departed early in the morning from the Takla Landing outpost and chugged slowly up the lake's eastern shore. The train meandered past the northern tip of the lake and along the wide valley floor of the Driftwood River, heading north until the tracks wound their way westward past mountains whose names Tom didn't know, Tatlatui Provincial Park somewhere to the east, the bush so dense and untraveled that the open windows of the coach caught the odd tree branch, snapping the brittle ones off. The loudest sound was the rolling *cachungcachung* of the train's weight going over the ties, like the heartbeat of some sleeping bull moose.

A few days had passed since the night in the trailer with Nix, and Tom, Matt, and Matt's crew were cramped together in the coach; the planters were at the windows, staring into the heart of the bush and joking about losing their minds the deeper they went. Their destination was a logging camp in the seat of the mountains, where the only roads were the potholed dirt tracks that led from the small camp to the cutblocks, and the felled trees were lifted out by helicopter. They would be there for a week.

Dozing, Tom thought about Erin and the steam train. This was in the time after Elka left, when he still believed he might find her and bring her home; when, for the sake of his kids, he wanted so much to see her that he mistook strangers for his wife. Erin was two years old and the fair was in town. A kiddie train steamed and whistled round and round a track by the riverbank for fifty cents a go, and he and Erin sat in the caboose, his knees up to his chin. The wind was up, and as they were coming past the small wooden platform of the station for the second or third time, he watched a folding chair tumble past the hot dog stand, past the candy floss drum that spun rags of pink sugar into the wind. The chair came to rest at the feet of a woman who, for one glance, was Elka. Slim, with dark waist-length hair that blew across her face. She wore a red skirt that was blowing too, and as she bent over to right the chair, he turned in the small awkward seat and strained his neck to see her, but the little train continued its cycle and he was looking at the river. When they came around once more, the train stopped at the platform and Erin said, "Again." Tom passed two more quarters to the conductor and settled into his knees and didn't look for the woman in the red skirt because damned if he was going to be fooled by need.

Now the diesel train wound down, shuddered, and stopped. Tom and Matt woke up those who were sleeping. The planters climbed wearily off the train and threw their bags clear of the tracks. They spent the next two hours unloading the seedlings and covering the cache securely with tarps. The conductor popped the whistle and wished them good luck, and as the train grumbled away they shouldered their bags and humped the few hundred meters into Camp Minaret.

The logging camp, in a dusty, rocky clearing, was small and functional; five long boxcars coupled together in a row, elevated on concrete blocks. A mesh steel gangway ran the length of the boxcars, accessed by a set of stairs at each end, with another set midway. From the other side of the cars came the powerful hum of a large generator. No one came to greet them. Accustomed to waiting, the planters dropped their bags to the ground, sat against them, and smoked. Someone strummed a guitar. Three mud-splattered trucks pulled into camp and parked side by side. These were the loggers, back from a day of felling on the high slopes of the mountain. With heavy boots they climbed down from the cabs and the flatbeds and crossed the clearing to the boxcars, glancing at the planters without much interest. They clanged up the stairs to the gangway and headed to their bunks, the showers. Tom climbed the stairs after them and walked toward the front car, past yellow bunk doors, the shower and toilet block, the mess. He found the manager's office, a stuffy room off the back of the kitchen, with a small window that looked to the rear of camp and, beyond that, a gentle, snow-brushed peak. From here he could see the manager standing by the tree line, hands on his hips, peering into the bush.

Small and sinewy, the manager smoked hard on a roll-up and spit into the dirt as Tom approached him. He looked at Tom and then looked back into the trees.

"I thought," he said, squinting into the green, "that you guys were coming two days ago. Don't know why I expected things to go as planned, but there you go. I've got thirteen steaks that need to be eaten tonight before they turn. I hope your tree huggers eat meat."

"Most of them do and they'll be glad to eat the share of those who don't," said Tom.

The manager cocked his head and put up his palm for silence. He and Tom listened. The manager ran a ropey hand through his hair, through to the ducktail at the back—molded most likely from decades of wearing a cap. His blue eyes were smiling even though his mouth wasn't.

"What's going on?" asked Tom, his voice low.

"Gray water," the manager said. He gestured for Tom to follow him and they walked to the back of the mess car, where in the dirt was a large puddle, a skin of grease on its surface pocked with gobs of food and dish soap. The puddle was fed by a plastic pipe coming from the kitchen.

"Can't you cover it?" asked Tom. "Barrel it?"

The manager rubbed his stubbled chin. "We covered it with sheet metal, weighted it with breeze blocks, and she tore that off like it was paper. We could barrel it, but then where do we empty the barrel? Thing is, it hasn't really been a problem so we just let her eat as much as she wanted. Bear's been coming early in the morning and then again after dinner. The boys call her Old Mrs. They stand out there on the gangway after dinner and watch her through the couplings. Few days ago, though, one of the boys opens his door up first thing, up there at the far end of the bunks, and Old Mrs. nearly falls into his room. She must've climbed them steps looking for more food and got comfortable and fell asleep right there against the door. Made herself right at home. She took off pretty quick but then she came back and pulled the same stunt this morning. She skedaddled again but not before she hissed at him for a good long while."

"She's getting too comfortable."

"Fucken right she is. No one here's got a bear tag. They're telling me we're going to have to helicopter someone in."

"I've got one," said Tom. "Didn't apply for it but I got it in the lottery with my deer tag."

The manager smiled broadly. "Well isn't that tidy? You can shoot her for us tomorrow."

"What kind of hardware have you got?"

"Ruger M77 okay?"

"That's all you've got?"

"That's it."

The manager assigned their rooms and then they gathered in the mess car to eat. The loggers filled half the tables, talking quietly over steaks and boiled vegetables and coffee. By their elbows were stacks of white sliced bread on plates, dishes of butter. Powdery gray pepper in plastic shakers.

Word of the bear had gotten around, and when they finished eating, the planters went outside to watch for her, or they crowded the windows of the rec car, where there was a mini pool table and a shelf of old puzzles and board games. A television that received four stormy channels.

Tom's small box room was exactly like the one he'd stayed in when he logged. Fabricated white board walls, a desk and chair, a mirror. One very small window, a thin yellow curtain on a plastic rail. He took off his watch and put it on the shelf under the mirror, unrolled his sleeping bag, and laid it on the cot. He sat on the edge of the cot and stretched his neck and rubbed his hands up and down the back of it. From outside

came the vibrations of people walking up and down the gangway, the sound of heavy boots on the mesh. He shifted back
and leaned against the cold wall, closed his eyes to the room,
and saw again small details of Nix: scabbed blackfly bites on
her neck and the backs of her knees, the burns on the insides
of her wrists, the fine hair on her legs. He sat up and swung
his legs over the side of the cot, and held his head in his hands.
There was no real need for him to be here. He pinched the
bottom edge of the thin curtain and held it up, peered out the
window. A half-moon shone brilliantly out of a clear evening
sky, darkening blue.

Since it was too early to sleep, he left his small room and
went down the gangway. Matt was there with some of the
planters, watching the bear as she lapped at the grease in
the puddle. Her coat was light brown and mangy. She was
skinny, which explained her daring, her desperation for food.
She looked old. Aware of the people watching her, and completely uninterested, she tongued up gulps of the rank water,
swinging her great head and eyeing them occasionally down
her long, dripping snout.

None of this was her fault; he didn't want to kill her.

One of the planters frowned. "He looks depressed," he
said.

"It's a she," Tom said.

"Can't they just fly it somewhere?"

"She's no fool," he said. "She'd find her way back."

# 15

**Early in** the morning, when the camp was empty and only Tom, the two cooks, and the manager remained, Tom went to meet the manager in his office and get the Ruger and a box of .223s. Tom balanced the rifle in his palms and felt the weight of it. Held it up to his eye and pressed his cheek against the cold stock, pointed it toward the window, and looked through the sight. He laid the rifle on the manager's desk and went back to the window and scanned the tree line. He wasn't confident in the rifle, and the caliber was hardly enough to safely take down a deer. He turned back into the room and put one finger on the barrel. "This gun had any intervention?"

"Few years back I bedded the action, floated the barrel. It's no tack driver but it shoots good enough."

"Okay, then." He slid the bolt and checked the magazine and loaded three cartridges.

Tom sat on the hood of the manager's truck, eyeing the tree line, with the rifle resting across his knees. The manager stood with him, eager to see the job done. He wore a trucker's cap that may have been blue once and kept taking it off, smoothing his hair and putting the cap back on again. The air was dry and warm, the morning sky white. The faces of the two cooks appeared at their small boxcar window and it seemed that the whole world was waiting to hear the crack of this shot. The manager took out a packet of tobacco from his back pocket and put it on the hood of the truck, and proceeded to roll a cigarette. He offered the tobacco to Tom.

Nothing about this was fair. By all rights they were trespassing on her land, and it was their waste that drew her. There wasn't even a need to hide, or mask his scent. She was habituated; she would come. He would shoot her because it needed to be done, and this was the way of men working the bush and he believed in the virtue of that, but he felt uneasy. They'd been irresponsible, had wronged her, and they couldn't take it back.

The manager finished rolling his cigarette and looked once more to see if Tom was going to help himself, and then folded the packet and put it in his pocket. He spun his thumb on a plastic lighter three times before it took and he lit the cigarette in a cupped hand, and began to speak. "I was surveying, me and this guy Gerry, way up near Liard River? Close enough to Alaska you could of crossed the border without knowing it. Come across a bear like this one, about fifteen years back. He was a grizzly, but he was skinny and mean, just like Old Mrs. We come up on him one morning—he was on high ground, other side of a meadow—he sees us and takes off fast as a shot. Few hours later, we're in thick bush, at the bottom of a draw, flagging a line with tape. We notice this same bear following us—we seen him up the side of the draw. He's keeping his distance but you can be sure he's stalking us. Gerry throws a rock up toward him and he takes off again. Later we're heading back to our truck and we come up to this boulder, size of a small house, and Gerry goes around one side of it and I go around the other. It's real thick bush and I'm ripping my way through some pretty thorny shit and I realize, eh, it's going to be easier to climb on top of this mother than try and get around it. So I grab on and I'm kind of hugging the thing, trying to find some kind of purchase for my foot. And then I hear this high hell—I don't know what kind of animal it is, right? Something screeching. But then it calls my name, and I realize it's Gerry screaming, other side of the rock. I figure the best thing to do is carry on up and over and when I get to the top, I kind of scramble to the far edge and look over and there's Gerry, hugging this big old fir, doing some kind of hokey pokey around it. The grizzly's on the other side and they're feinting each other out, eh, either side of the tree. Gerry's face is covered in blood, so I know the bear's already got a good swipe on him. I don't know how the hell he got on the other side of that tree and to this day, he doesn't know either." He looked at Tom as if Tom might know how he did it.

"Self-preservation is a powerful thing."

"Damn right it is. So you can imagine. I'm lying there holding on to this boulder for dear life and I look around me— what can I find, you know? From my vantage point I can see the white flag tape we tied at the beginning of our line, so I know the truck, the fucken road, is only about a hundred meters away. I can smell the bear; I can hear the sonofabitch breathing. Gerry is screaming the air blue and the bear takes another swipe and this one lands on Gerry's shoulder, rips half of it away, some of his back too." He stopped talking and drew on the stub of his cigarette, then held it away from his face and studied it as if he were deciding whether or not there was any puff left in it. He took another sharp hoot and ground the thing into the dirt. "Thoughts come to you in times like this that you're not expecting. Okay, I was looking for some kind of a weapon, I was screaming my head off, but really I was thinking how easy it would be to climb down off that boulder and get to the truck. Maybe I can rev the engine and scare him off, and I know there's a toolbox in the back full of shit that can do a lot of damage to a bear, but really, these are just lies I'm telling myself. If I can just get to the truck, I don't have to watch while my friend is ripped to shreds. And I know my ass is safe."

"None of us know what we'll do in these situations."

The manager nodded. "By this time, bear's got Gerry's head in his jaw and he's trying to drag him away. But Gerry's legs are wrapped in the underbrush and the bear can't get him out. There's some good-sized rocks on top of this boulder so I get one and chuck it. Miss the bear by miles. Get another one, a good ten-pounder, and hurl it and this time it bounces off his shoulder. He drops Gerry and goes up on his hind legs and huffs at me. That's when I see how skinny and mangy he is. And I can see Gerry's eyes are open; he's alive but he's playing dead. While the bear's upright I get another rock, and another. The rock that sent him running got him right in the nose."

"What changed your mind?"

"Eh?"

"You said you thought about making a run for the truck."

The manager shrugged. "I guess my ass wouldn't of been worth much to me if I hadn't saved his first."

He set to rolling another cigarette and Tom turned his attention to the tree line, a hundred and fifty meters away.

The sun climbed higher and beat down on them where they waited. One of the cooks brought mugs of coffee and asked Tom if he thought Old Mrs. could sense what was going on, because, he said, she was late.

"If she doesn't come this morning, we'll try again tomorrow," he said.

A snap resonated from somewhere close within the tree line, then another. Tom slid off the truck's hood and clicked the safety off the rifle and squinted into the trees. The dark mounds of her shoulders and haunch moved visibly in a stand of white alders, slowly rolling. The bear came to the edge of the trees and stopped, sniffing down her speckled snout, and then stepped out onto the clearing. Tom raised the rifle and secured it against his shoulder and rested his cheek against the stock.

"Poor fucker," the manager said.

Tom lined her up in the crosshairs and visualized the shot, straight through the heart and lungs. He wasn't happy with the angle. He wasn't happy with the caliber. She took a few more steps toward the waste puddle and he lowered the rifle and walked around the side of the first boxcar and down the row to get a better line of fire. Old Mrs. stopped and sniffed the air, watching him. He continued moving down the boxcars until he was at the right angle and he got down on one knee and raised the rifle to his shoulder again. She was close enough that he could smell her. He sighted her again and nudged the trigger with the pad of his finger, and waited for her to take a step with her left front leg, and took the shot. A crack and its echo punched the empty morning. The manager whooped. Tom knew he'd missed before he even let go of the trigger. Instead of dropping, like she would have if he'd hit the right spot, she lunged to the left and rolled, and when she pulled herself up, he could see the wound in front of her back leg. She scrambled in the dust and stumbled back toward the tree line, where she disappeared, leaving a ripple of quivering branches.

Tom slung the rifle over his shoulder and ran across the clearing. Spots of red-black blood made puckered holes in the dust and glinted on the leaves where the bear had crashed into the bush. He stopped and listened to the echoing cracks and pops of the injured animal running through the underbrush until there was nothing.

The manager trotted up to him and stood at his side. "She'll bleed out."

"I think I got her in the gut. It could take hours, maybe even days, and it'll hurt like a bastard."

"You going to track her?"

"Shit." Tom rested his hands on his knees and peered into the inky green. Several meters in, a staff of sun broke through a gap in the high pine boughs. He put the safety on the rifle, secured it over his shoulder, and stepped into the bush, into a veil of mosquitoes.

"You want a radio?"

"She'll gain too much ground. I'll go now."

For three hours, he plowed deeper into the bush, following and losing and finding again the bear's trail. She was moving clumsily because of the shot, and though they were few, her marks were obvious: leaves black and wet with blood, the vulnerable white ends of broken branches, a fresh pile of scat. The land eventually sloped down and he came to a creek, and where the sun hit the water, the creek widened to a sandy pool. By the side of the pool, a blood-filled divot in the sand where the old girl must have rubbed her wound. Tom poked a stick in the blood and drew it out, and the blood veined into the pool and stopped, a cloud. He leaned the rifle against a pine and sat. Whatever had happened to the sow to get her to the point of scavenging the camp's dirty dishwater—an injury or habituation or just plain old age—he'd made it even worse. He had to do right by her, but if he went much farther into the bush, he risked getting lost. Great legs of sunlight shifted delicately through the trees, playing the shadows. He mistook a black mound of dirt from an uprooted tree for the bear and had the rifle off his shoulder before he realized his mistake. The fractured shadow of some large bird swept across the ground.

He picked small stones out of the sand and tossed them underhanded into the marbled pool, cupped water in his hands and wet the back of his neck. Blackflies burrowed behind his ears and he killed them there, and flicked away their carcasses. He didn't even need to be here, had come only because of Nix. Now that he'd had his hands on her once, he didn't know how to stop.

Bear could be anywhere, thirsty, tired, and in pain. And even if she didn't soon die from blood loss, or infection, she would be less able to feed herself than she had been, and an even worse death would come in weeks instead of days. A branch snapped behind him and he turned to see what animal it was but saw nothing. Mosquitoes droned in his ears. He stood and got hold of the rifle, secured it over his shoulder, and walked a few paces up the creek from where he'd seen the blood. He stopped, blew the mosquitoes from his face, and listened. Eventually he came to a wall of rock, meters high, slimy with moss, where the temperature seemed to drop by degrees. He turned and stood and listened to some kind of small bird on a high branch calling to its mate. Where the land rose slightly to his left, something jumped off a rock and darted beneath the underbrush. It could have been a marten or it could have been something else.

And here he was again, searching for someone who didn't want to be found. A wind came up from the stillness and the tops of the pines swayed eighty feet in the blue, rearranging the stretched patches of sunlight where he stood. Deep in the murk he saw the shadow of a bear stand and turn and roll away, but there was no disturbance in the underbrush and he knew it was only a shadow. His need for it to be her.

The evening meal had been cleared up by the time he found his way back to camp. He begged a sandwich and a piece of lemon cake from one of the cooks, who peeled carrots over the sink and asked Tom for details of the chase. He took his food to the rec car and ate in front of the television, ruts of static running through the picture, one eye on his food and the other on the news. Something about a hit-and-run death in another part of the province and the expectation of a record-breaking winter, and he wondered why they even tried to predict a thing like that in June.

# 16

It took eight days for the crew to finish the contract up in Minaret. They boarded the diesel train early in the morning, and while there was never any chance of Old Mrs. returning, Tom watched the trees for her rolling black back and, like before, was shown the shadow of the bear, but never the bear itself. He said good-bye and hoped against common sense that her death had come quickly.

They got back to Takla Lake just as the evening campfires were being lit, and he found Roland and Sweet eating chocolate cake and swigging rum from the bottle in the back of Sweet's truck. Licking their fingers, they told him that the new reefer had arrived, but the seedlings were still partially frozen and couldn't be planted.

There were three separate fires that night, and Tom went to each one and told the planters that after five weeks in the bush, they would head to town tomorrow for a few days off, give the seedlings a chance to thaw. He warned them not to get too drunk and antagonize the locals, and reminded them that when they weren't in the bush, it wasn't okay to drop their pants and piss wherever they liked. Now everyone was in a good mood. Tom sat at a table at the back of the mess tent and wrote out paychecks for whatever amount they wanted out of what they'd earned so far.

"A thousand, please, chief." This came from Luis, drinking from a can of Coke.

Tom put down his pen and looked at him. "A thousand? You sure?"

Luis gazed at him through his thick glasses.

"Most people just want a few hundred bucks to get drunk and do laundry."

Luis shrugged. "Don't sweat it, Mom."

Later, Nix sat at the table in Tom's trailer drinking a mug of coffee and whiskey. She asked him about Minaret and he told her about the bear. She asked him why he cared so much about a bear, and why he did stupid things like risk getting bitten for that hawk, and he said it was a hell of a thing to leave an animal to die. He didn't tell her that the problem wasn't the bear. The problem was that he was getting tired of fixing what wasn't his to fix.

"I think you went to the other camp to get away from me," she said. "To forget about what we did."

"You could be right."

"Did it work?"

"No."

Her hands were warm on his skin, warm from the mug she'd been holding. Warm on his face and his chest. The first kiss tasted like coffee but after that it was only her. He needed to be in control, but like before, she seemed to be writing the terms of the thing and he was maneuvered up and down the bunk, her grip on his ankles, his wrists, his hips. She used her teeth, bit his lip and he tasted blood. He tried to pinch her in retaliation but couldn't find enough fat to get a grip.

Afterward, he lay with his head on her belly, his arms draped loosely along her sides. With eyes half closed, he listened to the coffee and whiskey passing through her gut and was melted, buzzing, disturbed by his own lack of decency and willpower.

"When I was little," she said, "like three or four or whatever, my dad used to take showers just after I went to bed. I loved that. I loved hearing the sound of the water falling into the tub. I guess I could pretend it was raining, you know, so I felt all cozy in my bed. And sometimes, even better, he'd play the piano. You say tomato, I say *tomahto;* you say potato, I say *potahto*. I think he only knew a couple songs. We had this massive house with two living rooms and his piano was tucked away in this dinky little side bit off the bathroom. Not much bigger than a walk-in closet." She inhaled deeply. "My parents fought a lot."

Tom nestled his cheek deeper into her stomach.

"Now you go," she said, the words rumbling deeply through her body. She drew lines in his hair at the nape of his neck.

"Hm?"

"It's your turn."

"To do what?"

"Tell me a story."

He turned his face to the other side, eyes wide-open now. The carpet under the cupboards was curling up from the floor.

"This is what people do, Tom. They fuck each other and then talk about personal shit."

He moaned. "Really?"

"Tell me something from when you were a kid."

"Like what?"

"You haven't been a stick-in-the-mud all your life. You must have been fun once."

He pushed himself off of her and fell to the side, leaned back on the bunk. He reached for his underwear from the floor and pulled it on. "I don't know what you want me to tell you. Life was pretty normal for me as a kid. My mom is tough as hell, brought me up alone. Pretty much left me to it when I was growing up. What else. I always had a dog? Is that what you want to know?"

"What about your dad?"

"You want to know about Albert, eh?" He rubbed his hand flat across his chest. "Women always want to know about Albert. He was around a bit. Not enough to make it count, I guess." He looked at her sideways and she was turned to him, propped up on one elbow, waiting for more. "I've got a lot to thank him for, though. He taught me to hunt, how to recognize my ass from my elbow. He wasn't a bad guy. Just not the type to stay in one spot. I think he ended up in Saskatchewan or someplace."

"When did you last see him?"

Tom scratched the hairs at his jaw, chewed his thumb. "I was about fifteen." He rolled away from her, onto his side. Hoped she would want to sleep in her own tent.

After a few minutes of silence, she jabbed his back with her elbow. "By the way," she said, "first time we did this you told me it was never going to happen again."

He looked over his shoulder at her. "You complaining?"

"No. But does this mean I get more? I want more."

"Now?"

"Fuck, ya."

\*     \*     \*

First thing Tom did when he got into town was go to the grocery store and buy the fixings for pizza. Ingredients for the dough, ham and a can of pineapple chunks, peppers. He bought ice cream and chocolate syrup that was meant to harden as soon as it hit the cold. He took all this home and put it away, and checked that everything was secure in the house after it had been empty for five weeks. It was as he'd left it, the only thing out of place being the lack of dog.

He mixed the flour and salt and yeast for the dough and left it covered with a damp cloth to rise. When it was ready, he knocked it back and wrapped it tightly in cellophane and put it in the fridge. The local newspaper showed the movie listings and he sat at the kitchen table with the entertainment page folded open, phoned Erin at Samantha's, and went down the list with her. He didn't know any of the titles or the actors starring in them so he let Erin choose.

The movie was mindless and he fell asleep partway through and stayed that way until she elbowed him awake at the closing credits.

"I've got some food at the house," he said as they walked back to his truck. "I thought you could sleep at home tonight."

"I'm meeting friends."

"Now?" He looked at his watch. "It's almost nine."

"Congrats. You can tell the time."

"Varmint." He pushed her sideways, and they walked quietly to the corner. "Which friends?" he asked, crossing his arm in front of her as she stepped off the curb while a car passed.

"I wasn't going to get hit," she said. "Jesus."

"Who are you meeting?"

"Just people from school."

"I guess you guys go to bars these days, eh?"

They were at the truck now. She grabbed the tailgate with both hands and hopped up on the bed.

"What are you doing?"

"Let me ride in the back."

"No."

"Why."

"Because I said so."

Something close to a roar rattled at the back of her throat as she pulled the passenger door shut and crossed her arms. "You're faking it," she said, looking out the window.

"I'm faking what?" He pulled out into the road.

"When you do something like not let me ride in the back of the truck. You're pretending to give a shit."

They were in the middle of an intersection, waiting to turn left, and he watched car after car go by until the opposite traffic stopped and he had enough time to make the turn. He thought about what he could say and decided that, given the way she misunderstood just about everything he did, there was pretty much nothing in the world that could answer a thing like that.

At home, he rolled out the pizza dough and covered it with the toppings he'd picked for her. He ate at the kitchen table, finishing the pizza and leaving the ice cream untouched in the freezer, and went to bed.

A ringing phone pulled him up through the haze of sleep and left him searching for a sense of where he was. The red numbers next to his head told him 3 a.m. He let the phone ring until the machine clicked on but whoever it was hung up and rang again. He walked down the dark hall with the heels of his hands pressed to his eyes.

"Who is this?" He leaned his shoulder against the wall.

"It's Nix."

"It's three in the morning."

"Sweet's got us all in a bit of trouble."

She explained, her voice slow and thick, that a bunch of people had gotten into a fight in the bar and Sweet threw a beer bottle onto the dance floor, and it hit a girl. A few of them had been taken to the police station and things got a bit rowdy and now the others were in the drunk tank for the night and she needed a ride home.

"Can't you get a taxi?"

"You really want me to get a taxi?"

She was slumped in a metal chair with one heel tucked on the seat and her other leg stretched out arrogantly in front of the police reception desk. Tom addressed the man behind the desk first.

"You've got some of my employees in the tank. Anybody hurt?"

Nix rose from her chair and hung from Tom's shoulder. "I told you he was coming," she said.

The officer looked at Tom. "I gather you're the chief?"

Tom rubbed his hand up and down his face, tried to shrug Nix's weight from his arm, but she held on tight. "Do you know what happened?"

The man watched Nix, amused, and then looked at Tom. "I can't tell you what happened exactly, but my colleagues tell me one of your guys thought it would be smart to throw a glass bottle onto a dance floor. You can imagine all hell broke loose, so we're keeping the young men overnight. Let them cool off."

"He didn't think it would be smart," said Nix. "That's a gross insinuation."

"You can take her home now, please."

The low, pale light in the eastern sky filled Tom's rearview mirror as Nix slept in the truck on the way back to the planters' hotel. When he turned off the engine, she sat forward and leaned her head against the dash, then slowly turned her face to him and smiled sadly. "Is it that early I can hear the birds?" she said.

"I'll walk you in."

She sat up and rubbed her face and looked out the window, frowned. "Here? Can't I come home with you?"

"I've got my girl at home."

"I'll be quiet."

"Nix, how bad was it tonight? What happened to the girl he hit?"

She yawned and stretched and leaned her head against the window, spoke with her eyes closed. "I think she cut her foot and her redneck Prince George boyfriends went apeshit. Those cops were only pissed off because Sweet embarrassed them. You can't throw someone in the drunk tank for being more intelligent than you."

"You think he's so intelligent?"

"I think he's a reprobate. You're pretty smart, though."

"Hate to break it to you, but I'm one of those Prince George rednecks."

"Your neck is beautiful."

"I'll walk you in now."

"No. I'm coming home with you."

He got out and went around to her side and opened the

door. He held out his hand and she ignored it, turned her back to him, and curled into a tight ball. Her body shook as if she were crying, but what he heard was a low, stuttering giggle. He reached across and gripped her shoulder and tried to turn her around, but she resisted, clung to the upholstery and curled into a tighter ball.

Tom stepped back and crossed his arms over his chest and waited. "You're embarrassing yourself," he said.

She stopped shaking, slowly unfurled, like some kind of dawn flower, and looked at him as if he were a stranger. Keeping her eyes on his face, she stepped down from the truck and quietly clicked the door shut and then turned toward the hotel entrance.

"I'll see you up to your room," he said, catching her arm.

But she shrugged her shoulder against him and pulled away, and yanked on the door. It was locked.

"Try your key," Tom said.

Swaying, she dug into her back pocket and took out a hotel key. She missed the lock with her first attempt and then guided the key slowly in with both hands. White-knuckled, she tried, and failed, to turn it.

"Here. Let me," Tom said, and reached for the key.

She pulled it out of the lock and held it up like a tiny sword. "You try and open that door for me, I will make you choke on this fucking thing."

He backed away and watched her until she unlocked the door. She pushed through it without looking back, and he was left for the second time that night wondering what he should have said.

\* \* \*

In the morning a woman sat behind the desk at the police station and told Tom that his people had been released without charge. He drove to the hotel and, in the first room he looked, found LJ and Beautiful T sitting opposite each other on one of the beds, playing cards. On the other bed were arms and legs and twisted blanket.

LJ's hair was dripping and she wore a towel, and the air in the room was humid and blue with cigarette smoke.

"Good night?" he asked.

LJ turned her head to him slowly. "A typical bash."

"You know where Sweet and those guys are?"

"In jail, aren't they?"

"They were released this morning."

She shrugged and turned back to her cards.

The hallway was cold and dark and smelled like stale beer and pot. The sticky carpet sucked at his boots. Tom looked through the doorways that were left open, but the silence, the lack of Sweet's monologue, could only mean that they weren't back yet.

He waited in the lobby, sitting on the edge of a single brown sofa by the window. Across from him, a cigarette vending machine glowed pale yellow. The street was mainly empty. When Sweet eventually came through the doors, he walked past Tom without seeing him and bent in front of the cigarette machine. He stood up, rummaged for coins in his back pocket, and swayed a little as he counted the money in his palm before slotting it into the machine. He pressed a button but no pack of cigarettes dropped, so he nudged the machine with his boot, hit the side of it with a flat hand, and stood as if he were considering something. He collected the hair at his neck in his fist, strangling the curls.

"Hey, Sweet."

"What?" He didn't turn.

"Hey."

Sweet looked over his shoulder at Tom, snickered. "Chief. You're like a little tree elf hiding over there." He gave the machine another kick and strode over and stood by the couch. His hair had fallen over his eyes again and he flipped it back. "Fucker took my money." His t-shirt was stretched at the collar and torn and spotted with brown blood, as if it had dripped from his nose. The knuckles on both of his hands were raw, bloody, and swollen.

"What happened last night?"

"We've just been discussing everything over breakfast, going over it with a...ah, shit." He snapped his fingers by his temple; his face tightened, then relaxed. "With a fine-tooth comb. Yes! A fine-tooth comb. We've just been going over it and I've come to, what with the frivolity and the ganja and the beer. And the tequila. I mean I'm not a violent person by nature, but at some point in a man's life, things have got to get physical, right? There's bound to be damage to his psyche if the brute is never released from its cage."

Tom relaxed into the couch, crossed his arms loosely between his legs, and looked up at him.

Sweet shifted his arms, as if he didn't know where to rest them, and settled on hooking his thumbs in his front pockets.

"Why throw the bottle?"

"Can you think of a better way to start a fight in this shit-hole town?"

Tom looked out the window at an empty intersection, a red traffic light.

"Frankly, I'm confused as to why you're here, boss—you've got nothing else you could be doing today?" His lisp was more pronounced, a wind blowing off the edges of his words. "You don't own me on my days off—not here. You've been hitting heavy on me all season but what happened last night has got nothing to do with you. Just can't help yourself from swooping in. Mr. fucken Fix It."

Tom stood up and Sweet smiled, grinned. "I'm just fucking with you, chief. Look at that face you've got on, that grim old face. It's okay. Why don't you go upstairs and let Nix take it all away?" He slapped a big hand on Tom's shoulder. "I'll even hold the elevator for you."

One of the other planters came into the lobby and took a half step toward them, then looked at their faces and stopped, mumbled something, and left.

"Your hand hurt?" Tom asked him.

"Eh?"

"It looks pretty bad."

Sweet took his hand away from Tom's shoulder and held it up, extended his swollen fingers, then made a limp fist. "That's just from the fight."

"Your knuckles didn't get torn up like that in any fight."

"Course they did."

"Nah. You've been punching a wall."

Sweet smirked, chucked a low laugh.

"Isn't that right?"

Sweet shook his head and went to the elevator, pushed the button hard with his thumb, over and over.

"Because whatever it is you want, you can't get it. And you know it."

The elevator doors opened slowly and Sweet put a hand on

each to force them wider. He stood inside, his head down, and the doors closed.

In the parking lot, Tom walked up the side of his truck and kicked the front tire. The planter who had passed him in the lobby called out from the other side of the street and Tom waved with a straight arm, without turning his head. He got in and turned on the ignition and looked at himself in the side-view mirror, bit his lower lip. That thing about letting go the brute, in spite of all the rest of it—he couldn't deny that part of him agreed.

# 17

**On his** last day in town, Tom wanted to see Carolina, leaving it until the end because he wasn't sure he should do it. One look at his face and she would call him out. When she kissed him, she would taste what he had done.

He called her in the morning and she asked him to meet her at the university library. Before leaving home he stood under a hot shower and scrubbed a layer of skin from his body, shaved, clipped his nails.

He hadn't been to a library since he was a kid, yet the hush of the place was familiar. Like in the bush, the silence at first seemed total, but once his ears adjusted he heard soft feet climbing stairs, leaves of paper, the characteristic call of the photocopier. On the wood-paneled, two-story wall of the open foyer hung a great fabric Haida print, a bear-faced moon in a purple sky, reflected in the sea.

Carolina had told him to go up to the second floor and straight to the back, behind the math and sciences stacks, where she would be camped in a cubicle by the window. He found her with her head down, asleep. He pulled a chair up beside her and sat, and watched her for a moment before he put his fingers on her back, softly drawing them up and down.

She sat up and wiped her mouth. "Oh fuck. I drooled all over this." She pulled her shirtsleeve down over her hand and blotted the piece of paper in front of her. "Why do libraries have to be such somnolent places?" She frowned. "I've ruined this girl's work."

"She might take it as a compliment," he whispered.

"That I fell asleep?"

"No, the drool. It was that good."

She scanned the area around the cubicle and then put her hands on his neck and drew him close, and kissed him, kissed his nose, the corner of his jawbone, under his ear. She pressed her cheek against his. "I'm sorry I don't have more time."

"This is good," he whispered. His hands shook. "This is enough."

"It's not. Not nearly."

"I get to see you in your natural habitat."

She wore her hair in two messy braids behind her ears. Glasses doubled the size of her eyes.

He pointed to her face. "Have I seen you in those before?"

"What? My glasses?" Her hands rose to them as if she'd forgotten they were there. "I wear them for reading. You've seen them plenty."

He took them from her and put them on his own face and his vision swam. "I never noticed."

"Well. You should pay better attention."

"I like them," he said.

She rubbed her eyes and stretched, pulled a sweater from the back of her chair, and put it on. "If I'd known you were going to be in town..." she said.

"I know. I messed up. I had all this stuff to do." His eyes

ached and he took off the glasses, and gently tucked the arms back over her ears, settled the frame onto the bridge of her nose with the tip of his finger.

"I swear," she held his face with both hands, "if thou come not forth I will love thee no more."

He held her knees, leaned toward her, not caring anymore if she could smell or sense the other thing on him because he badly wanted her close.

"Sappho," she whispered.

"Hmm?"

Someone moved quickly past their cubicle, looked in, and moved on. A coughing fit erupted a few seats over. She stared at him with her eyes in glass and he remembered he had seen this before, in a tent somewhere, while she read, entombed in her sleeping bag in the morning. If he told her about Nix right now, she would understand. She'd be hurt, she might even hate him for it, but he'd be able to make her understand. And he could tell her about his plans to build her a desk under the window in Smithers, because up until then he hadn't been sure if he should. Instead, he asked her if she wanted to meet him at the lake when he next had days off.

"We'll have more time," he said. A fluorescent bulb in the ceiling stuttered.

She looked away from him and out the window to the campus field as if she were searching for someone. "It'll depend," she said.

"On what?"

"What do you mean on what? On my life."

"I'll give you plenty of notice."

"No you won't."

"I will."

\*    \*    \*

He ate lunch at his mother's house. Sat at her kitchen table and watched her spread butter and mayonnaise on bread and felt like a boy again, home only for as long as it took to pound back a sandwich, with burrs clinging to his shoelaces and scraped knuckles sticky with tree sap and blood.

"You remember Diane," Samantha said, setting a plate in front of him. "Sissy's friend who got her realtor's license."

"She's got the lazy eye, right?"

"You should let her handle your place." She put a pot of coffee and another plate of sandwiches on the table and called Erin into the kitchen.

"I'm still not sure I'm going to sell it."

"You can't afford to keep two places."

"If I sell the business I can."

Erin came in and sat down. She wore a pair of shorts over a bathing suit.

"You going to put a t-shirt on?" Tom asked.

"She's only going to the river," said Samantha. "They float down the current on inner tubes."

"We used to do that," said Tom. "But there was always a shed-load of beer. There going to be beer?"

Erin shrugged. "Probably."

"I think it's crazy, owning two places," Samantha said. She took the top piece of bread off her sandwich and shook pepper generously over the ham.

"If I can, I will. Erin and Curt need somewhere in town."

"You're really going to move to the middle of nowhere?" Erin asked him. "Am I supposed to live alone?" She reached for her glass of water. The angles of her shoulders, her collarbone under the delicate blue straps of her bathing suit, her frame—each part of her still as perfect as when she was small.

"It's not the middle of nowhere and I haven't figured it all out yet," he said. "You still need to decide about university— where you want to go."

"I'm not deciding today."

"Applications need to be in by September," Samantha said, more to her food than to Tom and Erin, as if this were a thing she had promised not to say anymore.

"What if you choose Vancouver?" he said. "Or Toronto? Jesus and hell, we won't recognize her when she comes back. What if she chooses Toronto?" He went for her hair and she ducked out of his reach.

"Maybe I will," she said.

He wondered what that would be like, if she did end up at a school in Toronto, or even as close as Vancouver. He'd stopped trying to find in Erin that erratic behavior that Elka used to display. Winter walks at four in the morning, baths in the dark. A cupboard full of bags of rice and nothing else. He trusted now that it wasn't going to come. But still, the thought of Erin moving to the city dropped something hard and hollow in his chest that he hadn't been expecting.

On his way out of town, driving past the cul-de-sac that Sean lived on, Tom slowed to a stop when he saw a brown Suburban that looked a hell of a lot like Curtis's. He parked and crossed the street and looked at the license plate. It was Curt's, all right, but Tom still looked through the windows and took confirmation from the dent in the tailgate. He stood on the sidewalk with his thumbs hooked in his belt and looked up and down the street. Sean lived in a basement apartment; Tom had been inside once but couldn't place the house. He looked down driveways, searching for a battered shed that he remembered, concrete steps leading down to a side door.

He found the right house and went up the drive and suddenly felt hesitant and stopped. It was the same law that had always stopped him years before, when his kids were young, from driving by their school playground at recess. There was a balance between what a father should be part of and what he should not, and when it came to his kids, he respected this above just about everything else. Whatever the reason Curtis was in town and not staying at home, it was none of Tom's business.

He turned to go but the door opened and Sean came out and climbed the steps with a garbage bag knocking against his knees.

"Hey there," said Tom.

Sean stopped and cocked his head at him. "Oh. Hey."

"I was driving by and saw Curt's truck. Is he here?"

"Yes. Ya, he's here." He carried the bag to a can in front of the shed and dropped it in. He came back down the drive and stopped at the top of the stairs, and shifted his eyes, red, the lids slightly puffed, from Tom's shoulder to his face. "You want to come in?"

"You sure?"

Inside, it was dark; the small, cubbied windows close to the ceiling let in little light. Curtis was sunk into the couch like a button, a beer resting in the crook of his legs. The smell of weed was strong and the flicker of the television harsh.

With slow, underwater movements, Curtis turned his face to Tom and sat up. He squinted at him. "How'd you—?"

"Saw your truck outside. I'm just heading back up to the bush. Had a few days off. I wish I'd known you were here."

Curtis's eyelids hung thickly, low over his eyes that darted like minnows. The table in front of the couch was messy with empty bottles, rolling papers, drifts of weed.

"You got a cold drink?" Tom asked Sean. "A Coke or something?" He sat in an armchair next to the couch with Curtis watching him, his mouth curled in a half smile.

"It's fucken weird that you're here," Curtis said, his voice croaky. He bent over the table and slid a rolling paper out of its envelope, swept the loose weed into a pile with the cupped edge of his hand.

Tom laid his hand on Curtis's arm, could feel the boy trembling. He tried to move Curtis's hand from the table but the boy resisted and continued rolling. He shouldn't be here, shouldn't be seeing this—whatever it was. Curt was right: it was weird.

Sean handed Tom a glass of water. Curtis sat back into the couch, evidently abandoning the joint. He seemed deflated. Tom sipped his water, tepid, and looked around the room, at a pile of clothes in the corner, a pair of skis leaning against the wall, pizza boxes stacked by the front door. "You guys are hunkered down here like a couple of bandits or something. Curtis, did you lose your job? Something like that?"

Curtis shook his head.

"Is it that girl? You still upset about her?"

Curtis stared at the television, his smile the stroke of a pencil, partially rubbed out. A repetitive drip-plonk sound came from the tiny kitchen, a room not much bigger than a closet, opposite where they sat.

"Have you got a tool kit?" Tom asked Sean, pushing himself out of the chair by the armrests.

"Out in my truck."

"Go get it for me."

Curtis shifted, glanced at Tom, and then looked toward the television. A man in a yellow shirt on a putting green against a low, gray sky. The arms of his t-shirt ruffled against a strong wind; the spectators stood with umbrellas.

In the kitchen, the sink was full of cloudy water, its skin broken into concentric rings by the leak. Tom knelt in front of the sink on cold tiles, opened the cupboard. He moved a black plastic bucket out of the way of the drainpipe. In the bucket, a full bottle of window cleaner and an unopened can of Comet. A bottle of bleach and yellow dish gloves still in the wrapper, and a blue cloth dried and molded into a twisted fist. The kit was probably an offering from Sean's parents when he moved in.

Sean came in and placed a heavy green box carefully on the floor next to Tom and left. The television volume gradually rose with the low and steady voice of the golf commentator, the hollow *thwop* of metal launching a plastic ball, polite clapping like rain.

Tom emptied the bucket and maneuvered it under the drain. The couplings on either side of the J trap were rusted into place, and with gritted teeth, he loosened the first one with a pair of channel pliers. In the box was a new can of lubricant spray, which he used on the second coupling. He put a little extra grip to the pliers and soon the coupling loosened, pulling away from the drainpipe like a scab. He removed the trap, and the water from the sink gushed into the bucket. He searched the floor behind him for the dish gloves.

Curtis shuffled into the kitchen and sat on the floor, his back against the fridge. He drew up his knees and draped his arms over them, and looked at Tom.

Wearing one of the gloves, Tom dug his fingers into the J trap. If Curtis had anything he needed to say, he would say it when he was ready. Tom excavated from the trap a coagulated mass of spongy pasta and bread crust and fat, like a lump of brain matter. After dropping this into the bucket, he tightened the trap back into place. He turned the spigot under the sink, shutting off the main water supply, then stood up and turned on the tap to let the last of the water drain.

Curtis put his head between his knees and rocked back and forth. Tom searched through the tool kit for a Phillips head, finding five in various sizes.

"A guy with a tool kit like this should be able to unclog a drain and fix a tap," he said. "Eh, Curt? Shit. He's got everything in here." Tom was careful not to look directly at him, to give him space to raise his head and speak. Tom leaned through the doorway and waved to Sean, dappled in television light. "You think you've got any replacement washers?"

"Huh?"

"There's no reason for me to go any further just now if you haven't got a new one."

"For what?"

"This is you, Dad, how I see you when I close my eyes," Curtis began, his voice muffled. He raised his head and rubbed his temples. "You've always got some tool in your hand, bolts in your pockets, fixing shit. It's like you go around looking for things that are broken." Curtis looked directly at him and smiled. "You remember when Erin fell through the ice?"

"Of course I remember."

"That didn't faze you at all. You had the same look on your face that day as you have right now. Nothing touches you."

"I'm sorry if it seems that way to you."

Curtis closed and opened his eyes slowly, snickered.

"What is it?"

Curtis licked his lips; his tongue smacked dryly. "The energy in here is much better now that you've got your head into some mechanical snag."

"Nothing here to do with mechanics. This is straight-up plumbing. Doesn't get much simpler either. I can't believe you guys just left this."

"Whatever."

"Sean," Tom called. "How about it?"

Sean poked his head into the kitchen. "You need a washer?"

"Yes."

Sean blinked and looked hard down at the floor, frowning, squinting, his lips hung loosely open. He spoke in a voice that sounded as if he were trying to recall a dream. "I can see a bag of them, in my head." He brought his hand to his hat and pulled at the visor. "I can see the bag so clearly. Where the fuck is it? It's somewhere." He turned from the doorway and walked away, mumbling.

"You guys need to get out of this slack house, go for a walk," Tom said, shaking his head. He selected the right Phillips head, a pair of grips, and pliers. He laid them out on the gold-flecked counter next to the sink. He unscrewed the head of the tap to get at the copper valve underneath. "Pass me that cloth."

It looked as though Curtis had fallen asleep. But then he leaned over, picked up the cloth, and passed it up.

Tom wrapped the cloth around the tap's spout and clamped over it with the grips. He tightened the pliers around the valve head and began to wrench it loose.

"I think I killed someone."

The valve head was stuck fast. It wouldn't budge.

"Dad."

He squeezed harder with both hands, put his whole weight behind the pliers.

"Dad."

He let go, lay the pliers gently in the sink. He turned and leaned against the counter and looked down at his son, still on the floor. "What do you mean?" He sat down and faced Curtis. "You must be the first guy in history to care this much about an abortion. You're young; enjoy it."

Curtis looked at him, his face pinched and confused. He shook his head. "No."

Tom studied the boy's face. The older he got, the more he looked like his mother. When Curtis was born, Elka couldn't hold him straightaway. The labor had been difficult, lasted close to two days. In the end, they cut her with a tool that looked like garden shears and used forceps, like a set of salad tongs, yanking the kid unceremoniously into the world by his skull. They took ages stitching her up, and so the mewling pink thing (are they meant to be this small? he asked) was put into his arms. A matronly voice at his shoulder advised him to unbutton his shirt. "They want to be against your skin," the voice said. In a world incomprehensible, he did as he was told, pressed the warm, wet creature, its sticky skin like putty, to his chest. He was struck by the swampiness of the thing; a mugginess and odor rose from the baby that was utterly un-expected. The baby opened its mouth in a sort of grimace, and he was surprised to see that it had no teeth. Its motions were slow and fluid, as if it didn't realize it had left the womb, and it pushed the backs of its hands to the side of its face and slowly wagged its wrinkled fingers. As if, already, this was a game of make-believe, and here was a squid. The crevices in its skin were filled with a white paste; there was a dollop of it swirled with blood on the top of its head. The fingers were long, abnormally long, he thought (until Erin was born, and he learned it was just a matter of proportion). The tips under the nails were a deep burgundy. There was nothing else in the world to compare this to—it was something you couldn't prepare for. At the beginning, even holding him in that irretrievable moment, Tom didn't want him.

"It was an accident, Dad. There was no one there, and then there just...was."

"These things happen, Curt. It was her decision."

Curtis looked up at him, a weight tugging at the corners of his mouth.

Tom chewed the tough skin at the side of his thumbnail, tasting the lube oil. "I'm not going to get into some sort of thing with you here, not in the state you're in. You're not even making any sense. You need to get back home and to your job and forget about this girl." He stood and took the pliers out of the sink, a solid, cold weight in his hand. He rewrapped the cloth around the spout and took hold of it again with the grips, and took another shot at the valve with the pliers. He kept pressure on it until a growl rose from his throat and the valve popped. He exhaled.

Curtis was slumped on the floor as though he was under a weight he didn't believe he could lift. It was her, all over again, sitting on the floor against the bed that night of the bathtub. It wasn't right, not fair on Curtis that this was all he was left with from the woman who had given him life. Because she had been more than this shadow. It occurred to him for the first time that Curtis might be sick. That all the time he'd been watching his daughter, Elka's illness had been creeping up on his son.

"What the fuck do I do, Dad?"

"There's nothing you can do. She already went ahead and did it. Think about what you do have control over, and concentrate on that—you can't let this bring you down to a place where you can't get up again."

Curtis regarded him as if there was some obvious joke being told and he'd missed the punch line. It was a look he was used to getting from Erin. So, both of his kids thought he was a jackass. He could tell Curtis now what it had been like, when Elka pissed on that little stick in a locked bathroom and came out crying. How suddenly the thing they had together went from rolling around in the backseat of his truck (then whispering, entangled, until the sun came up) to looking for an apartment he could afford and driving all over town collecting secondhand chairs and dishes and whatnot to furnish the place. But right now, Curt wasn't in the mood to listen. Tom went at the valve again, dug out the washer head, like a miniature tire, and inspected it. The rubber was too hard to bend and crumbled around the edges.

"Sean, you located those washers yet?" he called.

Sean came in and pressed a plastic bag into Tom's outstretched palm, and sat next to Curtis on the floor. Tom dug through the bag for a new washer of the right size, found one, and slid it into the bottom of the valve. He fit the valve back into the body of the tap, then tightened it with pliers.

"Thanks for doing this," said Sean.

"No sweat," said Tom. He fixed the handle into place and drove the screw tightly into the top, turning it until it wouldn't turn anymore.

In the weeks after Curtis was born, Tom often dreamt of survival, like some sort of ancestral echo, like hearing a wolf call. Climb the mountain, follow valley, pebbled riverbed, and game trail until you reach the place where a person didn't have to think of anything else, didn't have to speak a word, only had to look after himself. Where he could take back what he'd lost the day his son was born—no, the day he met Elka, this girl with a forest of long brown hair, bony, frantic fingers, and a tiny glass gem piercing her nose. At seventeen, she had left her island home and was working at the pizzeria near his high school.

"Where are you from?" he asked two weeks after he'd first noticed her. It was his last day of school and he was a week away from starting full-time at the mill.

"Aguanish," she said. She was living at the YMCA.

"Why'd you come all the way up here?"

"Because it's nothing like Aguanish."

Later in the day, he picked her up from the pizzeria and took her fishing. He packed the back of his mom's car with blankets, a bag of chips, peanut butter cookies, and a stolen bottle of rum. He asked her how long she was going to stay in town and she told him she'd stay until she wanted to leave. He told her he was working to save money for a truck with enough room for his bike, his hunting rifle, a canoe, and his tent. They talked by the river until the northern lights domed the sky, shifting purple and white like liquid running down glass. It was the first time she'd seen them, and she rolled herself into the blanket and lay back in the grass, and pulled him down beside her. She reached behind her head and unfastened a clip from her hair and pressed it into his hand. It was digging into her head, she said—"Hold it for me or I'll forget it." On the clip was a small Haida salmon, carved from wood.

He admired her courage to leave home with nothing, and survive pretty much hand to mouth. All she'd brought from home was a small bag of clothes and some tapes and a portable tape player, which didn't play. He tried to fix it for her but couldn't. She was already pregnant by the time he learned that it wasn't courage but fear and depression that drove her to leave—that she wasn't on a journey; she was just running.

And only a year after meeting her, when his new baby cried in the night, Tom dreamt of shrugging that life from his shoulders like a wet coat and taking off with his rifle, some paraffin oil, and a good knife. Because he hadn't learned yet—the thing in the bathtub hadn't happened yet—that it would be his job, and a worthy job, to take care of this child for as long as he needed it. He hadn't learned yet that the mountain could wait.

# 18

**The four-day** break had been enough time for the seedlings to thaw, and the planters rolled back into camp with clean socks, new rolls of duct tape, batteries, chocolate. The season wasn't new anymore, and some kind of rhythm fell into place over the next several days in camp. Sweet, it seemed, had been cowed enough by what had happened in town to keep his mouth closed and work. The frosty mornings were finished, and now came hot, dry days of blue sky and little wind. Tom spent his time walking the blocks and dividing maps and taking the fuel bins to be filled at the outpost. He spent the evenings repairing the vehicles, battered by ditched roads that were either rutted with mud or clogged with dust. If there was time, he swam, and before bed he sat quietly at the fires and listened to the conversation and the music. There was word of an eagle nesting somewhere up the Old Driftwood road, west of the river. Both Roland and Sweet had seen it, and if Sweet could be believed, it had followed his truck a few klicks up the road. Tom drove out there at sunrise to see if he could spot it, but the bird stayed hidden.

Early one morning, while Tom drove to Roland's new block, the checker's voice came over the radio, asking him to meet her at the three-hundred-kilometer mark on the Sitlika road. When he got there, half an hour later, she was waiting in her truck. He parked across the road and went to her window.

"I hope this isn't too much out of your way," she said. She was without hat today and wore her pale hair in a braid that hugged her skull from the top of her head to her neck. She fiddled with her side-view mirror, adjusting it by the smallest fractions. The engine was off but she kept one hand on the wheel. "I was on my way to one of Daryl's blocks and I didn't know where you were going to be today."

"What do you need?"

She looked up at the sky through her windshield, squinting. "Weatherman says it's only going to keep getting hotter and drier. We'd like you to move to fire hours."

"In June? You're not going to see any fires up here now."

"It hasn't rained for two weeks and there's none expected."

He stared at her.

"You guys were lucky last time, but your planters smoke like truckers. I've seen them dropping their butts all over the place." She cupped her hand to her mouth and flared her fingers and, with eyes wide, made a little explosion noise.

"We don't know how that fire started."

"Regardless. We don't want the seedlings to be handled in the middle of the day when it's baking. Your planters carry too many in their bags as it is. Don't want them drying out." She started her engine. "We'll need you off the blocks by ten. That makes it a, what, 2 a.m. start?"

"I'll talk it over with my foremen and we'll decide what time to start."

"But you'll want to get full shifts in."

"I'll talk to my foremen."

Tom arrived back in camp as the crews were returning. He'd told his foremen to wrap it up early so the planters could sleep before their first predawn shift. Some people lounged by the lake, its surface dead calm and milky, but most hid in their tents. Tom took up his maps and sat in the mess tent, studied what was left to cover on the blocks farthest from camp. This move to fire hours was an act of distrust, and it was a message. He had thought the brush fire was long forgotten, but now this, and with the checker hanging around more than he'd ever seen before. If he didn't leave things on more than perfect terms with Nielson, his outfit would be worth half of what he had hoped to get.

Matt's canoe rested on its side on the beach, half in the lake, a few inches of cloudy water pooled in the hull. Tom flipped it over to drain it and then launched it with both hands on the gunnels at the stern. He paddled a few strokes and turned the canoe south, the shore on his left. The pulse of the water was almost imperceptible. Beyond camp the bush was thick and came right to the water, broken every now and then by small, pebbly beaches and sandbars. Twenty minutes of steady paddling brought him to an inlet where the water was glass. He lay the paddle at his feet and let out the broken chunk of cinder block that Matt used as an anchor, took off his shirt, and made a pillow of it at the stern. He lay back and crossed his arms over his face and settled his back into the flat bottom of the hull. The sun pressed his body down into the boat, which moved only with his breathing. Or it could have been the motion of the water; it was hard to tell. Birdsong wove with a buzz and creak that echoed over the water from the woods.

Curtis had asked him if he could come up and work, and Tom should have told him yes. Or should've taken him that day from Sean's, kept him close. No reason not to have just hauled him up from where he sat, utterly beaten, on the kitchen floor.

Tom shifted his weight, his back hot and sticking to the varnished cedar of the canoe, tried to close his mind, if only for a while. He looked up to the cloudless sky, at the blue that could somehow be flat as paper and unfathomable at the same time. Some small bird flew so quickly past his line of vision, he wasn't even sure it had been there. Maybe he should have said more to the boy, opened him up like some piece of machinery and taken the wires out. Switched a cable from one power source to another, eliminated all the possibilities until he found the fault, and maybe then he would have figured him out. But he had done the thing that came most naturally to him—played down whatever it was Curtis was upset about because that's how he, Tom, would have wanted to be treated. Sometimes it was hard to remember that other people didn't go by the rules you set for yourself.

He gave up on the idea of solitude for now and rose from the bottom of the boat, hoisted the wet anchor rope, and took up the paddle.

As he came around the last bend in the shoreline before camp, he saw the checker standing alone by the water, one arm crossed over her body and the other elbow resting on it; she was smoking a cigarette. Even from the water Tom could see impatience in the way she was standing, in the stiff way she bent her arm to bring the cigarette to her lips. It was almost six o'clock. The shadows fell long across the clearing and no one was around. Music drifted anonymously from somewhere in the surrounding bush, but other than that the only sound was the gentle suck of water on the stony shore, the buzz of a horsefly, his paddle. He brought the canoe right to the shore and let the bow drift up onto the sand before he hopped out. He pulled the boat out of the water completely and bent to get his shirt, pulled it over his head. The checker came over to him, her mouth screwed tightly.

"You take off like this often?" she said.

He watched her, waited for her to continue.

She looked at her watch. "I was hoping to be lounging in a cool bath by now."

"Did I miss something? Did we agree to meet up later?"

"I told you I was checking a whole bunch of blocks today. I thought you'd assume we were meeting."

"A whole bunch, eh? How'd we do?"

"Not so good."

He turned the canoe over, resting it on its gunnels, and lay the paddle next to it.

"I'll show you."

He followed her to her truck, which was parked at an angle just at the camp entrance, blocking it. She shook a cigarette out of a crushed pack from her back pocket and offered one to him, stopped walking to dig a lighter out of her front pocket, and then cupped her hand over the cigarette to light it. He waited a few steps ahead, tempted to remind her about what she'd said, the thing about his planters smoking like truckers. She exhaled and continued walking, her boots kicking dust.

"Those blocks down the Sitlika and Driftwood—those gnarly ones. Those were the first ones you planted in May. Is that correct?"

"Yep. Most of those have been checked, though. A few were done while I was out at Minaret, but my foremen do solid checks."

At the truck, Tom leaned with his elbows on the hood while the checker opened the door and stretched inside, retrieving a pile of dusty maps from the passenger seat. She nudged him out of the way and opened one of the maps flat on the hood.

"I'm afraid you've been misled. The whole place is a disaster. I found whole acres of J roots." She jabbed at blocked-off sections of the map with her finger, nail painted orange and lines of dirt in the knuckles. "Microsites ignored, the whole back section of a draw left unplanted. Why weren't you on this?" She slapped a mosquito dead against her neck.

"I told you. My foremen do their own checks. That's their job."

"Are you seriously passing the buck?" She wiped her forehead with the heel of her hand, drawing a pale smudge of dirt across it.

He leaned over the hood and looked at the places she had indicated, and spread the map smooth with his palms. "My foremen run their crews better when they're left to it."

"Oh really?"

"People don't learn anything if you're always on their backs."

"How profound."

"It's not. It's simple."

"Well. Your little system has failed you because this is beyond the pale. Frankly, I've never seen anything this bad."

"If it's what you say it is, then yeah, it's bad. I won't deny that. But it can be fixed."

She studied him, working her lips back and forth, and then gestured for him to follow her to the back of the truck, which was covered by a blue tarp. She lifted it gingerly, as if she were rolling back a shroud. Piled in the back of the flatbed were dozens of seedling bundles, still wrapped in cellophane. They were mangled, bent, dried out, black with the soil that would have covered them in whatever deep hole they'd been stashed. Tom rubbed his fingers over his mouth, down the sweat of his neck to his collarbone.

"This is straight-up theft," she said. "Some asshole got paid to plant these trees, not chuck them in a hole." She waved her hand around her ears, warding off mosquitoes.

"Exactly which block did you find these on?" His mouth was dry.

She went back to the map, pointed to a section along the Driftwood. It was one of Sweet's blocks. Without his own maps Tom couldn't be sure, but it looked as though all the problems had occurred on Sweet's land.

"We don't want to get ahead of ourselves here," she said, "but the company may see this as reason enough to end the contract now. They'd be within their rights to boot you out of this camp and transfer what remains of the trees and the land to another outfit."

He walked away from the truck and stood in the road, his back to her, then turned and gave her a long look. "This is my second season with you guys. Haven't set a foot wrong till now."

She raised her eyebrows and folded her map precisely, smoothing down the creases. "Not entirely accurate."

He kicked the dirt, slapped the dust off his thighs.

"Of course it's not up to me," she said. "I'm only giving

you the worst case. But you know what these guys are like. Loads of competition for this contract. They've got crews lined up who've bid lower than you." She stepped up into her truck and closed the door heavily, rested her elbow on the window frame.

Tom gestured toward the back of the truck with a cocked thumb. "Any of those salvageable?"

"Doubt it. Have a look."

She stayed in the truck while he inspected the bundles. Most were completely dried out, but a few looked as though they might make it if they were planted right away. He stacked them carefully by the side of the road and approached her window.

"So you'll start the replant tonight, then," she said. "All those bits I showed you. Every tree needs to be dug up and every one of those plugs needs to be straightened." She looked out her front window and turned on the ignition. "You will start tonight, right?"

He nodded.

The truck lurched forward in a half turn, then stopped, reversed. She backed up too far into the ditch and her wheels spun in the loose dirt. He went around to the back of the truck and pushed until she popped out, then watched as the truck bounced over a deep puddle bed that was caked and dry.

# 19

**One frozen** blue eye, one brown. Like a husky. The picture they showed on the news was a close-up, her head cocked to the side, laughing as if her mouth were full of food, or as if she were about to say something. The police urged the driver to come forward and the reporter spoke about her life. She was nineteen and had younger brothers, she rode horses, she was home for the summer. In a front-lawn interview, wind lifting white hair off a broad forehead, an uncle reported that her parents were destroyed.

"Did you know her?" said Sean, in the dark, eating macaroni and cheese out of the pot with a wooden spoon.

In the blue light of the television, Curtis shook his head, but what he could see was this: Days before, in a bright kitchen full of people, a girl stood in front of him with one blue eye, one brown. She had those bruises on her legs, like a little kid. He gave her a sip of his beer and then he forgot all about her.

And after countless empty hours on the couch, numbed by the marijuana coursing through him, Curtis started to notice the damp of the earth creeping through Sean's basement walls. And though he tried, he couldn't smoke it away. Then somehow, from out of a dream, his dad had punched his way onto the scene. He came and fixed a dripping tap and then he was gone. In the fog of the kitchen, Curtis had told him that he killed a girl, but this was for nothing. When his dad walked out the door, the absence of the tap dripping into greasy water was the loudest and emptiest sound in the world.

He left the apartment early in the morning, after Sean went to the mill, pulled into his dad's driveway, and left the engine idling. He thought again about Tom at the barbecue, grilling chicken. That had been before, when all he could think about was Tonya. He stared at the dark front windows of the house and started in on something he'd been doing a lot since the accident: rolling the *ifs* in his palm like dice. If he'd left the party minutes earlier. If he'd taken a different route home. If his tin had been in his pocket. If, when he met her in the kitchen, they'd kept talking, and maybe she liked him a little, and maybe he walked her home.

He didn't have the key to his dad's house, could picture it in the bowl of loose change he kept on his dresser in Whistler. He went around the back of the garage and lifted the bald tire up onto its edge, but the key that had always been there was not. Only a flattened ring of damp yellow grass and a scurry of hard-shelled potato bugs. He tried the back door and the kitchen window, then lowered himself into one of the basement wells, but those windows were locked too. He looked around the backyard for something he could use, but typically, there was nothing, nothing loose or out of place. Other than the old tire and a rusted swing set under the cedar, the backyard was trimmed and organized, no hockey stick or shovel or abandoned tool in sight. He lowered himself into the basement well again and put his boot to the window until it broke, and glass rained into the darkness.

\*   \*   \*

The first dream came that night, while he slept in his old bedroom. There was clear water and she was down deep in it, frog-kicking up to the surface. On the palm of his hand, a deep, perfectly shaped bite, the crescents of each tooth mark welling with thick, dark blood. He opened his eyes and couldn't at first make out where he was, was confused by the bar of streetlight shining through the gap in the curtains. But there was his dresser against the wall, just a bulky piece of furniture he'd never considered before. The top left-hand drawer always stuck. The bottom drawer was missing one of its polished wooden knobs. The mirror was black. The dresser began to tilt. Its shadow climbed the wall as it fell forward and the mirror on its hinge stayed erect. A creak of pained wood, the drip of water. He was unable to move and she was under the bed, scratching softly at the wood panels, the opaque, waterlogged nails having peeled off her fingers long before.

The second night, he dreamt that his mouth was full of eggshells. He sucked and spit out the tiny fragments, tongued the powdery shards from between his teeth, and cleared the back of his throat, only for his mouth to fill again.

He woke at some unknowable hour to blue-glass light in the room and stared at the ceiling, thinking for the hundredth time about the road. On television they could always identify a car by the skid marks made by its wheels. He couldn't remember seeing any in the road, but then he hadn't been paying much attention—he couldn't even remember driving home that night. Now he rolled over and thought that maybe he should wash his truck again. He'd looked, so closely, his nose to the bumper, the hood, the lights. But they had those infrared beams or whatever that could detect even the most minuscule traces of blood. He rolled over again, kicked one jigging leg out from under the blanket. There must have been marks on the road; he had seen them, like shadows. He could smell the burning rubber.

Panic was like a band around his chest, so he wrapped himself in his blanket and went out to the backyard, curled his toes in the cold, wet grass. He dropped his blanket and stood naked, feeling the cool air mostly on his dick, where he wasn't used to it. Long, blue-bodied, reptilian skin in the cruel dawn light. Cruel because each day stretched endlessly ahead of him like the long road, the curve up ahead that he couldn't get beyond.

The spring when he was twelve, he went to Black Pond, in the woods out near Sean's place, with a bunch of older boys to collect tadpoles. It had been raining, and his shoes slipped in mud and wet leaves. At one point he fell and landed on his palms in a rosette of thistles. The pain seared up to his elbows but he managed to keep pace with the others and hold on to his bucket too. When they got to the pond it started drizzling again, the mist collecting into silver beads in their hair. One of the boys lit up a joint and passed it on, and by the time it got to Curtis it was tea-colored, sticky, and soggy. The earthy smoke gripped the back of his throat and he coughed to his knees, thinking the coughing would never end.

He stood alone in the wet bulrushes by the edge of the pond and looked across its rain-cratered surface to the overhanging tree where, the winter before, a craggy hole had opened up in the ice and taken his sister. He'd been scared; he thought she was going to die. It took his dad ages to get her out of the water, and he got angry when she didn't do what he said. And he told Curtis to shut up, as if he was pissed at both of them, as if the crack in the ice was their fault.

When Curtis stood there with his bucket, the edge of the pond was thick with furry clouds of unhatched frog spawn and wriggling tadpoles, heads heavy, budded with legs, as slick and black as drops of oil. He dipped his bucket into the water and then watched them butt their heads against the plastic. He would take them home and feed them lettuce. One of the boys said that's what they liked to eat. The tadpoles thrashed their tails and swam zigzags across the bucket, like shrapnel.

When he climbed back up the bank, he could hear the other boys laughing and shouting somewhere off in the woods. Their buckets were all there, standing in the tall grass. Full of tadpoles. He followed the sound of their laughter and found them crowded around the hollowed-out trunk of a long-dead cedar, its south-facing side covered in thick moss. Five frogs, one for each boy, had been impaled against the trunk with nails. One of them was already dead but the other four still struggled, webbed feet softly hooking the air, trying to swim away. They had taken bets to see whose frog would survive the longest. The boy whose frog was already dead had lost interest and stood to the side, pelting a tree with stones. Curtis watched the other boys and pumped his arms as they did, and made a careful O shape with his mouth and hooted. There was very little blood, but what did drip from the wounds was clumped and snotty. Two more frogs died and then another, leaving one alive, twitching slightly, throat bulging for air, thin white membranes floating over its eyes.

The boy who won took a quarter from each of them and

said he was going to spend every penny of his winnings on red shoelace licorice. Before leaving, Curtis waited for the others to go first and then emptied his bucket of tadpoles back into the pond.

Now, shivering in the early morning cold, he inspected himself. One tidy cut at the base of his wrist, from the basement window. Rib bones rising up to the surface of his pale skin. Neck pain with no known origin when he turned his head from side to side.

In the kitchen, with the blanket tied loosely around his waist, he held the two pantry cupboard doors open with his arms stretched wide. His dad kept the place well stocked with cans of beans and meaty soup, tomatoes, peaches, potatoes that tasted only of the brine they floated in. Curtis wasn't exactly hungry but opened some beef and vegetable soup and, leaning against the counter, ate it cold from the can with a teaspoon. Then he went on to peaches, letting the syrup limp down his chin. It was the first food he'd eaten in days. The phone rang until the answering machine clicked on. A friendly voice he didn't recognize echoed down the hallway. Curtis could feel his heart beating in the soles of his feet, where they pressed flat on the linoleum. It was a detective something or other, and could you please give me a call as soon as you get this, it's concerning the whereabouts of your son, Curtis.

Curtis went down the hallway to the small desk where his dad kept the phone and the answering machine, now pulsing a red light. He listened to the message again and tore the phone jack out of the wall socket, flipped up the machine's lid, and removed the miniature cassette from its bed. He went into the bathroom and pulled the silky brown tape from the cassette until it snapped and the end curled up, wilted. He dropped the handful of ribbon into the toilet and watched it snake out of sight with the flushing water.

He got dressed and went down to the basement, where his dad's collection of tents, sleeping bags, thermal mattresses, and flashlights was stored neatly on the shelves by the stairs. Cooking pots and small gas stoves that looked like moon-landing pods. All maintained, looked after, loved. He packed a sleeping bag and tent, a pot, a stove, and a mattress roll. He found some plywood stacked neatly under the stairs and boarded up the broken window.

His first thought was to go west into Alberta, hike up Mount Robson to the alpine meadow and pitch his tent by the side of Berg Lake, where the water was the milky blue of a throat lozenge. He could stay there until the snow came. Nothing but mountain pine and waterfalls, marmots and the odd trekker. He could sit out on the shale beach and listen to the thunder of ice calving off the berg, chunks the size of cars, of houses, splashing blue into the lake in apparent, slow-motion silence until the sound of their fall caught up to the light.

He made it down Highway 16 and was getting close to the Alberta exit. Here the steep and striated granite of the Rocky Mountains prodded the faultless blue sky. Topped with summer snow, brush cut with pine. Any other time, these mountains made him feel as though he could fly, but now they folded in on him. The curves and undulations in the road seemed to breathe; they played tricks. He had no confidence that the asphalt continued beyond the bends, and he half ex-pected to either plummet into the valley or plow head-on into the mountain. With fingers gripped white on the steering wheel, he drove past the turn to Robson and continued south-west on Highway 5 toward flatter land, where, if something was coming, he might have time to react.

That night, he pitched his tent next to a cattle fence in the dusty hills around Kamloops—hills so old and worn they were like great piles of dirty bedsheets. He lay awake most of the night, sweating. Could smell the sour yeast of pulp mill, which made him think of home. The next day, while drinking black coffee in a greasy spoon in Merritt, it occurred to him to go to the island where his mother had grown up. It was small, and hard to get to. The islands down there were over-grown with dense rain forest and sometimes banked with fog. It would be like crawling into a hole, or under a blanket. And maybe his grandmother was still there. He knew from his fa-ther that she was twice as crazy as she was mean, and Curtis hoped that this was true.

**20**

**Curtis couldn't** leave his Suburban in the ferry terminal because if the police really were looking for him, they would find it there and know he was on the island. So he left the truck on a residential street in Nanaimo and walked north the short distance to Nanoose.

The small passenger ferry moved slowly and heavily through the water. Curtis sat on the upper deck with his bag between his knees, his head down. The sun beat on his neck and the voices of the people around him swung with the wind, so he only caught patches of what was said: something about film for the camera and a bike pump and what had been packed for lunch. Seagulls screamed in retreating loops and somebody was laughing and a girl asked what time the last ferry left the island because she didn't want to be trapped for the night. As if any of this mattered. They had everything they needed for a picnic but they couldn't see the dirty membrane that divided their world and his. They didn't even know how free they were. The sea air settled like a shell on his skin.

When the ferry docked at Owl Bay, Curtis disembarked last. He had a feeling that little had changed since his mother lived on the island, and could picture her waiting by the passenger ramp for the outbound sailing. A few buildings clung to a horseshoe of rocky land sloping up from the bay: a bed-and-breakfast, cabins, a coffee shop. Walking up the one road that led from the terminal, he came to a small kiosk selling cold drinks, sandwiches, and island maps. He bought a bottle of water and looked at a map. It showed a campsite at the opposite end of the island on the southeastern tip, a few kilometers' walk from the road.

A farmers' market occupied a clearing at the top of the slope. The food was all handpicked, home-cooked: carrots with dirt still clinging to hairy tendrils, bulbs of garlic like hard little fists, hand-butchered meat, cakes of strange combinations like ginger and zucchini. Curtis chose food randomly—a bag of apples and plums, bread, ground coffee, and cured ham—not because he was hungry but as an act of duty to a body that, each day, seemed more remote, like something he was tethered to.

He caught a lift in the back of a muddy flatbed, huddled next to a pallet of cedar shingles, and got out at the campsite trailhead. Tightening the waist strap on his pack, he started at a hard pace, estimating that he had to cover three or four kilometers. The Douglas fir, tall and spongy with moss, grew thickly, and under this the rocky track stayed cold and dark. The way was straightforward and easy to follow, and without thinking, he fell into a rhythm that the girl could quietly invade. Under a high white sun, he could see her walking on the side of the road where he had hit her. The light was so bright that he could barely make out her form. She was there on the road ahead of him, a slender figure shimmering in heat. In this dream he wasn't in his truck but instead on his feet, working his legs to catch up to her and then walking by her side, matching his step to hers. Maybe she looked a little bit like Tonya, a little bit like his mother. Hard to tell. Her hair was long and dark, at least. But not soft. It was wet and clumpy and didn't flow over her shoulders when she turned her head and stared at him with eyes like the open mouths of dead fish.

The trail petered out and he scrambled over lichen-covered rocks and mossy logs to find it again, where it rose over more rocks up a steep incline. In his life before now, this would have been a decent trail to ride, and he counted how many days it had been since the accident. Twelve. Hardly any time at all, considering how much had changed. The ghost of his bike materialized under his body, and he watched himself pump the pedals up the incline and disappear over the top.

The campsite was on a pebbly beach in the bend of a small inlet. There was an outhouse, a freshwater creek, and a painted sign on a wooden money box asking for two dollars a night. Three other tents were pitched close together at one end of the beach, alongside three sea kayaks. Milling around the tents was a trio of guys who were hanging clothes on a line, building a fire.

It was close to six o'clock when Curtis finished pitching his tent under a latticed stand of flayed arbutus, the bare, smooth wood of the trees the color of a bull's tongue. He walked down to the water where the sea gently licked at the pebbles, falling back under a lip of white foam. To the east, the coastal mountains on the mainland floated on the horizon. Those were his mountains, and now they were losing their hold too. The thought of it overwhelmed him and he sat down and covered his face with his hands, the pebbles biting into his backside.

The guys with the kayaks were calling to one another about the orcas they had seen—unexpectedly in this part of the strait in June. For one of them, this was his first time seeing a killer whale, and he announced, inviting laughter from his friends, that his life would never be the same again.

Curtis unrolled his sleeping bag and pulled on a sweater. He ate an apple, sparked up the camping stove, and boiled water for coffee, which he brewed in a sock. Gnawing on a hunk of bread, he went scavenging for wood to build a fire and found a neat stack of logs behind the outhouse. Another painted sign and money box, asking for payment for the wood. He filled his pockets with kindling and stacked the crook of his arms with five or six chunks of wood, promising the sign that he would pay later.

Carefully, he built a small pyramid of kindling and stuffed it with the paper bag that had held the plums. He lit the paper and blew at the pulse of fire until the whole structure caught. He sat back and surveyed his setup: tent ropes pegged tightly against the rain, a pile of dry wood, this fire built the way he'd been shown as a child. His dad would be proud that Curtis was well enough equipped to live like this.

When the kindling was going steady he balanced two bigger chunks of wood on top of it, careful to set them at the right angle, and then the girl came back again, nestled into the base of his fire. With her knees drawn to her chest, she sat and pulled savagely at a fistful of bread as if she were desperate for the last strands of meat off a bone. She asked Curtis what he knew about her and he told her what he'd learned on the news. She was three years younger than him and eldest to a couple of brothers. She went to a university at the top of a hill in Vancouver and was home for the summer, working for her parents. Something to do with furniture. She was unexpected in this part of the strait in June.

He lit a stale, flattened joint that he'd found in one of the pockets of his backpack and watched a troupe of wood mites sprint in panic over the burning logs. The smart ones made their way to the edge of the pit while the dopey ones ran in circles and back into the flames, where they burned to white ash.

The guy who had seen a killer whale for the first time came over and asked Curtis if he wanted to have a beer and join him and his friends at their fire. He was saying something about orcas, but Curtis was thinking about the thing the guy had said earlier, about his life being changed forever. The guy had no idea. What if Curtis sat with them now, under the watch of stars, and told them everything? Maybe they would tell him that it was her fault for walking next to an unlit road at three o'clock in the morning. Yes, they would tell him that an act was bad only if you meant it to be. In fact, they would say that none of it mattered, none of it, because fate had had it in for him all along. But he didn't think he could stand it, sharing the soft glow of their fire, while the blood pumped so healthily through their bodies that it bloomed in their cheeks like flowers. They might have decided he'd done a terrible thing and he wouldn't be able to stop himself from crying, or screaming, or from booting the embers of their fire to the wind.

"Maybe next time," he said.

Sleep that night was angry, prodding. Rain began to fall steadily; it fell and fell until the tent, filled with the damp smell of mildew, lifted from the ground and pitched toward the sea on a slide of mud. Ice-cold water rose around the edges of Curtis's body, creeping into the spaces between his fingers, rising up his neck, one hair at a time, and spilling over his shoulders into the ditch of his collarbone. He brought his hand up close to his face and saw that the skin was covered in maggots. His whole body was writhing with them, milk white and pulsing. Now he hovered at the apex of the tent, watching the larvae consume a body that had become the girl's, the skin so tight over swollen limbs that if he were to touch her, she would explode like a blister with congealed, black blood.

He woke and, not wanting to sleep, sat up. Some comfort could be found in the pattern of rain drumming the tent, a chorus of fingers. If he listened closely he could keep her out of his head, and wait, almost in peace, for dawn.

When he crouched out of his tent into fine morning rain, the kayakers were already gone, their camp tied tightly against the weather. He packed up his wet tent and the rest of his gear. Today he would look for his mother's old house, where possibly his grandmother still lived. The little he knew about his grandmother had come from his dad in small, torn pieces. Her head was in the clouds, he often said. She lived like a hermit and made her own soap. She was selfish, and incompetent, the latter an unforgivable flaw in his dad's book. She had come to Prince George to meet Curtis when he was born, and had, for some reason, rubbed his infant body with weeds from the backyard. She came again a year later, and then after that, Elka didn't want to see her anymore. In his life, he hadn't given his grandmother much thought. But now, looking for her was the one thing keeping him from chewing his own fingers to the bone.

On the trail, the rain had freed the smell of earth and rock into the humid air. Water dripped heavily onto his shoulders from the lofty fir boughs and from the engorged leaves of maple saplings and birch, while the undergrowth, mainly fern and stinging nettle and something tall with salmon-colored flowers, slapped wetly at his thighs. Once he reached the road it was easy to find a lift back to Owl Bay, where he hoped someone would be able to tell him where the house was. He stopped first at the marina coffee shop and sat by the window, looked out over the ferry dock and the boats in the choppy bay. A fishing boat with a blue wheelhouse and crane-like arms at its stern nosed heavily through the waves. On deck, a man wearing a dirty yellow raincoat walked expertly with a coil of rope over his shoulder, and Curtis envied him his balance, and the simple, purposeful weight of a coil of rope. A fresh downpour pelted the window and he looked out beyond the bay into the Georgia Strait and watched the gray water shifting under rain and wind. He ordered a black coffee and asked the girl who brought it if she knew Roberta Sirota, his grandmother, and where she lived. She didn't but suggested he try the art gallery on the north end of the bay. The man who owned it, she said, had lived on the island for decades. Curtis swallowed the hot coffee and left a few dollars on the table. He circled the top of the bay to the gallery, head down against rain that was now driving in horizontally from the strait.

The gallery was housed in an old cottage of warped, silvered cedar and half hidden by fir trees. He peered through the wide front window into a room with an empty desk and a tabby cat sleeping on a sofa in the corner. Picture frames hung from the walls; a lone plinth in the middle of the room displayed a wooden sculpture. Curtis leaned in closer to look at the sculpture, and it occurred to him that if he did find his grandmother, he wouldn't have a word to say to her. And she would want to know what he was doing on the island. He squinted, couldn't make out what the sculpture was supposed to depict. Interlocking waves were carved out of a deep-red wood into a tall, slender figure that could have been a woman. He let his focus drift from the sculpture to the cat to nothing, and stood motionless with his hand cupped loosely over his mouth, unsure of what to do next. When he focused again on the room, there was a thin, bald man standing in the middle of it, smiling and beckoning for him to come in.

"It's so fluid, isn't it?" said the man, nodding toward the sculpture as Curtis came in and shucked his wet bag to the floor. "The artist is local. He knows wood like you wouldn't believe." The man, in his sixties, wore jeans and a light-blue t-shirt printed with a picture of the earth and the words "Love your mother." He was so skinny that the t-shirt swayed like a curtain from his bony shoulders. "You look like you've been sleeping rough, man. You down at the campsite? Can I get you a tea?"

"I'm all right."

"You sure? I make it with lots of milk and twice as much sugar. Good energy." He nodded at the paintings. "These are all done locally too. I've got more in the back."

"I'm actually trying to find someone who lives here. The girl in the coffee shop said I could ask you?"

"Who are you looking for?"

"Roberta Sirota."

"You a friend of hers?"

"I'm her grandson."

The man leaned forward and searched Curtis's face for a long time, and then smiled slowly. "That's beautiful, man," he said. "You look just like your mother."

"You knew her?"

He smiled warmly. "I knew Elka well." He made a frame around his eyes with his fingers. "It's all here, just the same."

This was something he had been reminded of all his life, mostly by his dad's mother. His dad must have seen it too, but never said. Samantha, though: she would stop Curtis in the middle of things, like when his fork was halfway to his mouth, and point out that the set of his jaw was just like Elka's. Or she would knuckle his dark hair when he let it grow and accuse him of looking more like his mother than he usually did. Sometimes he thought she was trying to be kind, as a grandmother should be—sneaking him pieces of Elka like candy before dinner. Other times he felt as if he were being blamed for some shameful thing.

This man was the first person he'd ever met who, at the mention of Elka, didn't look angry or uncomfortable.

"I'm Dan," he said. "I knew your mom from when she was born. God, you're like a carbon copy, man." He rubbed his scalp with both hands; the skin moved loosely over the bone. He closed his eyes as if he were remembering something. "I met you once, a long time ago. Your mom brought you here when you were a baby."

"I didn't know that."

"Well, that's understandable—you were just this tiny little baby, man!" Dan shook his head. "I had a feeling something was going to happen today."

So Curtis had been to the island before. His dad had always told him otherwise, and used to say that if their grandmother wanted to see them there was nothing stopping her from coming up to Prince George.

"Here's what," said Dan. "I've been meaning to go over there for a few weeks; Bobbie makes the most amazing sesame paste, and I need more. Why don't you let me run you over? She'll be pleased to see you; I know she will. But you showing up with that face of yours is going to scare the shit out of her. You can use me as a kind of middleman, you know?"

The gravel lane to Bobbie's house wound through open bush of aspen and birch. Dan pulled up to a low gate made of driftwood, which opened onto a path through a thicket of blackberry. He turned off the engine and looked at Curtis, as if to check that he was okay, then asked him to wait in the truck while he went in first.

The rain had stopped and Curtis rolled down his window. A banana-yellow slug, as fat and long as a finger, glided evenly along the top of the gate, feeling its way with slick tentacles. Curtis thought about the girl. From the time she was born, he decided, the moment of her death had been marked on the side of the road. Which meant that from the time he was born, the moment of her death was marked for him too. All the decisions he had ever made were leading him to that dip in the road. Their meeting at the party had been short and at the time seemed insignificant, but now he saw that it was all part of a plan. They would have talked to the same people, smoked from the same resin-black pipe that had been passed from mouth to mouth all night, their paths slowly converging toward the moment of impact. If there were such a thing as agents of fate, then they were tiny, rat-faced goblins scripting people's lives like jokes. They would have been lurking somewhere at the party—in the houseplants, behind the drapes—rubbing their thorny hands together and laughing their balls off.

Maybe his grandmother, Bobbie, would let him stay, maybe even until the snow began to fall in the mountains, and then he could go back, not to his mountain in Whistler but to some other one. Back to the safety of snow, powder so airy it looked blue, covering every leaf and rock. Filling every ditch. Until then he could hide on this spongy island, where the weeds grew so fast you could almost hear them climbing.

Dan beckoned to Curtis from the gate and then disappeared behind the blackberry bush. On the other side of the thicket, a wild lawn climbed a gentle rise to a small brick house that looked as if it were being consumed by the vegetation around it. Ivy climbed the walls and draped over the roof, fingers poking through a second-floor window. A bed of twiggy lavender bowed over the top of the porch railing. Plums and cherries hung maturely from hard-looking trees; the fruit that had fallen was rotting in the grass. Dan stood on the porch, holding open the screen door for a tall woman in a shapeless, flowery dress, with straight, bushy white hair parted down the middle. She squinted angrily in Curtis's direction.

"What did I tell you?" said Dan. "He looks just like her." He turned to Curtis. "She thought I was fucking with her. But you see, Bobbie? Here he is in the flesh."

Bobbie took a step forward and gripped the porch railing with both hands. Her eyes were heavy-lidded, sleepy. She tilted her head back and peered down her nose at Curtis.

"But he looks like his father too," she said. "The cocky way he's standing there." Her voice rang loudly, biting through the humidity.

"You going to invite him in?"

"Might as well." She retreated into the house, and Dan waited for Curtis, holding open the screen door.

The house was stuffy, with low, exposed beams gray with dust. A blackened stone fireplace gaped from the left-hand wall. Damp spread up the walls in patches, leaving blooms of plaster, bubbled and flaky. Toward the back, Dan stood in the small kitchen filling up a kettle and Bobbie sat at a table in an adjoining, windowed nook. She glanced at Curtis and gestured with her head for him to join her. He made his way to the table, stopping at a crowded bookshelf to study a photograph of his mother in a tarnished silver frame. The picture showed her clinging with young arms and legs to a rope swing, suspended over water and riverbank. Her clear eyes were focused intently on a spot where she was probably intending to land. His image of her had been conjured from the few pictures that his dad had, mostly in shadow or out of focus, more like the negative of the photo than the photo itself.

He took a seat opposite Bobbie. From a fold in her dress, she took out a pack of rolling tobacco and cigarette papers. She squinted at her work, shaking a pinch of tobacco into the crease of a rolling paper. Closer up, she appeared boxy and strong, the muscles in her arms solid under thick, old skin.

"Bobbie," Dan said, turning slowly in the middle of the kitchen. "Where do you keep your cups?"

Bobbie looked up, and all the tobacco fell from the paper

she was mincing between her fingers. "On top of the fridge. Why? Where do you keep your cups?"

"Just brewing some tea," Dan said, smiling.

"I've only got dandelion. I wasn't expecting anyone." She put her hands flat on the table, exhaled slowly, and started again on her cigarette.

"Mind if I?" Curtis said, pointing to her bag of tobacco.

"Be my guest."

"Since when do you smoke, Bobbie?" Dan called from the kitchen.

"About two months now. I can't believe I left it this long. It's frigging marvelous."

Curtis deftly rolled a well-packed smoke and passed it to her while she still concentrated on her own. She waved his away impatiently with her elbow.

"The ritual of rolling the damn thing is why I started," she explained, working the cigarette inches from her nose. She licked the paper and smoothed it down with her thumbs, gave the whole cigarette a twist, and held up the wrinkled thing for inspection. Nodded at it. "I have to earn the right to smoke each one."

Dan brought in three mugs and sat down.

"You like that picture, eh? Of your mom?" she asked Curtis. "Her dad took that one."

"She looks so different," he said.

"Different from what?" Bobbie stared at him. "You barely got the chance to know her, you poor thing." She tilted her head at him, and her smile was sad but also, though he couldn't be sure, a little smug. "When my daughter was little, she used to tear dandelion stems into strips and put them in a bowl of cold water." She tucked her cigarette in the corner of her mouth, and with her eyes still on him, she searched the folds of her dress and produced a book of matches. "You know what happens when you do that?"

Curtis looked at Dan.

"They curl up, perfectly, into these tight little springs. They take on this pearly, silvery sheen. She would make dozens of them and tie them into her hair. My daughter was very good at that sort of thing, making things beautiful." Bobbie lit her cigarette and inhaled deeply, and watched the smoke rise and curl from the cherry as if she were testing its quality.

Curtis blew across the surface of his tea. "I don't remember," he said.

"Well, no, you wouldn't. Would you?" Bobbie adjusted her dress and pushed her brittle hair behind her ears. It fell back over her eyes. "I suppose you want to know why I haven't been in contact with you?"

He took a sip of tea, which was oily and coated his teeth and the edges of his tongue.

"My daughter brought you here to me when you were a baby. I don't know what went on in Prince George, but she was getting you away from your father. The two of you were going to stay here, and for a few days it was, as I recall, idyllic. We foraged together, with you tied to her back in a sling. I rocked you to sleep in this very kitchen. You were a cute kid. But then your dad came looking for you, with his dirty boots and his face all stony. He blamed me for everything, and convinced her to go back with him."

"It wasn't really like that, was it, Bobbie?" Dan asked, his forehead creased.

"How the hell would you know?" she said.

Dan raised his palms apologetically, winking at Curtis.

"He hated me," Bobbie said. "And I wasn't going to go into combat with that man."

"He never told me any of this," Curtis said.

"Well, no shock there. Not much of a talker, is he?" She looked out the window and delicately picked a shred of tobacco off her lip. When her gaze met his again, it was skeptical. "What were you expecting to find here?"

Curtis didn't know what to say. What he hadn't expected was for her to be so solid, to be so unnerving. And he hadn't expected to like her, but he thought that maybe he did.

"Is there something you want from me?" she asked.

"I need somewhere to crash for a bit," he said, judging that it was better to be straight with this woman than not. "I could help you out around the yard or whatever."

"It wouldn't hurt, Bobbie," said Dan, coaxing. "Your fruit trees are breaking my heart, man. The Rainier is choking to death."

Bobbie looked slowly from one of them to the other. "What in the hell are you people talking about?" She jutted her cigarette at Curtis. "You show up here out of the blue and I let you stay, and tonight you strangle this old woman in her bed!"

"Get off it, Bobbie," Dan said, laughing. "This is Elka's kid here."

"I don't need anyone's help."

"I've got my tent," Curtis said. "I don't have to stay in the house."

To his relief, Dan got up and took Curtis's full mug to the kitchen. "You could use the company, Bobbie," he called over his shoulder.

She stared at Curtis and sighed heavily. "Looking at you, I can't deny it's like I'm looking at her. She was perfect, you know, in every way. I suppose I could tolerate you for a short time because, some would say, your ever-loving father most certainly would say"—she closed her eyes and they fluttered under the heavy lids—"that I owed it to her. I'm sure she loved you dearly, though this was something we never spoke about. But I loved *her* dearly, so I know how it feels." A thread of tobacco fluttered to the table as she brought her cigarette to her mouth. She squinted against the smoke. "Now. What do you know about rapeseed oil?"

He shrugged. "Nothing?"

Her top lip curled and she pushed back her chair, and stood up heavily from the table.

# 21

**Tom watched** the checker's truck retreat down the road and he watched while the dust rose and then settled to nothing but a haze. A band of noseeums hung around his head; mosquitoes landed on his neck and shoulders and he slapped them off. His anger seemed to be concentrated in his mouth, in his teeth.

First he woke Roland, then Matt, giving them five minutes to be in his trailer.

"How many bundles did he bury?" Matt asked, looking at the map Tom had spread on the table. His meaty hand was cupped over his mouth, his eyes glittering. He and Roland sat side by side on the bench; Tom stood at the other side of the table.

"Enough to fill the back of her truck."

"Shit, boss."

"What do you think she'll do?" Roland asked. He was peeling an orange and carefully building a stack out of the concave disks of peel.

Tom shook his head. "Both of you look at the map one more time," he said. "Before I do anything, I need to be sure."

Roland and Matt bent over the table. Roland drew his finger over the red lines that delineated the blocked land that the company had already planted. The foremen's names had been penciled into the blocks that their crews had worked.

"I know this is right because Sweet was stuck in that draw for the first week and a half. You remember?" Roland said. "That's all we heard about every fucken time we sat down. Me and Matt were over here." He pointed to the other end of the map. "Then Sweet moved his guys to that big block up the Sitlika. And I put him on that creamy one right next to it when you guys were in Minaret so I wouldn't have to listen to his babble all week." He stretched out his chest and hung both hands off the back of his neck. "I don't know what to say."

"That's where she found the stash," said Tom. "That last block. He must have done it after we got back from Prince George."

"You think he did it? You don't think it was one of his guys?" Matt said.

"I think he did it when we got back from town." Tom leaned over the table and drew back the curtain by Matt's shoulder and looked out at camp, fallen to the color of sand under a dusk-white sky, the lake so calm it almost wasn't there. They would all be asleep now, ready to pull on their boots at 2 a.m. for their first night of fire hours. He was going to have to tell the people on Sweet's crew that they'd be working the next three or four nights without pay, replanting the seedlings that had gone into the ground so sloppily. Maybe Sweet had even encouraged the lazy work, but then he wouldn't have had to go that far. These were long, arduous days, one rolling into the next, broken only by the lacing and unlacing of boots, the taping of fingers, the washing of tin plates. Every day, slotting one or two thousand trees into the hard ground, trudging through unsympathetic terrain—it was easy to cut corners if you weren't being watched, prodded a little. Natural, even. Tom moved away from the window and leaned on the counter next to the sink. "Between the two of you," he said, "you think you can handle his crew?"

"You're going to give him the boot?" said Matt, his voice hoarse.

"That's the only thing for it," Tom said. He reached for the map and folded it.

Sweet's tent was pitched at the back end of camp, at the top of a grassy rise behind the cook van. His tent was an expensive-looking, four-man dome, around which he'd dug a deep trench for keeping back the rainwater. Two tightly bound tarpaulins were strung up to the surrounding alders, providing extra cover as well as an overhang, like a porch, which was furnished with ground sheets. There was enough room for two deck chairs and his bike, locked. Not a beer can or piece of garbage in sight.

Tom sat in one of the chairs, set at a friendly angle to the other. The view was good. The apex of the mess tent cut off some of the camp, but there was a clear view of the lake, and you could see more of the planters' tents in the trees. The low, resonant rhythm of deep snoring came from inside the tent like an underground train. Tom unfolded the map, shooed blackflies from his eyes. For a long time, Sweet had been part of the landscape here, same as the bugs and the thistles and the threat of fire. Maybe that was why Tom always asked him back. And sitting here now, he felt he had arrived at a place that was inevitable.

"Sweet. Wake up."

The snoring continued, and then snagged.

"Sweet."

The swish of a sleeping bag, then, "Fuck off."

Tom looked across the water to the mountains, only a blue outline now under a darkening sky. "It's Tom. Come out here for a minute."

"What do you want?"

"I want you to come out here for a minute."

Sweet cleared his throat, farted. Then came the muffled sounds of sleeping bag, of clothes being pulled on. Then silence. Tom was being made to wait. He sat back and breathed deeply.

"What time is it?"

Tom looked at his watch. "Just after eight."

The tent flap zipped open and Sweet emerged, his eyes red, the top half of his hair pulled up tightly in an elastic band. He wore an orange hooded sweatshirt, jeans, and thick wool socks. He closed his tent flap and sat in the other chair, stretched out his legs, and dug his hands protectively into the front pouch of his sweatshirt, puffed mosquitoes from his face with his bottom lip. His eyes flicked to the map in Tom's hands and then he stared out at the lake.

"The checker's just left, irate."

"Old Camel Toes?" Unsmiling, Sweet kept his gaze forward. He slowly raised his hood over his head and pulled the tie strings, then crawled his hands back into the pouch.

Tom leaned over and spread the map on Sweet's thighs. "She found J roots here, and here, and here." He jabbed his finger at points on the map. "And she found a huge stash" — he pointed again — "here. A few thousand seedlings, at least."

Sweet's mouth twitched, as if he were trying not to smile.

Tom took the map back. "This is funny?"

Sweet opened his arms wide, shook his head. Evidently it was too much for him, though, and he laughed, a crack opening in ice. "Boss," he said, shaking, "I've always, ever since I was a kid, whenever I catch shit for something, I can't help it. I've had women...literally punching holes in walls..." He pressed his fingers to the bridge of his nose and doubled over in his chair, drew up his knees. His back moved with deep breaths. A branch cracked far off in the trees, followed by the shudder of its echo.

"So you know these are all yours. This is no surprise."

Sweet sat up, rubbed his hands up and down his face. His knuckles were etched with dry brown scabs.

"Yeah. Those are my blocks." He had stopped laughing and was licking and puckering his lips, trying to straighten his face. "We'll do a replant, right? No harm, no foul." He removed his hood, watched Tom from the corner of his eye.

"I pay you okay, don't I?"

"Your percentages are good, boss."

"Treat you right? Treat you fair?"

"Well, now."

Tom sat up, watched him steadily.

"Do you think I get fair treatment around here?" Sweet's face screwed up and he wagged his head, whined in the voice of a child: "Dig the shit holes, Sweet. Here's your crap land, Sweet. And while you're at it, have some more. Roland is in charge, Sweet." With each point, he threw his hand like a conductor. He finished with a clap, looked at Tom, eyes wide. Something ticked a long way off in the bush.

"So you let this happen. You stashed those trees."

"And then you go around fucking the cook. Not very professional."

"Is this because of her?"

Sweet crossed his arms over his chest and looked away.

"You're ruining my company because of her?"

Sweet cocked his head to the side and winked. "You think I can't get what I want."

Tom came closer in that moment than he ever had before to hitting a man. The punch was there, waiting in his throat and in his palms. He wanted to rip the obnoxious fountain of hair from the top of Sweet's head. He stood up, knocking the flimsy chair to its side. They stared at each other and in Sweet's blue eyes Tom saw a deep and uncomplicated hatred. There was nothing left to say and he'd run out of all equanimity, so he gripped his trembling hands together.

"You've got until the morning," he said. "Once I've factored in what you've cost me, you'll get the rest of what I owe you by check. When we get back from the blocks tomorrow you won't be here. I see you again, I'll knock your head off."

Sweet stood up, the knobs of his fists poking through his pouch. "You can't take my money. I'll sue you, for unfair dismissal." His voice rose. "For intimidation!"

Tom headed down the hill into the quiet of camp, the only sound being the whine of mosquitoes at his ears.

He woke at two in the morning after four hours' sleep. He swung his legs over the edge of the bunk and stared ahead at nothing, rubbing his eyes, his head full of Sweet, as if there'd been no sleep at all. He stepped out of his trailer into the darkness and moved to the trees and pissed. The sky was clear and the stars were dizzy, a dome from end to end.

The lights were on in the cook van and the mess tent. Nix would have been up for at least an hour already. Someone stood at the water pump, in the band of light that spilled from the tent. Stood there in a woolly hat, spitting a gob of tooth-paste into the dirt.

The back door to the cook van was propped open with a plastic crate and Tom could see Nix through the opening in the warm light. She wore a yellow bandanna in her hair and a long-sleeved wool shirt, army pants cut off at the knees. Her muscular calves were dotted with swollen, angry-looking bites. She worked in a cloud of steam. He stepped up to the door and opened it and leaned on the frame. She glanced at him quickly but continued to work, wheeling back and forth between either side of the van, where the counters were piled with loaves of bread, jars of jam and peanut butter, boxes of cereal. Water steamed in a large pot on the stove and she la-dled whole eggs into it. She kept a cloth over her shoulder and stopped and wiped her face.

"You want some help?" he asked.

She turned back to the pot. "Nope."

"You sure?"

She took a deep breath and he thought she was going to speak, but instead she moved down the counter and reached for a knife, and began to chop.

"Nix. You going to talk to me?"

She coughed and moved farther away.

Outside, whoever it was who'd been at the water pump was gone. No sign of life over by the tents. No bobbing lights or movement. He went to where the vehicles were parked to-gether and saw that Sweet's truck was already gone. Tom sat in his own truck with the door open and, as a wake-up call, gunned the engine a few times, honked the horn. A flap of birds rose from the trees. In the dark he couldn't tell what kind, something small and fast—confused and angry at this invasion.

Within a few minutes, people stumbled dreamily from their tents. The first night was always the hardest. They ate, smoked, sat bleary-eyed at their tables. Somebody asked where Sweet was and it didn't take long for the news to spread.

Tom gathered Sweet's planters at one of the fire pits, white ash circled by stones black and cold. Some of them were complicit, he knew, but it didn't matter who. When he told them they'd all be working for nothing for the next few nights, one guy stood up, laughing, and quit on the spot. His laughter echoed across the camp as he made his way back to his tent. The rest sat slack-jawed, kicking the dirt. He sensed that some of them had known this was coming.

"This is a bastard of a situation," Tom said. "I know it. And I apologize for letting it get so fucked-up. Some of you guys have nothing to do with this, but we get in there tonight and tomorrow night and rip into it, and it's done." He looked at all of them and they stared back. And they looked at one another too. They would know soon enough, when they got back onto the land, whose hectares were planted badly and whose were done right. One of the other crew vans started up, the headlights beaming across the camp. "You think we could make a promise to each other?" he said.

Nobody said anything.

"Maybe we just get this work done and not talk about who's responsible for the bad roots, and who's hard done by? You guys think we can do that?"

"Probably not," said Amy. She was sitting on her water jug, hands on her knees. "People might promise you that but they're full of shit."

"It's got to get done. You either make it quick and painless or you stew in it. Your choice." Tom stood.

"I've never planted a tree wrong," Amy said, steadily.

"Fuck you, Amy," someone else called. "In all your hundreds of thousands, not one bad tree?"

This brought a soft, communal laugh.

Sweet's crew worked in morose silence under stars that slipped across the sky. Sometime after five, light began to bloom in the east, and what was black and indefinable began to take shape, lightening to pale silver. They worked with headlamps and the going was easier because they had no bags to carry. Tom separated the crew into four teams that worked in lines on different patches of land. They crawled slowly over the terrain, lifting each seedling from the ground, straightening bent root plugs. Tom brought his shovel, jumping from team to team, and found LJ and Beautiful T sitting on a charcoal-black log at the edge of a huge, sandy ashpit, an old site where slash had once been burned. They sat and smoked, their nostrils black with dust from the burn.

"Where's the rest of your team?" he asked.

LJ gestured with the back of her hand to somewhere beyond her shoulder and threw her head back, exhaled smoke toward the sky.

"Probably a bad idea to stop when the others are still working."

"We're only taking a quickie, chief," she said.

"You want to talk bad ideas," said Beautiful T. She had a

flat rock in her hand and drew on it with a piece of charcoal. She held it up: a face with angry eyebrows and a mouth full of fangs. "This is you."

"Come on," he said. He worked with them, stumbling through mist until the sun rose beyond the mountains and every twig, every pebble cast a long needle of shadow. LJ sang, and eventually Beautiful T joined in, their voices strong and resonant. It was not yet eight but already the morning air felt warm. They stopped to peel off their wool tops and pass around a bag of dry cereal. Tom pulled an apple out of his pocket and cut sections from it with his knife, and passed out the pieces.

"What's going to happen to Sweet?" Beautiful T asked.

"He's gone."

The two girls looked at each other. They were at the top of a rise, and to the east a group of planters picked their way slowly along the side of a draw, like insects trying to crawl out of a bowl.

"So who's going to be our foreman?"

"Roland or Matt. We'll split you up."

"This is like my parents' divorce," said Beautiful T. She took the bandanna out of her hair and sprayed it with bug repellent from a small, oily bottle, and then tied the bandanna tightly over her head again.

"Don't be an idiot," said LJ. She held her hand out flat and gestured with her fingers for the bottle of repellent.

"Are you ever going to buy your own?" Beautiful T said, slapping the bottle into LJ's palm.

"I'll make sure you two stay together," said Tom.

"Don't put us with Matt," said LJ. "He squeaks when he gets angry."

Tom cut the last of the apple and threw the core over his shoulder. He wiped the knife blade on his thigh. "How often did Sweet check your work?" he asked.

"Not a lot."

"Less than usual?"

Beautiful T turned away and LJ leaned on her shovel, her head down. She looked up at him. "I like Sweet, okay? I know he's a dick, and he's selfish, but he was selfish on our behalf too. You know? We've been working for him three years; we don't want to rat him out."

Tom flipped his shovel onto his shoulder and nodded at them. "Fair enough."

The going was slow. By 10 a.m., the sun on Tom's neck was strong and unhindered by cloud or wind. He told LJ and Beautiful T to plant their way back to the road and meet at the crew van. They ignored the first half of what he said, slung their shovels over their shoulders, and picked their way toward the road, scrambling over slash and weed-choked logs. He headed toward the other planters, some spread along the tree line, others hidden at the bottom of a draw, and called them to the end of the night's work.

## 22

**It took** Sweet's crew two nights of unpaid slog to straighten out the mess. Two more planters quit. Tom watched them pack their things in their car, while most of the camp slept, and grind down the gravel road, leaving a hanging pall of grit and dust like a ringing in the ear.

Working the bleak twilight hours had a way of twisting people's nerves. They could never get enough sleep; it was too hot in their tents at the height of the day, too light. So they spread blankets on the sand and played their guitars and their card games, swam in the lake, drifted in the canoe, trailing their feet in the cold water. The grunting and cussing from Sweet's crew had spread to the others and something ugly had settled over everything; when Tom pulled into camp on the second morning, the replant finished, it was with relief. He would give all the planters the night off, stay out of their way.

He headed to his trailer for a towel and a change of clothes. Nix cut a diagonal line from her cook van and stopped him.

"You owe me an apology," she said. "For what you said to me in your truck. That was mean."

"I could probably say sorry for a lot more than that, but this isn't the time."

"You've hardly said two words to me since we got back from town."

He cupped her elbow with his hand and started walking again to his trailer. "I've tried. You weren't interested."

"Well I'm interested now."

"Have you been paying attention around here? I've got a whole crew that wants to kick my ass."

"Well maybe I want to kick your ass."

"You'll have to get in line."

She stopped a few paces from his trailer. "Some guy called Kevin from the logging company radioed. Said it was important you called."

"How did he sound?"

"He sounded like it was important."

Tom knew the fallout wouldn't end with the checker, and before he picked up his radiophone, he sat quietly in his trailer for a minute, preparing for what was coming. A warning, maybe a probation period. At worst, the loss of the contract and his reputation destroyed.

He didn't expect to be told that the police had been in touch. Nothing to panic about, apparently, but they were looking for his son. They'd been given directions to the camp and would be there the following morning. And almost as an afterthought: he was expected, once his personal business was squared away, to come to the office and talk about what the hell was going on with his outfit.

He turned off the radio and stared at the floor. He thought about Curtis again in Sean's kitchen, his head between his knees, his shoulders hanging low.

With movements that were almost automatic, he sifted

through his things for a bar of soap and a towel, clean underwear, and a pair of jeans. He cut through the woods to a
small patch of beach out of sight of camp, peeled off his work
clothes, stiff with sweat and burn ash, and walked briskly into
the cold water, rubbing his arms vigorously as the water inched
up his calves, his thighs. He dove underneath and rubbed soap
into his face and hair. Curtis had never done anything stupid;
Tom had always been able to trust him. But the police? Tom
went over that last conversation he'd had with Curtis. Curt had
been trying to talk to him, and all he could remember now was
how hard it had been to get at that valve, how easy it had been
to avoid whatever it was Curt was upset about.

He dove again and spun underwater, tried to undo the knot
that was coiling in his chest, and when he surfaced he could
hear the planters' voices chittering over the water from down
shore and around the bend. He treaded water for the weight-
lessness of it; every hair, his diaphragm, his scrotum, floated
freely. He paddled to where he knew there was a flat rock just
under the surface and sat on it, cleaning the dirt from his ankles, between his toes.

"Hey. You."

Nix was on the sand, her arms crossed above her head in
the act of pulling off her t-shirt, the small pot of her stomach
stretched flat. He watched her tug her pants off and wade in,
shoulders raised to the cold, sculling her fingers along the surface of the water. "I'm sorry I behaved like that back there."

"You've got nothing to be sorry about."

"I acted like such a girl."

"You are a girl."

"Not that kind of girl."

He slid off the rock and she stopped in front of him,

touched his hip under the water. The hairs on her arms were standing up in a field of goose bumps and she was shivering. She took her fingers from his hip and hugged her arms around her body.

"Swim around a bit. You'll get warm," he said.

"What did the Nielson guy want?"

"He just wants to talk."

"You in trouble?"

"Yeah."

She looked across the water and then she looked at him. She frowned.

"What?"

She hit the water with a sudden backhand slap, splashing him. He ducked under and spun away, and then stood up, facing the shore. Laughing, she jumped on his back, arms around his neck, and he fell backward to get her off, throwing her into the water. By the time she came up, spluttering, wiping her face, he was trudging out of the lake. She ducked back under and surfaced farther out, and floated on her back, sprayed water from her mouth. "I take it that's it, then?" she called.

He wiped the towel quickly down his limbs and across his chest and pulled on his clothes, and rubbed the towel back and forth across his head. His left ear was plugged, so he hopped with his head thrown to that side, hitting his palm flat on the right side of his skull. The warm membrane of water stayed fast to his inner ear and the sound of his breathing piped loudly in his head. By the time he looked back at Nix, she had floated farther out; the profile of her face against the sunny lake was dark and sharp and distant.

\*   \*   \*

In the morning, Tom took his truck up the camp trail to the turn at the logging road to wait for the police. Sleep the night before had been hard to come by, and now he rolled down the window, leaned back against the seat and put one boot up on the dash, and tried and failed to close his eyes. A nervous scratch came from somewhere in the bush to his left, then a *titch* and a warble. Then, eerily, nothing. No such thing as absolute silence in the bush, but for a moment it was as close as it got. Then the faraway rumble of an engine. Too heavy to be a car. Up ahead at the bend, a few hundred meters away, he saw the dust first. Then, materializing out of it like some angry bull, the squared chrome nose of a logging truck. Twelve feet wide, fully loaded, bearing down. When it came closer, the driver, high in his cab, saluted. Heavy chains rattled over a towering stack of bucked logs. Tom rolled up his window, the air now thick with yellow dust. Dust in his teeth, the back of his throat. It settled onto the roadside trees, and the truck, and the dashboard where a few seconds before his boot had been. And then, in the grit that still hung all around, quiet again.

Through the dirty windscreen, he studied the empty road, chewed the skin around the edge of his thumbnail, and listened hard for the approach of the police car. Restless, he got out of the truck and walked along the ditch, kicking plates of dried mud. Pulverizing them. He came to a corrugated culvert and balanced on its ridges, pulled a bouquet of needles off a pine bough, and picked the needles one by one, tossing them into the road as he continued to walk. Fresh sap on his fingers. What had Curtis got himself into that was so important the police were bothering to come way the hell out here?

Eventually, the sound of a small engine. What came around

the bend wasn't a police car but what looked like a rented vehicle. And the driver was alone. By this time, Tom was sitting on the hood of his truck, his boots on the fender. The car pulled up nose to nose with his truck and he hopped down, walked around to the driver's side.

The man who got out was dressed in a short-sleeved dress shirt and suit pants. A loosened tie. Taking Tom's hand in his large, moist grip, the man smiled. "I gather you're Tom Berry? Detective Brendon Wythe. I'm late; I know. I took the opportunity this morning to drop in on your mother."

"What's happened to my kid?"

The detective waved his palms in front of his chest, as if trying to stop something coming his way. "No! No. They were supposed to tell you. As far as we know, nothing has happened to your son. Ah, hell. I bet you were worrying all night."

"You're not here for nothing."

"We're only trying to track him down. I wanted to come and talk to you in person, see if you know where he is. Or if you can help us find him." He slapped a mosquito off his arm.

"What's he done?"

"Probably nothing. I need to speak to him in relation to a hit-and-run accident that occurred down in Whistler. Listen, can we sit in the car? I'm getting eaten alive."

Tom sat in the passenger seat. "You mind if I roll the window down a bit?"

"As long as you catch 'em when they get in." Brendon switched on the air-conditioning, and dust and the smell of plastic blasted from the vents. "So here's the thing. Little over two weeks ago there was a hit-and-run incident on the highway in Whistler. You know about that?"

"Vaguely."

"It's all over the news."

"Don't get much of that up here."

The detective put both hands on the steering wheel, looked down the road. "Well. A girl was hit. Whoever hit her left her in the dirt, and after a few hours of what I'm told was pretty terrible suffering, she died. The only thing we know about the vehicle that hit her was that it was something high and heavy, like a van or a truck or some kind of SUV."

"She a friend of Curt's or something?"

"We don't know. We do know that they were at the same party, night of the incident. We're talking to everyone who was there, but we haven't been able to locate Curtis."

"I still don't see why you needed to come up here, for that."

"Thing is, he hasn't been at work since the day of the party. Or home. Nobody down in Whistler knows where he is."

Tom shifted in the seat. The air in the car was too cold, and stale.

"Have you seen him in the last few weeks?"

"I saw him in town."

"Prince George?"

"Yes. Just over a week ago." Sean's kitchen. Dripping tap, a life gone.

"Where exactly?"

"He was staying with his friend. But then he was heading back to Whistler. For work."

"He hasn't been at work."

"You mentioned that."

"Is this the type of thing he does? Go off like this without telling anyone?"

"He hasn't lived at home for a few years. Maybe he does this sort of thing now."

"How was he when you saw him?"

Incoherent. Sitting on the floor with his head between his knees.

"Mr. Berry?"

"It'd be better if you called me Tom."

"Did he seem upset? Anything like that?"

"He was upset about his girlfriend. They broke up. Maybe that's why he split."

"Do you happen to know when that was?"

"I don't know. Couple of weeks back."

The detective nodded. He had been looking through the front window for most of the conversation, and now he shifted in the seat so that he was facing Tom. "Mr. Berry. What do you think of all this?"

Tom rubbed the rough hairs on his chin and shook his head. He opened the door and got out and stood looking down the road, his hands in the back pockets of his jeans. The detective got out and stood next to him, crossed his arms and looked down the road, and they stood there as if they were both waiting for someone to come.

"I think," said Tom, "that there could be a hundred and one reasons why he took off."

"But you can see why we might be interested in talking to him."

"Yeah, I can see that."

"Any chance you can get away from here for a day or two? Maybe see if he's staying at home, or has been there? Have a talk with that friend he was staying with? You might have better luck than me."

Tom nodded.

"We're only trying to eliminate him at this point."

"Give me an hour to talk to my foremen."

Houseflies picked over open cans of food in the kitchen, and Tom knew that Curtis had been home. Had been hiding. Tom stood at the counter, motionless, boots still on, bag over his shoulder. White fear traveled clean through his body. It rose from his gut to the tips of his ears, turning them hot, and brought with it the truth, straightforward as milk. A mass of maggots butted wetly against each other inside a half-empty can of peaches. He opened the window above the sink and tipped the maggots outside just as Brendon came through the kitchen. He crossed to the back door and looked out the window.

"You got a nice big yard out there."

Tom pulled a plastic bag from under the sink and put the cans in it.

"You got a daughter too, right?"

"Erin."

"I met her at your mother's place. She looks like you. Got the red hair." Brendon's eyes moved to the bag of cans, then roamed the kitchen.

"Do you want a cup of coffee?" Tom asked.

"I would love a cup of coffee."

Tom pushed the bag into the garbage under the sink and got the tin of coffee out of the cupboard. He filled the percolator with water and looked out the window to the disused swing set. He dumped three scoops of grounds into the top of the percolator, spilling some onto the counter and the floor. Then, reaching for a spoon in the kitchen that he'd built himself, he opened the wrong drawer.

"Would you mind at all, while that coffee brews, just having a look to see if he's been here?" Brendon asked.

Brendon followed Tom through the living room, where the blanket from Curtis's bed lay on the floor like a windless flag, and down the hallway to Tom's closed bedroom door. Inside his room, the double bed was pushed against the wall, the tightly tucked bedding untouched. The only sign of life was from the pulsing red colon on his clock radio.

"He hasn't been in here," Tom said.

Across the hall, Erin's room. He pushed her door open against a pile of clothes and stuck his head in. He didn't know if anything had changed, if Curtis had taken anything or slept in there, because he couldn't remember the last time he had actually stepped beyond her doorway.

"This is your daughter's room?"

Tom nodded. "You got kids?"

"Hell no."

Tom moved past him in the narrow hallway and checked the bathroom, clean as he'd left it, except for the towel hooked on the back of the door. He looked at Brendon and shrugged, as if he were still unsure. "Nothing wrong with a boy coming home. Only thing you learn from him being here is that he's been here."

Brendon took a deep breath. "You can understand, I need to find out what happened to this girl. No stone unturned, eh?"

"I can understand that."

Curtis's door, opposite the bathroom, was open. In his room, some clothes on the floor, the curtains drawn, the bedsheet twisted at the foot of the mattress.

"Would that be his blanket on the floor in the living room?" Brendon asked.

Tom nodded. They went back through the kitchen and down the basement stairs. When Tom switched on the light, the room felt darker than it normally did, and then he saw that the window at the far end of the basement had been boarded up.

Brendon stood by the workbench, the shadows on his face elongated by the overhead light. He pushed the hammer on its hook on the wall, watched it swing. "Ditching your job, not getting in touch with anyone—this is the behavior of someone who is running. You can see that, right?"

Gaps on the shelves by the stairs, where the camping gear was stowed.

"You could say he's prone to drop things, I guess. But he's twenty-two years old, you know?"

"That about the age you were when you had him?"

"I was nineteen."

"Same age as Lindsay."

"Who?"

"The girl who died."

"That's a hell of a thing. I don't know what to say about that. Hard to even think about. What about her parents?"

"You can imagine."

"I can."

The moment of death—he'd seen it enough times. A buck's or a bird's or a dog's eyes dulled and half open. He'd dreamt it of himself. It was a sigh, an exhale, a pulling from underneath black water. And when it was you, he wondered, was there this thought? *My last breath, my last touch.* All those thousands and here is my last. When Elka did it to herself, when darkness pulled at the edges of her eyes and her breath began to fade, did she grapple for more? Was she conscious of the end? This girl, alone—there must have come a point when she knew it was happening. She must have been so scared.

The smell of burnt coffee hung in the kitchen, the room now blue with dusk. Tom sat alone with his elbows on the table and rested his chin on crossed fingers. He stared at the card, propped against the pepper pot, bearing Brendon's number, the address of his office. Tom would find the boy himself, before they did. Make him turn back before they could catch him from behind.

With no light on in the kitchen, the blue gradually darkened, and the percolator on the stove, the magnets on the refrigerator, and the two clean cups on the counter first lost color, then definition until everything blended into one plane. Out the window, one star pricked the purple sky, and then twelve and then forty and so on.

The familiar sound of the front door rubbing against its frame surprised him and he sat up.

"Curtis?"

"Nope," his mother called. Lights switched on in the living room and Samantha's head appeared in the doorway. "I've been calling you for the last hour. Why didn't you pick up?"

"The phone didn't ring."

She disappeared, her voice retreating down the hall. "I don't know what to make of all this, Tom."

Erin came into the kitchen and turned on the light and sat across from him. She picked up Brendon's card and read it and carefully leaned it back against the pepper pot. She looked startled, and full of color, and very beautiful.

"Did you see Curtis when he was in town the last time?" Tom asked her.

"No."

"You sure?"

"Am I sure that I didn't see him? Let me think. Yes."

"It didn't ring because it was unplugged," Samantha said, coming into the kitchen. She opened the lid of the percolator and sniffed inside, dumped the grounds into the sink and turned on the tap. "He could be trying to call."

"He's the one who unplugged it."

Samantha turned and leaned against the counter, crossed her arms under her chest.

"How'd you know I was here?" Tom asked.

"I called the camp. How do you know he unplugged the phone?"

"He's been here."

"That detective seems okay, doesn't he? He keeps a cool head."

"He's convinced Curtis hit that girl, all right."

"He is."

Erin shifted in her seat.

"You know anything at all?" Tom asked her.

"Last time I saw him was when he was here, Dad. Right before you went to camp."

"Tom," Samantha began, her voice thin, "if that kid hit a young gal with his car, on my life he would have stopped to help. He just would. All day since that policeman came I've been slipping into this panic, thinking, oh my god he's killed someone, and I let the thing take ahold of me right around the neck, and I imagine headlines and courtrooms and Curtis in a prison cell all alone and I can't breathe. And then I stop. I hit the reset button and I just stop. Think about it. This is Curtis here. He could never do that."

"Things happen. You don't know what you'll do."

"You think he's responsible?"

"Well, where the fuck is he?"

"He's taken off somewhere. That's all. Some poor girl died in a ditch and my grandson is missing. That's all we've got."

But Curtis had confessed to him and he'd missed it entirely: there was no one there, and then there was.

Erin watched him from across the table and he looked right back at her. Looking at this seventeen-year-old girl, with his eyes exactly, and the thin, white scar at her brow from a goat hunt she hadn't been ready for—he knew he was a fool. He thought he'd stuck around just about long enough, but he hadn't, not by a mile. Your kid could be the one driving or the one who was hit, and you would never know it was coming.

## 23

**The first** morning at Bobbie's, Curtis crawled out of his tent after he'd lain restlessly, watching the light change from blue black to the color of stone. He stood just inside the back door of the house and found Bobbie humming in the kitchen, standing at the sink. The night before, she had gone to bed without offering a meal. He'd searched the cupboards for crackers or bread or an apple, at least, maybe a bottle of home brew, but found only baggies of dried mushrooms and jars of grains and powders.

Today a multicolored scarf twisted her hair into a nest on top of her head. Her dress sleeves were rolled up and she plunged her arms up and down in some kind of liquid, elbow deep in the sink.

"The funny thing is," she began, her back to him still, "I used to have a recurring dream about you."

"Oh ya?" He wondered if he'd missed the first half of a conversation he was supposed to be a part of.

"Mind you, it was you but it wasn't you. Because I could only guess what you looked like." She continued to plunge, her wide back rolling. "You're much better-looking than I'd hoped, by the way. I always imagined you to be more like your father, all rusty-haired and hard knocks. He's attractive to some, I guess—that was half the problem—but you are a Sirota." She looked at him over her shoulder and smiled.

She lifted a mass of something dark and hairy out of the sink and twisted it tightly. Purple liquid cascaded from it and down her strong forearms. She carried it dripping over to the stove and dropped it in a deep aluminum pot. Wiping her hands on her dress, seemingly unconcerned about the watery streaks of purple she drew across it, she finally looked at him. "You'll eat some eggs, won't you?"

His throat tightened at the thought of eating an egg, but fear of displeasing her overcame his disgust. He nodded and sat at the table, looked out the window. Outside, the grass grew unchecked, choking a rotting stack of roughly chopped logs. A metal chair lay on its side, rusting into the ground. "Have you thought of anything I could do around the place?" he asked, fiddling with a clay bowl of peppercorns. "I can paint. I can do pretty much anything in the yard."

She lifted an iron skillet from its hook on the wall and set it on the stove. "What's implicit in your offer, you realize, is that my house is a dump. And my land has gone to seed." She flipped butter into the skillet and palmed three eggs from a bowl. "Before I met your grandfather, I taught on a reserve near Prince Rupert. Did you know I used to be a teacher?" She stared at him and he was about to answer but then she turned away and cracked the eggs into the skillet, then wiped her fingers on her dress. "I lived up there for the better part of two years, taught grade one in the new schoolhouse they built after the original one was burned to the ground. They were great kids. A bunch of rapscallions, but tough as nails. Independent little buggers. Some of them dirt-poor,

and they'd come to school in patched-up clothes, shoes falling apart. I was a stupid fool and when I think about this
now…I just burn with shame. I started a clothing drive in
Prince Rupert—you know, for the kids. I had this vision
of myself presenting the clothes to their parents, like I was
some kind of saint. Like I knew better than them. One of the
fathers—he was a band councillor—he came to the classroom one day after school and he sat down and at first he
didn't say anything. Just stared at me until I was this close to
tears." She pinched a centimeter out of the air. "Then he said,
'We all got a job to do. My job is to fish, and when I'm not
fishing, my job is to stand up for the people of my community. My kids' job is to go to school and my wife's job is to
look after me and my kids. Your job is to teach, and I suggest
that's what you stick to.' "

"You were only trying to help."

"Balderdash! You think you care about other people's
needs, but mostly, you're only acting on behalf of your own.
Altruism's for the birds."

He pushed the peppercorns around the walls of the bowl,
grinding them into the pottery with his thumb.

Steam rose from the big pot on the stove and she stirred its
contents with a wooden spoon. "Can you forage?" she asked.

"What, like, pick stuff?"

"Your mother was a little wood urchin when she was
small. I used to send her out alone and she would come
back with her skirt full of the most useful things. Watercress
and sheep sorrel. Oh gosh: peppergrass, pickleweed, burdock.
She'd be out in those woods or combing the beach for hours."

"I might pick the wrong kind of mushrooms or something,
and poison us."

She scoffed. "I hope you like scrambled." She handed him a plate of phlegmy eggs. "After you've eaten we'll go to the beach. I need kelp."

He followed her through to the back of her land onto a well-worn trail that climbed gently through low-lying juniper before it sloped down to the sea. She walked, panting, her fist white-knuckled over the head of a walking stick. Wisps of hair grew wet against her neck, and every now and then she stopped and put her hand against a tree and rested.

Curtis tried to imagine Elka as a child, creeping along this trail, gathering nettles or mushrooms or whatever it was she hunted for. But it was hard to picture. Memories of his mother amounted to very little: burying his face in the warmth of her lap; standing on the toilet lid in a steaming bathroom while she was in the shower, throwing toys over the top of the curtain that she threw back; crawling over her sleeping body and prying open her eyes with his fingers, saying, *Don't sleep*. And her thick reply: *I'm just resting my eyes.* The soft curve of her earlobe, the punched hole where the earring went.

What he remembered about her leaving was sitting in the grass in his grandma's backyard. Samantha had just cut the lawn and there were clumps of wet grass everywhere, and his knees were stained green. His dad came and stood next to him, and then knelt down and pulled Curtis into his lap, and crossed his big arms together over Curtis's legs.

"Mom's gone," his dad said. "And I don't know when we'll see her again."

"Where'd she go?"

He didn't remember there being an answer to that question,

or if he'd even asked it in the first place. He assumed he must have, as that would have been the natural thing to say, but mainly he only remembered being angry. Angry because there had been the promise of a sleep-out in the tent, but then there was something wrong with Erin and she wouldn't stop crying and everyone except him forgot about camping out.

The beach here was exposed and windy, crisscrossed with driftwood logs as smooth and rounded as old bones. Carpeted with blue and yellow and purple stones, it was littered with knots of dried kelp. Curtis picked up a rubbery tangle of the brown, tubular tentacles, each attached to a spongy head, disturbing a horde of sand flies living in its folds. They rose into his face, bounced against his eyes and lips. The kelp smelled like wet sand and rotting fish.

"Is this what we want?" he called to Bobbie, puffing the flies away from his mouth. She was making her way down the back of the beach toward a driftwood hut that had been constructed up against a shrubby bank. Suddenly the tired old woman from the trail was agile as a fox, almost leaping from log to log. She ignored him and disappeared behind the side of the hut. He followed her, clumsily, to where she stood next to a tubby, faded red kayak leaning against the log wall. A long crack that had been scabbed over with amber-colored epoxy resin ran the length of the scratched hull. She was smoking and tossed him a lighter and a small leather pouch of her cigarettes. He took one and lit it. "Is that the kelp we want?" he asked again, holding up a reeking strand.

Smoke blew back into her face and one eye squinted against it. "Only if you want to produce a mother lode of shit," she said. She pointed with the cigarette between her knuckles at a small island beyond the mouth of the bay, six or seven hundred meters out. It was no more than a swipe of land and looked as if it were moments from being blown for good from the face of the sea. "That's Stoney Island. Other side of it there's a small bay. In that bay there's a bull kelp bed so rich in gold it would make you weep. There's a knife in that bag. It's all you need."

Curtis looked out at the waves, not high, but galloping white-capped and misty up the beach. Together, they dragged the boat over the lattice of driftwood to the water. The kayak was heavy and he worried that she might twist an ankle, but the wind off the sea seemed to steady her.

"How do you do this when you're on your own?" he asked after they had finally cleared the driftwood and laid down the kayak just short of the wet tide line.

"I've got no one in this world, boy. I can do most things you can do with one hand tied behind my back. It's slow and it isn't always pretty, but I've scraped through this far without killing myself." She pulled a white fiberglass paddle out of the kayak's cockpit. "I gather you can swim? My life jacket blew out to sea years ago."

He took off his shoes and socks and rolled his jeans up to his calves, and walked into the aching cold water. Bobbie waded into the low-breaking waves to hold the boat for him while he attempted to get in, and was pushed back toward the beach as a bigger wave broke under the boat. He offered the crook of his arm to her and she took it, her dress heavy and dragging behind her, and held on until she'd regained her balance. Then she let go of him and held on to the boat with both hands, at its widest point behind the cockpit. She kept it pointed into the waves while Curtis wedged the tip of the paddle into the stones for leverage, and clumsily sat in the cockpit. He pressed his knees against the sides to center himself and gripped the paddle with both hands.

"Cut no more than a meter off each strand," she called. "Take more than that and you'll kill the plant. And harvest as much as you can fit into the boat."

The waves pummeled him sideways, whitecaps like obnoxious birds. He tried to paddle. Seawater sprayed coldly off the blades into his face, into his mouth. The principle seemed easy enough: left side in the water, then right, then left. But the two blades of the paddle were set on the shaft at different angles, and every time he paddled on the left side the blade sliced uselessly into the water, like stepping onto a step that wasn't there. He would lose his balance toward that side, arm submerged to the elbow. The boat drifted broadside to the waves, pushing him back onto the beach. He threw his leg over the side to stop rolling over but the boat capsized, coughed him out like meat stuck in the throat. The cold water took his breath and he ground the balls of his feet into sharp rocks trying to right himself. It was futile. The kayak bobbed away from him hull side up, a dead thing.

Bobbie splashed ankle deep up the beach, her laugh a deep brass horn. "I assumed you were made of greater stuff than this!" she boomed. "Goddamn mother of earth I wish I had a video recorder." She clasped her hands together at her chest. "You were flailing around like two retards in a pillow fight!"

She waded out and grabbed the kayak by the tip of its stern, and again pointed the boat at a right angle to the waves and then held it by its middle. "Come here and help me turn it over!" They flipped it, heavy with water now and sunk to the gunnels. She directed him to take hold of the stern with both hands and push the end under, and then, in one swift motion, lift it out of the water and flip it so it could drain. She didn't stop laughing throughout the whole procedure. "You need to twist the paddle, child. Twist it with your right hand just before you take the left stroke. And keep your goddamn knees together for balance. Press them up against the gunnels like that and you're finished. You can do it. All you need to do is point your nose into the waves, keep readjusting, anticipate where the next wave is coming from. You'll be fine."

Shivering, he got back in and gripped the paddle. He tried the twist and this time caught the water strongly on both sides. He paddled hard on the left side to turn the kayak into the waves, and when he got it right, the boat cut steadily through the water. When he got beyond the break and into the calmer swell, he turned to see how far he'd gone. The boat bobbed gently now, the water clear to several meters down. Back on the beach, Bobbie was making her way determinedly toward the driftwood shack, her scarf unraveling into a plume blowing off the top of her head.

The bay on the other side of the small island was protected by a soft arm of lichen-green rock. Curtis paddled into the glassy calm water, where the swell was no stronger than a deep breath. Creamy yellow ribbons of kelp swayed with the motion of the current, so densely that once he reached the bed, the plants twisted around his paddle and stopped the boat. He stowed the paddle and took up the knife, then grabbed a stalk of kelp by the throat and estimated a meter from its end. The boat jerked under him with the first cut and he almost lost his balance, but it didn't take long to get a feel for controlling the movements, and soon, his head empty, the work became easy, the boat steady.

Bobbie was a trip, like a highway or a river or something, and he could either merge or be lost. She didn't seem to care. There was no empty kindness or small talk or making up for lost time. There was only this new existence—him in this red kayak in the Pacific Ocean. And maybe he'd figured it out. Maybe if he kept readjusting, a little to the right, a little to the left, always a few steps ahead, the dead girl, bloated black as a plum, would go away.

He continued to cut and stuffed the lengths of kelp between his legs and in the hollow space behind his seat. It was smooth and rubbery, and plastered itself wetly to his legs and back. The sway of it under the surface of the water was inviting and also forbidden, like a sacred place from which you couldn't come back.

Behind Bobbie's house there was a little mushroom-shaped hut, like something out of a dream. Cedar-shingled roof and mud walls. She called it her cob house. Inside, shelves of small glass bottles—powders and oils. There was an old camping stove and canisters of fuel. Glass beakers, pipettes. Dried herbs dusted the floor. Curtis helped Bobbie hang the strands of kelp from clotheslines until the room was like a rubbery wet forest. When the work was done, she left him there and he took one of the bottles off the shelf and uncorked its rubber stopper. His nostrils shut to the sharpness of the inky black liquid inside. He tried another bottle, this one containing an odorless powder the color of ashes. Another bottle smelled like cat piss.

He felt the lightest pulse of breath on the back of his neck, heard the soft lick and hiss of something moving toward him. Slowly he put the bottle back on the shelf and turned around, and saw only the sway of the dangling, spiraling yellow strands.

The next day, Bobbie got Curtis to pick blueberries along the road in front of her house, gather nettles, and chop wood. On the third day, he found her at the sink again, wringing out the purple mass that she'd been cooking before, which she'd left to soak in a bucket. He stood at the back door until she noticed him.

"What?" she asked, not turning from the sink. "You hungry or something?"

"No, no. I'm just...Is there anything else you need help with? I know what you said before, but I don't think your land is a dump. Dan said something about pruning trees?"

"You can't prune trees in the middle of June." She put the thing she had been wringing in a large plastic bowl and came toward the door where he stood. "Scoot," she said, and moved past him. She smelled like farm, like goat.

He followed her to a splintered wooden picnic table, where she began to spread the purple stuff flat. He could now see that it was wool.

"You going to be under my feet like this all the time?" she said, pulling apart the wool and securing it to the table with straight pins.

He shrugged.

She stopped what she was doing and squinted at him, chewed her lower lip. "And what happens when the jobs run out, eh?" She pinched a fan of straight pins and tapped them against her thigh. "I don't know what it is you're stewing

about but there's something. I can read you, son. You're just
like your mother. I don't care what's bothering you. Most
likely you've been humiliated by some coquette." Her voice
caught and she coughed into her fist. "But you can't follow
me around like some kind of lost duckling. Go read a book
or something. Take a walk in the woods. Does wonders."

# 24

**The parking** lot in front of the Nielson office was bleak and empty at seven in the morning. Tom turned off his engine and waited. The logging company's office was one cinder-block building out of a series that occupied a concrete lot near the airport. Tom watched the entrance to the lot, willing each passing car to pull in. Eventually a red pickup drove in and parked a few spaces away. A woman in a brown suit got out and walked around to the other side of her truck and took a bag from the front seat. She headed toward the Nielson building but walked past it and unlocked the door to an outfit that dealt in the rental of heavy machinery. Three more people arrived and three more times he was disappointed. Finally a yellow Škoda pulled in and he recognized the driver to be the Nielson receptionist. He waited for her to go in before he approached the heavy glass door, which she'd locked again from the inside. He knocked and waited while she switched on various lights and opened the window blinds, turned on a computer at the front desk. She looked at him and walked out of his line of sight and he thought he might go crazy having to wait before she came to the door, unlocked it, and opened it partway.

"We're not really open yet," she said.

"I'm with the planting company," he said. "Kevin's expecting me."

"Well, he's not in yet."

"It's just that I'm leaving town today."

"But he's not in yet."

"What time does he usually get here?"

She looked over her shoulder at the clock on the wall. "Anytime now."

"Can I wait?"

"I guess."

He sat in a metal chair next to a plant that he couldn't determine to be real or fake until he pincered one of its dusty plastic leaves with his thumbnail. A framed poster on the wall showed a guy leaning out of a harvester, the machine's insect-like arm extending toward a stand of pines. Tom got up and helped himself to a paper cone of water from a cooler. The water was cold in his throat and tasted like the paper cone.

Someone he didn't recognize came in, and then someone else, and finally Kevin, one of the three company managers. He boomed a hello to the receptionist and paused when he saw Tom and smiled at him with his teeth. He gestured with a lift of his chin and Tom followed him down a blue-carpeted, white cinder-block corridor to his office.

Kevin hung his jacket on the back of the door and asked Tom to sit. "I need a coffee. You want one?"

"I'm all right."

Kevin gripped the doorframe, leaned into the corridor, and called for the girl to bring him a coffee. He then settled himself into his chair. "Everything okay with your son?"

"Nothing that can't be fixed."

"Who's looking after your camp right now?"

"Two of my guys. They're good."

"This Daryl Sweet has really hung you out to dry," Kevin said. He flipped through a stack of papers on his desk and pulled out a folder and opened it. "All the problems occurred on his blocks?"

"He's been fired."

Kevin laughed a low laugh and nodded. "We know. He came here. Talks pretty fancy, eh? He whined about discrimination and a bunch of other crap but I don't know why he would come to us. It's got nothing to do with us."

"I think I set him off. I'm sorry about that."

"And I understand there was an arrest in town a few weeks ago? A bottle thrown on a dance floor?"

"I took care of that."

The girl came in with a steaming mug and put it on the desk in front of Kevin.

"You don't want anything?" she asked Tom.

He shook his head.

Kevin rolled the mug between his palms and blew across the surface. "You should probably also know he's telling people that you've been knobbing the camp cook. I couldn't possibly care less what you people get up to out there. Hell, this is bush work, I get it. I been out there myself, but you can see how this looks from where I'm sitting."

"Thing is, Kevin, I'm not going to be around for a week or so. The two guys I've got out there know what they're doing. I was hoping we might be able to figure this out when I get back."

"You're not going back to camp now? With all that's going on? You're down a foreman."

"It's this thing with my kid."

Kevin took the first sip of his coffee. He shook his head. "I don't think there's anything else for us to figure out. We've been satisfied with your work, but I don't see how you can hold your end up just now. There's a lot of guys out there lining up for this contract. I'm thinking there's enough grounds here to terminate at the end of this season and we go our separate ways."

"But I told you. I've got it under control."

"Well, I told you. We don't think you do."

Tom went to look for Carolina at her house. She wasn't there, so he found his way again to the university library and through the warren of stacks and cubbyholes to the desk by the window, where he'd met her before. She wasn't there either. He asked someone where he might find the poetry teachers' office and was directed to another building, on the other side of the campus. Fine arts, he was told.

People lay in the grass with their books open and flapping beside them, and it didn't look as though they were doing much of anything at all. Smoking on benches under broad-leaved maples. A Frisbee arched toward him and he reached for it but missed. It bounced on the grass and rolled away.

Many wrong turns in a bright, clean-lined building brought him to the department he was looking for, where thick carpet swallowed the weight of his boots. Most of the office doors in the narrow corridors were closed. He found a woman with a mass of gray hair tied in a knot at her neck; she was pecking at a computer. Her back was to the door so he knocked lightly on the frame. She turned halfway toward him with a cocked eyebrow, her fingers still resting on the keys.

"Sorry. I'm just looking for Carolina Ferris?"

The woman's face showed no recognition. "Is she a student?"

"She teaches here."

She shrugged and smiled. "Haven't heard of her." She turned back to her computer.

Tom took a step into the office. "Maybe you could help me. I know she's a teacher here."

She tapped something on her keyboard and the screen went dark and she swiveled back to face him. "What does she teach?"

"Far as I know, it's poetry."

"She'll be over in the English department. In that cubist monstrosity on top of the hill." She jerked her thumb toward the window.

Nothing made sense in the building on top of the hill. There was no numerical order to the rooms, and corridors led off corridors where they shouldn't. Too many stairwells. Tom found the English department in a wing of the building that he was sure he'd passed before, and found a man who told him that Carolina wasn't there either.

So he waited in his truck outside her house. Bars of sunlight angled and lengthened along the road, stretching time. Whether it was help or comfort he wanted, he didn't know. Across the street, three men smoked on a bench in front of the Aboriginal Friendship Centre. Two of them gesticulated together in conversation but the third man sat alone. Small and weathered, with his head pitched forward as if he carried a great weight around his neck, the man caught Tom's eye and nodded gravely.

By the time the street had sunk into dusk, Carolina turned the corner on her bike. She rode right up to his window. Her helmet, as always, was crooked, and grocery bags hung by her knees, the handles twisted to rope. A sweater was tied loosely at her waist. She angled her face away from him and stared down the street.

"What are you doing here?" she asked, one foot on a pedal, one on the ground.

"What am I doing here?"

She put her other foot down and leaned the bike against her thigh. The tail of her sweater was dirty and torn.

"You get that caught in the spokes?" he said. He pointed at the sweater.

"What?"

"Your sweater."

She picked at the torn fabric and then left it.

"Will you get in the truck please?"

"What for?"

"If you've got something to say I'd prefer it if this door weren't between us."

"Then maybe you should get out."

He got out, and she leaned her bike against the front porch of the house and sat on the curb next to him. He crossed his arms over his knees and knocked his legs against hers and waited for her to speak.

She stared at the gutter on the other side of the street. "Your friend Sweet came to see me. You know why?"

Looking down the road, he swallowed dryly. The bench in front of the aboriginal center was empty. "I think I know why."

"Ya?"

"Carolina, I'm sorrier than I have words for. But there's something going on with Curtis."

"So he was telling the truth?"

Sweet's face stuck in his mind. "I'm sure it was the truth and then some," he said, "but the truth is bad enough."

"I know better, but part of me hoped he was lying. The vitriolic way he spoke about you, and about her. He was loving it." She rubbed her forehead under her helmet, then took it off and rested it on her knees.

He almost said to her that out in the bush, things were different. That the thing with Nix was nothing more than skin and pulse and happened in a world that wasn't part of this one. That he was an idiot. That none of it was important because none of it was. Not anymore. "I think Curtis might have done something stupid. Right now, I need to find him."

"Were you going to tell me about her?"

"What, Nix? No, I wasn't."

"What kind of an asshole name is that."

"It never came into my mind that it would do any good to tell you. I thought it would just go away. I guess that's stupid."

"You guess."

He tucked a loop of her hair behind her ear and she drew back.

"I need to find my son," he said.

"So go and find him, then."

"I want you to come with me. I don't want to do this alone."

She looked at him sadly. "I'm afraid you don't understand."

He watched her face, the soft down on her upper lip that almost wasn't there.

"My friends said I was a sucker, hanging around with you. But I liked how we were—that's the bit they could never get. I wasn't waiting for you to get down on one knee; I've got no intention of spending my life in this town, or halfway up a mountain shooting rabbits. I wasn't any good at being married anyway. But you've ruined this and I don't want to touch you anymore; I don't want your hands on me."

She got up and he watched her unlatch the side gate to her backyard and wheel her bike through it, and he watched her shut the gate without looking at him, and he stayed there until she was gone.

At home, he walked through each room, opening the windows to let the heavy air move freely, to lift the dust. He checked the boarded-up window in the basement, where Curt must have broken in, and hammered a few more nails into the boards. This was something he could fix later. In Curtis's room, he sat on the edge of the bed. Stared at the oblong square of yellow cast on the wall by the streetlight and thought about what needed to happen next. Tonight he would find Sean, and in the morning—no, before that: at dawn—he would drive to Whistler. Grill the housemates, the girl, Tonya, who'd had the abortion. Curtis wasn't like him: Curtis talked to people. Somebody would know where he was.

He looked around the room. Under the bed, a stack of snowboarding magazines and a dusty hockey stick. In the closet, three naked hangers and a scrap heap of shoes. Pajama bottoms and single socks in the drawers, broken CD cases, one ticket stub slotted in the mirror frame. Nothing on the walls, no boxes of letters or photo albums. There wasn't a lot of history here. Was this Tom's fault? Should he have taken more photographs, told more stories? Wasn't a boy's room supposed to be full of stories? The curtain rail had come down on one side and he stood on the bed to reconnect it to its binding. He retrieved the blanket from the living room floor and came back in and pulled the bedsheet tight up to the pillow, covered the bed with the blanket and squared it neatly with the sheet, folded them over together, and smoothed the whole arrangement with his palms.

Sean's apartment windows stood dark and listless. Tom knocked anyway, his nose inches from the door. He knelt down to the mail slot, opened it and called Sean's name, and waited there in silence, a draft from inside cool on his face.

He took Giscome Road out toward Tabor Lake and went on memory from there. When Curtis was young, Tom used to come out this way all the time to pick up Sean from his parents' house and take the boys riding. Sean was a good kid. He changed after the accident in his uncle's truck, after they took all the hardware out of him and he started walking again. It was as if he was never quite sure what he'd come into the room for. Some of the kids around the place got mean but Curtis stayed close, and Tom loved him for that.

Sean's parents' lane was hard to find in the dark, especially now, with all the new houses on Giscome, but Tom did find it. Their place was the same, a timber build that fit naturally into the side of the hill, mostly hidden by grandfather cedars.

Sean's father answered the door just as Tom remembered

that he'd forgotten the man's name. He was thinner than he had been before, and faded, more scalp. His face was cocked as though he was waiting for Tom to say something. He didn't know who Tom was.

Tom took his hand out of his pocket, offered it to him. "It's Tom Berry. Curtis's dad?"

The man slapped his forehead, squeezed his eyes shut, and then opened them wide. "Of course you are. I thought I knew your face, when I opened the door...I was expecting Sean. Come in."

"Oh," Tom said, and rubbed the back of his neck. "I'm actually just trying to find Curtis. I thought Sean might be here."

"He's supposed to be." He looked past Tom and down the road. "His dinner's ready, at least."

"Hey, you're eating. I'll come back."

"Don't be ridiculous. He'll be five minutes. You hungry?"

He led Tom into the living room. A room with thick carpets, warmly lit by standing lamps that were reflected in the expansive glass of the front wall. He told Tom to sit down on the couch. Tom sat, looked at his watch.

"He really will be here any minute," Sean's father said. "You want a beer?"

"A glass of water would be fine."

Sean's father disappeared behind a wall that was covered in photographs in mismatching frames. Somewhere a clock ticked and the house smelled of Sean's dinner. Tom had forgotten to take off his shoes.

Sean's father came back in and put a wooden coaster on the coffee table and put Tom's glass on it. A wedge of lemon was caught under the ice. He sat down opposite.

"So how long's it been?" he said. "A decade?"

"At least." Tom drank and rested the glass on his knee so it wouldn't drip on the carpet.

Sean's father looked at the clock on the wall and then to the floor and back at Tom. "Things going okay with Curtis?"

Tom drew a line in the condensation on his glass. "Seems he's been ditching work. I want to know where he's got to before I head back out to the bush."

"Ah. You're still working up there."

"For my sins."

"It's good work."

"It suits me, I guess."

The sound of an engine came up the road and stopped in front of the house. Sean's father smiled at him as though a promise had been kept.

Tom listened to father and son talking in the hallway and stood up. Sean came into the living room and they shook hands and Sean avoided looking Tom in the eye. His father came in a moment later carrying two bottles of beer by the necks, like a brace of geese. He told them to sit while he put dinner on the table in the kitchen. Sean sat in the chair his father had just occupied and took a long gulp from his bottle, and Tom perched on the edge of the couch.

"You going to tell me what you know?" he asked Sean.

"You know some police detective came to see me?"

"I do, but listen: I need to know where he is."

"He was so messed up."

"Do you have any idea what happened? He tell you anything?"

"I don't know nothing. When he stayed over, all he wanted to do"—Sean looked over his shoulder and looked back at

Tom, and spoke in a coarse whisper—"all he wanted to do was get baked."

"He didn't say anything?"

"He didn't say nothing. He just toked and watched TV and washed his fucken Suburban, like, four times. I've never seen him like that."

"Sean? I need to find him now. Don't cover for him."

"He was fucked, okay? If I knew where he was, I would tell you."

On the insistence of Sean's father, Tom shared their meal of sausages, beans, and bread at the long glass table in their kitchen. Sean and his father spoke of things immaterial to Tom and it seemed obvious to all three of them that the meal was best got through as quickly as possible.

Tom was pulling his keys out of his back pocket when he heard the sound of the phone ringing through the empty house. He fumbled to get the house key in the lock and then left the door wide-open.

"You all right there, Tom?" It was Brendon.

"Just got home."

"Listen, we've found Curtis's Suburban in Nanaimo. People are telling us it's been there about four, five days. Does Curtis know anyone in Nanaimo?"

"Not that I know of."

"Anywhere around there? Gabriola Island?"

"He could. I wouldn't know."

"Ladysmith? Qualicum? I'm just trying to ring some bells here."

"Curt has a lot of friends. He could be any of those places."

"Or none of them."

"That's true too."

"Would you agree now that your son is possibly trying to evade us?"

"You won't get me to agree to that, sir."

"But you can see how bad it looks."

"What I can see is that a decision has already been made about my kid and so whatever happens between now and the time he surfaces is going to look differently to me than it does to you."

There was a pause. Tom's ears felt hot.

"You'll get in touch if you hear anything," said Brendon, his voice flat.

"I will."

So Curtis had gone to Aguanish. It made sense, Tom figured, as if Curtis were running home to his mother, as if some covert quality belonging to the island had been imprinted on him when he was taken there as a baby. The police wouldn't need more than a day or two to figure it out for themselves. He had to go now.

Tom filled the tank on the way out of town and drove directly southward, the lit and unchanging road slipping like sand under his hood. Bugs illuminated ghostly white for an instant, and then were gone. He drove through the night without stopping until he got to Lytton, a few hours north of Vancouver. The town was all dark windows, dream light, and chittering birds calling up the morning. He parked his truck at the top of a weedy dead-end lane overlooking the Fraser River and took a piss in the tall, dew-wet grass, and stood yawning and stretching his arms, watching the dark water flow south, like molten metal. This was the water that started with a trickle and spilled from the western flanks of the Rockies, meandering northwest, by some fault of topography, to Prince George. There the Fraser turned south and converged with another great river, where its water was used by the mills, and then continued south through valley and gorge, used along the way for irrigation, for transport, for power.

When Tom turned back, there was a buck in the road, its big, wet eyes on him. New, fleshy antlers white with fuzz, ears pricked and twitching, one foreleg raised politely. It regarded him for a moment and then bounded silently a few meters along the embankment, disappearing over the lip.

He watched the spot where the deer had passed from view, the tall grass still swaying, and it occurred to him how inexcusable it was, the thing his son had done—it was a feeling of plunging in after a bit of time had passed. Unanswerable. Somewhere along the line, he had failed this boy. The bridge of his nose stung painfully and the sting radiated across his eyes. He smelled something like ammonia.

He drove into the morning rush of a city that locked him in. He made his way slowly through the east end of Vancouver, like chewing gristle. The streets were papered, signs peeling off lampposts and walls. Vans were stopped in the middle of the road; guys unloaded boxes of fruit and pallets of bread into the open doorways of stores, and couriers on slick road bikes threaded the traffic, their city.

Tom crawled through the center of town in a daze, falling into stitches of sleep at every red light. He inched across the Lions Gate Bridge, thinking that this wasn't the first time he'd gone to Aguanish chasing Curtis. He thought about what happened the night before Elka took him there, when Curt was still small enough to sleep in the crook of his arm. And he thought about the land in Smithers. The hunter's cabin that stood on its southern border. The hand tools he was going to use to rebuild it. The well still drew water and the original, warped glass still filled some of the windowpanes. He knew a couple of guys from the mill who would have been willing to help with the heavy lifting, but mostly he'd planned to use winches and pulleys. He was going to put in a stone fireplace and a woodstove, and that broad desk under the bedroom window if Carolina had wanted it. There would have been enough room there for Curtis and Erin to come and stay whenever they could find the time.

His breath caught and he gripped the steering wheel with both hands, watched these things slip away, like getting one shot on the bear before it took off. All he had was a weak trail of blood in a darkening forest.

# 25

**"I don't** normally go to parties," Bobbie said, bludgeoning mustard seeds with her pestle and mortar. It had been four days since Curtis arrived. "On the whole, merrymaking irritates me and the food at these shindigs is always too rich, rots my gut. But Dan has suggested we join the shrimp hunt tonight, and I thought it might amuse you."

Dan drove them to the north end of the island, where they parked next to a jumble of trucks and vans at the edge of a wooded cliff, then toed a steep, rocky track down to a small beach, the quiet elbow of a cove. Curtis supported Bobbie's weight over the rocks; Dan carried a cooler and a couple of long-shafted nets. On the beach, a bonfire sparked and blew black ash and warmly lit the faces that seemed to float bodiless around it in the darkness, faces that belonged somewhere else, a place where people were content and unafraid. A circle of bongo drums lay in the sand like some archaeological find. A few meters down the beach there was a tent and tables and chairs. Paper lanterns hung from the tent ropes and barefoot children chased one another in and out of the soft pink and yellow light, their mouths greasy with food. A man with long, weathered dreadlocks sat in the sand, playing guitar, a sleeping baby strapped to his back. Bobbie planted herself in a chair and someone brought her a drink and a plate of food.

"Come with me," Dan said, draping his arm around Curtis's shoulders.

Now, nearly midnight, he was knee deep in calm water, shining a flashlight into the murky spaces within a cluster of underwater rocks, trying to catch out the shrimp by the light reflecting off their eyes. At first, searching the water with the yellow beam, Curtis saw nothing. But then there they were: two tiny red orbs, like a spider bite. After an hour of silent work, Dan went back to the fire with his bucket full, while Curtis had landed only a small catch—ten or twelve glassy shrimp curled sadly in the bottom of his pail. But the task was hard to resist. The light penetrated the water in a marbly, shifting kind of way that reminded him of a lullaby. Something cloudy, half remembered. Motes of algae, caught in the light's beam, were suspended in the water. For a few minutes he would forget what he was doing, but then he'd spot the eyes, glowing pinpricks in the shadows under a rocky nub, and he'd strike with the net. But the difficulty was judging where, exactly, the shrimp was. There was a trick to the way the light refracted in the water, and most of the time he misjudged the distance and jabbed uselessly at the sand, making little explosions of it. The process had sounded so easy when Dan explained it to him, but nothing—the water, the light, the shrimp—was behaving as he'd expected.

When the cold ache in his feet started to climb up through his calves, he walked back toward the fire on the wet packed sand where the tide was going out. The impressions his feet made were marked out with the glowing-green sparkle of phosphorescence, and he ran in circles, making starbursts out of his tracks. A dark-haired girl stood ankle deep in the water doing some sort of dance, expertly swinging two ropes that were alight at the ends, the fire drawing concentric orange tracers onto the black night. He stopped to watch and fell into the rhythm of those ropes the same way he'd fallen into the shrimping, catching firelit glimpses of her strong shoulders, her calves, and when she stopped and put out her fire and spoke to him, he couldn't at first understand what she was saying. What he saw was a face gleaming with sweat that shone like the phosphorescence in the sand.

They took two seats together at the tent and drank sweet red wine from the bottle, and continued to drink well after the hour that Dan took Bobbie home. Her name was Michelle. She was hanging out on the island for the summer, picking fruit on a farm. Too bad he didn't come the week before, she said, because he'd missed the car burning festival. She pinched a tuft of her hair, put it under his nose, and told him to take a whiff of the burnt upholstery and rubber smell that still lingered there.

He walked her home along the main road and then down a gravel path through a stand of alders, their peeling white arms like signposts. They stumbled across loose planks that bridged a deep gash of running water and passed through an apple orchard on the southern border of the farm, the apples just emerging where the blossoms had dropped, small and hard as nuts. In the gray light of 5 a.m., the trees were also gray, and Curtis imagined they would come into color only when the apples grew. He plucked one and dropped it in his pocket.

They lay shoulder to shoulder in her twin bed and smoked

hash from a greasy glass pipe until his head felt heavy as a planet. He took in the room. A gauzy orange material hung in front of the window. A poster on the ceiling showed a circle of people holding hands in the forest. On the floor by the bed, a dirty plate. Her hands crawled over his stomach, and when he kissed her, his mouth was dry and also thickly coated with something gelatinous. She straddled him and danced her hands above her head, sculpting the air, swaying her hips while her rib cage spread open like a fan. How easily those delicate bones would shatter. Her nipples and the dark hair under her arms stood out blackly, and so did the wine stain that bruised her lips. She leaned in to kiss him again and there was the smell of burning rubber, and his vomit came up fast, first as a mouthful of spit, then as bile on the floor.

"Oh," she said, and went away, then came back with a glass of water.

Sweat dripped from the tip of his nose onto his knees and he felt white. After wiping what he could off the floor with his t-shirt, he limped back to Bobbie's in the hard light of morning and collapsed, shivering, in his tent.

# 26

**The wool,** Bobbie told Curtis later, when he climbed out of his tent, shaky and pale, was for a hat. She was knitting him a hat. Once the wool had dried in the sun, she collected it in a frizzy bundle. Now she took it to her spinning wheel, which stood in the corner of the living room, next to the fireplace. She pinched a twist of wool between her fingers and pumped the pedal, and began to feed it onto a spool.

"This is going to be a guilt hat," she announced. "To make up for all the grandmothering I've never done. Nothing but guilt, in the dyeing and the spinning, and the knit. That should cover a decade. I suppose I should do one for your sister too. Just have to wait for some personal crisis to drive her here. How old is she again?"

"Seventeen."

"Should be coming soon, then."

Playing with her, Curtis asked, "Why not just buy the wool?"

"Ha." She told him where he could find a saw. "Make a nice healthy shape out of that Rainier cherry," she said. "If it dies, Dan will never forgive me. His grandfather planted it back in the day when there were only six families living on this island. Also, your mother's placenta is buried underneath it."

"Are you serious?"

"What? About Dan's grandfather?"

Curtis laughed. "I thought you couldn't prune trees in summer."

"Get out of my hair, boy."

Curtis leaned against the stepladder and studied the tree. He had no idea what he was doing so he started hacking at the lowest branches first, the ones that stuck out from the main body. The dense wood was hard to cut, and after just a few strokes with the saw his hands and arms were feathered with pink juice. A bank of cloud covered the sun and he thought about the work he'd done for his dad two summers before, out by Terrace. His dad's company had been contracted to exterminate an aspen grove that was growing on land that had been slotted for a spruce farm. The grove must have spanned more than a hundred acres. The crew worked in pairs, Curtis with his dad, moving like ghosts through the slender, white-trunked aspens, the trees so close together in some places that it felt as if the two of them were barred in. Couldn't see beyond the thousands of trees, few thicker than a man's arm, the world speckled with the flutter of silver-dollar leaves. The tool that Curtis carried was like a wrench, but with a double-clawed blade at its head, so that when he drew it around the circumference of a trunk, it stripped off an inch-high band, revealing the clean, green-white flesh beneath. His dad explained the principle to him: that an aspen grove, considered in silviculture to be a weed, was a collection of suckers all growing from one far-reaching root.

"She's just one big mother," his dad had said. "Largest organism on earth, or one of them, at least. The root system can go for miles; it can survive for thousands of years. And if there's a fire, she just hangs tight underground and, when the earth is ready, sends up her shoots again. More trees than there were before the burn. Tough little bastard, this tree. If we just cut them down one by one, mother would send up ten times as many suckers. Stripping the bark like this, we choke off the food supply to the roots, while they're still busy sending water up to the tree. Eventually, the system will exhaust itself. It takes about a year, but they'll all go."

"So basically, we're killing the mother," said Curtis.

"Yup," Tom said. "Straight to the roots. Waste of time if you do it any other way."

That was the kind of thing his dad said, without sentiment— straight to the roots. But that was Tom Berry all over: practical, emotionless, maybe even a little ruthless. It didn't bother him at all that they were choking these trees to death, the roots maybe hundreds of years old. The thing Curtis remembered most about this work was how, after only a few hours, the white flesh under the stripped bark bruised red, like a bite in an apple. Like evidence, or an awareness of the slow choke that would end with weakness and collapse at the point where the wounds were first cut.

Tom set off for Bobbie's house. The walk would do him good; he could stretch his legs and think about what he was going to say to Curtis. Because he hadn't figured it out yet. The whole way down from Prince George, he mulled over just about everything except how he was going to do this. Maybe, for once, the right words would just happen and he would be understood.

The weather was scatty. Sun in the morning, then dumps of rain from low clouds, then sun again, steam rising from wet wood. The air was oppressive. Tom threw his bag over one shoulder and then the other, walking with his head down, kicking stones. For three or four undulations of road he considered telling Curtis some kind of false story, just to get him to leave. And then take him to the police station. No. Curtis would never trust him again. What Tom would do was talk sense into him. Curtis would have to believe that going back was the right thing to do. Because they had to walk off this island together, and he couldn't drag him. Couldn't carry him either.

Curtis hauled the cut branches and stacked them against the back of the house, and then raked into piles the leaves and cherries and sticks that had fallen, until the ground under the tree was clean of any debris. He stuffed the piles into a garbage bag and took that around to the back of the house too, then stood away from the tree and cocked his head to the side to try to make it seem more symmetrical. He went inside and got a wooden bowl from the kitchen and filled it with cherries from the branches that he'd cut.

It had rained heavily while he was working, but now the sun was out, sending a ladder of light across the wet grass. He sat on the front steps with the bowl resting on his knees and slowly ate, sucking the flesh until each pit was bone clean, and then spitting the pits into the grass.

What if he went back? Who would that help? When he was younger, he used to make up stories about his mother's leaving. Someone took her, and kept her for years until she turned up frozen in that snowbank. It was comic-book aliens who erased her memory, or the circus, the navy. Or some other kid who wanted her for himself. And for a while he thought that his dad probably sent her off because she'd loved him the wrong way, or too much. In the version Curtis held when he was young, his mother was the kind of person who told you that she loved you, every day. She held your hand, and kept the stuff you made at school. Curtis's dad had never kept things like report cards or photos or letters. At Sean's place, his mom used to stick his crappy artwork to the fridge with magnets shaped like food. Photos everywhere. The house Curtis grew up in was empty walls and a bare mantelpiece. A dusty set of the Scholastic Canadian encyclopedia from 1970-something was on the bookshelf in the living room, along with a stack of topo maps. The shelf in his dad's closet (Curtis had once gone looking for something—anything—interesting) held spare blankets, neatly folded.

But the spring he turned thirteen, while rummaging in the garage for his baseball mitt, he found a box. Inside, a collection of photos wrapped carefully in cloth, a few of his parents together, but mostly they were of her, in shadow and out of focus. At the bottom of the box was a summer shirt. The silky material was flowery and so thin that when he pressed it between his thumb and finger, it was as if it didn't exist at all. The buttons were like pearls. He stuck his nose to the cloth but it smelled only of the cardboard box. There was a barrette, a cheap metal clasp with a wooden fish glued to it. This too had been wrapped in a piece of cloth. And tucked down the side of the box: yellowing paper folded neatly into a rigid square, a note. Four sad words scrawled in blue ballpoint.

*You'll do it better.* Curtis imagined his dad trying to preserve these things gently with his boxy hands, always, always with lines of grease on the knuckles and around the clipped fingernails.

And if someone came along now and offered to tell Curtis everything—where she went and what she did and whether or not she thought of them at all before she died—he would refuse. Because in his experience, once someone you loved was inexplicably gone, after a while it felt as though the truth would be worse than the stories you told yourself.

Bobbie's gate looked exactly as Tom remembered it: in utter disrepair and half consumed by the crooked arms of a blackberry bush. He opened the gate and shimmied past the thorns and was relieved to see the old house undisturbed. No telling when the police might turn up. He didn't know how long they had.

He stood at the base of the porch steps and first called out Bobbie's name, then Curtis's. When no one answered, he climbed the steps and rapped his knuckles on the doorframe. He waited, and then pushed open the screen door and poked his head in the dark front room, calling hello. Inside, there was the feeling that someone had just left. A breeze came through the open kitchen window. On the dining table, white smoke rose and curled from a bowl of some smoldering dried herb. He went back out to the porch and sat on the top step. At his feet there was a bowl nearly empty but for a few sulky cherries floating in juice. He toed the bowl away from the edge of the step with his boot. The rumble of an engine approached the gate and he stood up, cocked an ear toward the road, and stood there, clenched, until the sound subsided and was gone.

"Dad?" Curtis was standing on the other side of the screen door, both palms pressed into the mesh. A shadow over his face. He pushed open the door but didn't step out. Tom turned, unsure of what to do with his hands. Standing here in front of him was a different kid. Hair greasy and falling over his eyes, his eyes rimmed and tired, his skin bloodless. Not even two weeks since he last saw him but the boy was skinnier; his chin and the hollows of his cheeks were roughened with wiry black growth.

"Look what you've done to yourself," Tom said.

Curtis stepped onto the porch and suddenly his arms were around Tom and here was this trembling boy. Curtis held on to him as if he were sinking and Tom put his hands on the boy's shoulders and pushed him back so he could see his son's face.

"Was it you? Did you hit that girl?"

Curtis looked down.

"Did you?"

"I tried to tell you at Sean's. You remember? You were fixing a tap." He moved away.

Tom reached out and Curtis moved farther into the house, letting the screen door slam shut. Tom followed him in and over to the couch, where he sat next to him. He wanted to touch his son but didn't, and through the cushion between them could feel his convulsive shuddering.

"It's okay here, you know," Curtis said. He fiddled his hands together in his lap, cracked his knuckles. "Bobbie said I could stay as long as I wanted."

"Where is she?"

"She's not like you said. She's knitting me a hat."

"Did you tell her?"

"Why would I do that?"

"Is that how you're playing it?" Tom put his hand on the back of Curtis's neck and held it firmly, feeling the tension there. "I can make this better."

"How the fuck you going to do that? You don't even know what this is." Curtis looked at him, the whites of his eyes stark. "She's inside my head."

Tom nodded. "Mine too."

They sat quietly. Curtis held his head in both hands, gripping his hair. Tom stared into the cold fireplace.

Eventually Curtis spoke. "How come you never told me I was here before? When I was a baby?" His voice shook.

"Curt."

In the darkening room, the flaking plaster on the wall opposite where they sat looked like a snow angel. Other than on the night Curtis was born, Tom hadn't had much to do with the baby, this alien, lamblike thing with a neck so delicate you could break it just by looking. He was completely afraid of the boy. But then, the night before Elka took off with the baby, Tom found Curtis alone in the bathtub, braying on his back, pumping his mottled fists in the cold water where she'd left him. Clouds of yellow baby shit floated around his head, which was turned to the side, his mouth partially submerged and spitting. Tom picked him up, and the back of Curtis's neck, just under the curve of his skull, was blotched a raging purple.

Elka was sitting on the bedroom floor in the dark, her back against the bed. Tom turned on the light and searched the dresser for a clean diaper, warm pajamas. He carried Curtis in the crook of his arm back into the bathroom and laid him on a towel. Curtis hollered with all of his red body. Tom emptied the tub and turned on the hot water and waited for it to steam, and cleaned the tub with bleach powder. Then he filled it with warm water and lowered the baby in, supporting Curtis's head and neck with his forearm, the way he'd seen Elka do. And then she appeared next to him, on her knees, gripping the edge of the tub as if she were trying not to fall.

"Sometimes I imagine what it would be like to let the stroller roll into traffic," she said. She was crying now, her upper lip wet. "Or...maybe just let him sink under the water."

"Elka?"

"Sometimes I think about it."

He held her in bed all that night, and in the morning put in for a few days off at the mill. After trying to get her to eat breakfast, he left her for twenty minutes to pick up his mother, and when they got back, Elka and Curtis were gone.

So he drove. Methodically up and down streets, to the river. He checked parks, restaurants, the movie theater. He sat up in the kitchen until four in the morning, drinking coffee, and woke at seven with his head on the table and an almighty crick in his neck. She called two days later, from an Aguanish pay phone. When he got to the island the following afternoon, his heart beating three meters outside his body, he held his baby tight and whispered fiercely into his ear, *you're mine.*

"It wasn't a nice story to tell," Tom said now, his hand still on Curtis's neck. "I never wanted you to know how bad she could get."

"You should have just left us here. It was your ticket."

Tom nodded slowly. "You really believe that's what I've always wanted."

Curtis shifted away from him, hugged the pillow tighter to his body.

"Maybe one day you'll see it differently." Tom turned sideways so he could face Curtis directly. A loose spring in the back of the couch jabbed at his knee. "But we need to figure out what we're going to do now."

"There's nothing to figure out. This is what I'm doing."

"How long you think you can keep this up? You've got to go to the police."

Curtis got up from the couch, shaking his head. "I thought you were here to help me."

"I am."

"You gotta fucken help me hide."

Tom stood, clenched, hot breath coming out of him like a bull. "You must have mistaken me for somebody else, thinking I'm going to help you hide. How could you leave her there? How could you do that? I've been going over this the whole way down here and I don't know when you became such a coward." They faced each other in the middle of the room. "I'm not going to let you crawl under some rock," he said, his feet hot in his boots.

"Thomas Berry!" Bobbie stood in the doorway wearing a green rain poncho and gripping a large, white-bellied salmon by its tail. "You're never far behind this boy, are you?"

"Bobbie."

She slapped the fish on the kitchen counter and struggled to get her poncho over her head, and then came and stood between them, drying her hands on her dress. "Fish is big enough for three, Tom, if you're staying until dinner. Just traded it with my neighbor for hard labor. Curtis, you're helping him reshingle his garage roof tomorrow."

"We won't be staying," Tom said.

"I'm not going anywhere," said Curtis. He stood by the

fireplace now, holding the mantel with one hand, holding his stomach with the other as if he'd been punched.

Bobbie looked at Tom and then at Curtis. "What in hell's going on?"

"Tell her," said Tom. "I'd like to hear you say it out loud."

"Tell me what?"

"What the fuck, Dad?" Curtis said. "You suddenly give a shit?"

"Tell me what?" said Bobbie, her eyes large.

"Curt. Tell her."

"Can you hear yourself? You? You want me to talk about my feelings while I'm at it? How about you listen to this? Only thing I can be sure of when it comes to you is that you've been trying to get away from me and Erin since we were born. Well, here you go: I release you. Now fuck off and let me figure this out alone." Curtis stood there, breathless, eyes lit.

"I don't know what's going on here, gentlemen," Bobbie said, "but you know, Tom, he's fine here, with me. How about this time you just let us be, eh?"

The sun had sunk below the trees now and the room was growing dark. Bobbie switched on a lamp in the corner and sat down at a spinning wheel. She threw the wheel into motion and began to pump the pedal, feeding dark wool onto a spool through pinched fingers.

"Just go," said Curtis. "I already told you, I like it here."

"He likes it here, Tom. You can't take him this time."

"I can't go without you."

"It wasn't my fault," Curtis whispered.

The creak of the pedal under Bobbie's prodding foot and the hum of the wheel spun the thick air in the room until Tom felt that his ears might implode.

"What wasn't his fault?" asked Bobbie.

Tom looked at her. More than ten years had passed since he had last seen her, when he came down after Elka died, and she still blamed him. As he blamed her. He looked back at Curtis, clinging to the mantel. Shivers moved up the boy's body, like wind on water. "He hit a girl with his truck," said Tom, his eyes steady on the boy's face. "And left her by the side of the road. The police tell me she lived through the night. If he'd stayed, got help, she wouldn't be dead."

The wheel stopped spinning and Bobbie turned on her stool to face them. "That's why you look so haggard, boy."

"You're lying," said Curtis, his voice small, curled up at the back of his throat. "They never said that on the news." He let go of the mantel and covered his face with his hands, and swayed. He leaned with his back against the wall and slid down it until he was sitting, pulling with him flakes of plaster.

"And I was beginning to think you were just generally feral." Bobbie jutted her chin at Tom, her voice accusatory. "Why on earth would you tell him something like that? If he'd stayed, got help... Why make it worse than it is already?" The wheel was back in motion, her leg moving rhythmically under her big dress.

"Bobbie, he needs to turn himself in. The cops'll be knocking anytime now."

"What good will it do to ruin his life over this? He's not a criminal."

Curtis shook his head.

"If you hand this child over to the police he'll be slammed in a concrete box, not much bigger than a coffin, festering and totally disconnected from the world. And he'll hate you. I'm sure you want him to redeem himself in some way, but I don't see why it couldn't be accomplished at home. What he needs is a good lancing, like a boil."

"I've been doing all kinds of work here, Dad. Bobbie needs me."

"I wouldn't go that far, son," she said, her hand raised. "But I've gotten used to having you around."

"So tell me what he could do," Tom said to Bobbie. He sat on the couch again, leaned forward with his palms on his knees.

"What do you mean?" The wheel wound down like a clock.

"You claim to have some sort of recipe for homemade redemption."

She rotated toward him on the stool and shrugged as if these things were obvious. "Sweatbox. Vision quest. Community service. A vow of silence?"

"What the fuck is a vision quest?" said Tom. "How's that going to make it up to the girl? And what about her parents?"

"You're talking nonsense. There's nothing that can be done for that girl. Her parents, they don't need anything from him."

"Curt, is there somewhere we can be alone?"

"I'm not going anywhere with you."

Curtis's face locked. Some kind of haunting hung off the bones of his sunken cheeks. In the low-lit room, Tom could see what would happen to him, what was already happening. Curtis's young body shrinking until there was nothing left and you could pass your hand right through him. If he kept running, he would always be alone, he would always feel cornered, and the thought of your kid, scared and alone—well, he couldn't live with that. The thing to do now was step back and give Curtis an open pathway to the door. Tom relaxed back into the couch and turned his gaze around the room.

"I think he's made his decision, Tom," Bobbie said, her tongue pushing at the corner of her mouth to block the smile. She moved behind him and into the kitchen.

"And I think I will have some of that fish," Tom said, "if you don't mind cooking it."

"Don't mind a bit. I was thinking of steaming it with lemon and thyme and salal berry. Elka used to put salal with everything."

"Sounds delicious."

"I thought it fitting."

Tom ate voraciously, mopping the juice from his plate with a hunk of bread. Curtis had gone out to his tent and Bobbie told a story about sending him out to Stoney Island to collect kelp.

"Do you remember what I told you about Stoney?" she asked Tom. She was bent over a bag of tobacco, tucking a cigarette paper into her fingers. "That's where I spread her ashes. You remember? Over the kelp bed."

"Does Curtis know that?"

"No. I wanted to see if he said anything."

"Said anything about what?"

"If he felt anything. If he felt her."

"He hardly knew her."

"She was his mother."

A light with a burnt orange shade hung low over the table, casting shadows. "You got any coffee?" Tom asked.

"How about some huckleberry wine? Made it myself."

"I'd prefer coffee."

She made him a pot of bitter coffee and set it on the table in front of him with a bowl of sugar.

Tom cleaned and dried the dishes and wiped the counters, and then went out to Curtis's tent. It was a cool night; low clouds quickly sailed just beyond the tips of the tallest trees, lit by a high three-quarter moon. Tom knelt in the damp grass by the tent flap. "Can we talk?" he asked.

When no answer came, Tom opened the flap to a dark interior without any warmth. He stood and looked around the yard, at a long blue shadow at the foot of a silver cherry tree, an overgrown bush hung with ripe, black raspberries.

Back in the house, Bobbie lay on her back on the couch with a book open on her chest, a pair of glasses perched on the end of her nose. Next to her, on the floor, a mug of what could have been huckleberry wine.

"He's gone," Tom said. He stood in the middle of the room. "Any particular place you think he might go?"

Bobbie hoisted herself upright and took off her glasses, carefully folded the wire arms, and slipped them into the pocket of her dress. She closed her book and put it on the floor while he waited, flexing his toes in his boots.

"Any ideas?" he asked.

She rubbed her eyes and squinted up at him, smiling. "He's your son."

"This isn't a fucking joke," Tom yelled, the bark of it a surprise to them both.

Bobbie, her eyes wide, put a finger to her lips. She stood and moved past him and into the dark kitchen and pressed her palms against the counter and looked out the window, her face pale with moon. "Good news is, he can't get far."

\*    \*    \*

Curtis seemed to float over the trail to the beach, the rocks and the roots lit by the moon's pearly light. The island was helping him get away. It was all coming together now: with his tent and most of his belongings cast off, he could move faster. It didn't matter that he had no place to go, because, when the time was right, the destination would present itself. He tripped on an exposed root and landed on his palms, and wiped the grit and blood on his thighs as he ran.

The driftwood on the beach glowed, pulsed like embers, and the hush of the ocean and the tin can smell of it came up to meet him. He stumbled toward the little lean-to hut, wrenching his ankle in the lattice of wedged wood and rock. The red kayak, with its scar running down the hull, was propped against the back of the hut as before. The paddle lay on the ground. He turned the kayak over and set it on the rocks, hull down, and stuck the paddle into the cockpit. He tried to lift it by the gunnel but the boat was too heavy, so he wrapped his fingers around the looped bow rope and began to pull, dragging the boat over rocks and wood, the scraping of its plastic bottom a dry, hollow sound. Several times he had to stop, drop the boat, and shake his fingers to push the blood back into the joints where the rope bit deeply.

The water was calm, and surged slowly and rhythmically onto the stones. He could just make out the black shoulder of the island where he had gone to cut the kelp. He took off his shoes and slid them under the deck behind the cockpit, and pushed the boat off the beach. He clumsily sat down in it, taking on a gush of cold water, and began to paddle. Wondered where he would end up if he followed the moon trail on the water, that silver, shifting road that lay always just out of reach. He was hemmed in here, and no matter where he pointed the bow he would hit either the mainland, or Vancouver Island, or some other small, rocky island in the strait. It was disorienting, paddling in the dark, with the bow bobbing unpredictably back and forth. As he got farther from the shore, the wind picked up, and the harder he looked at the kelp island, the less it appeared to be there. One moment it was clearly in front of him; the next, a cloud would pass over the moon and the island would be shadow. The water he'd taken on when he got into the boat sloshed at his feet and his backside. He watched the white blade of the paddle as it went through the stroke, like some whale diving down to feed.

He approached the same side of the island that he had been to before and leaned forward, looking for the arm of rock that sheltered the kelp bed. Could hear the suck of the sea coming off the barnacles and mussels stuck to the rocks. He dipped the paddle tenderly into the water, moving slowly until he could see the arm, and then pointed the boat toward it. He paddled a few more strokes and then the bow reared up and a low scrape reverberated under his body and he was stopped dead in the water. He dug the paddle in deep and pulled hard but the boat didn't move. Tried the other side, and rocked from left to right, grabbed hold of the gunnels and shot his weight forward and back. The boat didn't budge. He stuck the paddle between his legs and dug at the water with his hands. He rested his head on his knees, pressed his skull hard against the square bones of his knees, and closed his eyes and listened to the night, which in this place was composed of wind, and suck, and, in the water lapping against the side of his kayak, the dead laugh of a girl. Pain shot through the bridge of his nose and he cried.

The level of water in the boat was rising. At first he thought he'd imagined it, but no, the water had been at his heels and seat but now it was past his ankles. It climbed like something amphibious, alive and cold, up the hairs on his thighs. He pressed his palm against the hull between his legs, and his arm was submerged to several inches above the wrist. All he could do was watch. After a few minutes, the kayak began to list to the side, and water flowed over the gunnel freely, and when the bow dipped under the surface, Curtis allowed his body to slip out of the cockpit. Barking the cold out of his chest, he swam toward the arm of rock, but when he got to it, he saw how steep its edges were and that he wouldn't be able to hoist himself onto it without slicing his hands and feet on the barnacles. He would have to swim through the kelp bed to the beach.

Afraid to submerge his face, he swam a mix of dog paddle and front crawl with his head up, gasping. He reached the kelp bed, and at first it wasn't too bad—a nibble against his toes, a lick of the thigh. But as he got farther in, the kelp began to wrap itself around him; his hands were full of it. It got so thick that Curtis could barely move. A strand drifted around his neck and he felt the gentlest of pulls and stopped swimming. His fingers were numb and had curled into claws that he couldn't open; his skin was alive and tingling with the frigid water. For a moment, the kelp held his body afloat. A pulse ran through the strand around his neck and he felt it move and tighten like a snake, warm and fleshy and inevitable. He closed his eyes and lay back so that only his face was above the water, and a shudder passed through him. It

was as if all this time since the accident, he'd been strapped
into a car going too fast on a potholed road, and now the
seat belt was unclipped and his body was rising above the car,
above the road, and he could look down and hear the stress
and wrench of metal parts that no longer had anything to do
with him. He exhaled whatever air he had left into the sky
and sank under the surface of the water.

A ticking. A quiet rush in the ears. Minuscule sea life and
sea dust suspended in moon-bright water. Below him: no
light, no sound. A cold hand on his ankle. He screamed and
his mouth and throat filled with salt water and he thrashed
back up to the surface, coughing.

He lay on his back and kicked frantically toward the beach,
stopping every few kicks to check his direction. Eventually
the kelp bed thinned and then ended, and he flipped onto his
front and swam until his fingers plunged into sand and stones.
He pulled himself up onto the beach and lay on his stomach in the sand and began to shiver. The shivering turned into
spasms, and he stripped off his clothes, curled himself tightly
into a ball, and held on. When he was able, he wrung out his
clothes and hung them from a sturdy, wind-bent beach pine.
He climbed into the island's thick underbrush and collected
whatever loose, dead foliage he could find to make a nest. He
knew that he would wake up itching.

It was just past 10 p.m. when Tom and Bobbie stood on the
porch of Dan's place. The large picture window showed a
dark front room, but there was light coming from down a
back hallway. Tom knocked on the door and waited, looked
in the window again for movement but saw none. Could
smell coal smoke. Bobbie pounded on the door with her fist.

"Don't do that," said Tom.

"Chill out."

A skinny, bald man in a robe answered the door, his eyes shot with alarm.

"Curtis here by any chance?" Bobbie asked.

The man blinked at Bobbie, then looked at Tom, and back at Bobbie. "What?"

Tom held out his hand. "I'm Tom Berry, Curtis's father. Sorry to be putting you out like this, so late at night, but Curtis has taken off somewhere. We thought maybe he'd come here."

Dan held his robe tight to his body with one hand and shook Tom's with the other. "I haven't seen him since we went shrimping. Come in." He stood back from the door and Tom followed Bobbie in. As they walked through to the back, Tom passed his fingers lightly over a tall sculpture on a plinth in the middle of the room, its surface cool and smooth. In a small, well-lit kitchen, Dan motioned toward two chairs at the cloth-covered table, took a kettle from the stove, and filled it at the sink. He turned and leaned against the counter. "Maybe you want something stronger than tea?"

Tom held up his palm. "I'm all right."

"What're you offering?" asked Bobbie.

Dan opened a cupboard and pulled out a bottle of something amber. He filled a glass halfway and set it on the table in front of Bobbie. "You sure?" He angled the spout of the bottle at Tom.

Tom shook his head.

Dan dropped scoops of something that looked like mouse turds into two mugs and filled them with steaming water. "You working him too hard, Bobbie?" he said.

Bobbie rolled her eyes and took a drink. Her top lip was beaded with sweat and it occurred to Tom that she probably didn't venture from her house very often, and he appreciated the fact that she was here now.

"Kid's on the run," she said. "Nothing to do with me." She looked at Tom. "You going to tell him what for?"

"You don't need to tell me anything," Dan said, handing Tom a mug.

"I appreciate that."

Dan locked his fingers around his mug and held it against his chest and looked thoughtfully toward the floor. "Would he have gone for the ferry?"

"He left after the last sailing," said Bobbie.

Dan continued to look at the floor, and then he snapped his eyes at her. "You try that girl from the beach?"

"Eh?" she said, head back, squinting at him.

"The gal working over at Blue's place. One of the feathers and bones kids."

"Why in hell would he be with one of them?"

"Feathers and bones?" said Tom.

Dan smiled at him. "Kids come out here just for the summer. They squat out in the woods or get fruit-picking work on farms. Sometimes you see them with bones piercing their ears, feathers hanging from their hair."

"Hippies," Bobbie spat.

"Anyway, I heard from one or two wagging tongues that Curtis left the shrimping party with this girl," Dan said.

"You know where she lives?" asked Tom.

"Yep. Take my truck."

"Appears the boy isn't as traumatized as he's making out to be," Bobbie said, eyebrows raised, filling her glass again.

*    *    *

Blue's farm was a few kilometers up the road from Bobbie's house. Behind the single-story, stucco house, which was dark and bedded for the night, there were a few acres of orchard: cherry and peach and apple. Dan had told them about a cabin at the back of the property where Blue's pickers stayed. Tom and Bobbie walked through the trees, long bars of shadow and silver-blue bark, stepping in the dead, slippery mulch of dropped cherries and peaches, to find a dark cabin with the door unlocked and no one inside. Clothes lay on the floor next to an unmade bed, and a plate of something crusty balanced on the end of the bed, and there was the smell of thick-oil incense, but this feathers and bones girl was not home. And there was no feeling of Curtis about the place at all.

Bobbie lifted a bra hanging over the back of a chair by its strap and dangled it, inspected it as if it were a clue.

"Put that back," Tom whispered close to her face.

"Big tits," she declared, impressed. The bra rotated a half turn.

"We'll go back," he said, rubbing his chin. "Likely thing he'll do is go for the ferry in the morning."

"I think you're going about this all wrong," Bobbie said, tossing the bra to the floor.

"And your solutions make a whole lot of sense? A fucking sweatbox?"

She put her hand on his shoulder. "Repentance comes from within, Tom."

He could only look at her.

*    *    *

It wasn't really like waking—more like giving up on a very light and fitful sleep. Curtis rose to a pale, oppressive dome above him and mist in the trees. He was beyond cold, his fingers stone white, and when he brushed the feeble covering of leaves and sticks from his body and went for his clothes, he found them to be almost as wet as they had been when he hung them. Regardless, he pulled them on, jerking with discomfort. What a stupid, stupid idiot. How much of an asshole did you have to be to maroon yourself on an island? He couldn't see Aguanish from where he was, so he picked his way through the thick underbrush to the other side of the island, stooping as he went, in search of berries. He came to a thicket of blackberry and grabbed at the clusters of fruit, just beginning to turn purple. They tasted tart but Curtis ate anyway, thorns snagging his skin, and he continued to eat until he felt the berries' weight in his stomach.

When he eventually broke through the trees to the low, rocky drop of the other side of the island, he saw only mist— a dark and blurry impression of Aguanish through the mist. He would wait for it to clear, and when it did, he would swim back. As soon as the sun was up and his body was warmer. For now he sat on a rock, shivering, holding his knees to his chest. He had to readjust everything, hadn't been thinking straight the night before, and now he needed to rethink what he was going to do. It still made sense to keep to the islands but of course he was going to need another boat. He would steal one if he had to. He could go back to that campsite and wait for more kayakers to come.

A soft rumble began in his lower back and his stomach clenched. Some kind of darkness moved through his body, and he remembered that the only thing he'd eaten since the day before was cherries and blackberries. The thought of all that fruit brought spit up the back of his throat. Everything suddenly became very loose and he barely had enough time to pull down his pants.

When he finished, he lay on his side, thirsty, his thighs throbbing, and stayed very still, trying to see Aguanish through the white. He lay like that until the looseness in his bowels brought him up to his haunches again.

A small collection of people waited by the fencing at the top of the ferry pier in the morning. One old man with a bike and a dirty backpack, a woman in a toque with a wicker basket in the crook of her arm, a family of three, only the hint of a baby wrapped tightly against its father by a sling. It was a white and heavy morning that had settled wetly over everything. With Bobbie at home still in bed, Tom waited behind the wheel of Dan's truck, halfway up the hill from the pier. He drummed his fingers softly on the wheel. He heard the ferry's deep and off-key horn before he saw the boat, and then it appeared out of the mist at the wide mouth of the bay. Tom turned to look up the hill. He got out of the truck and kicked stones down the road and looked up and down it, even though something told him in a voice louder than hope that Curtis wasn't coming. He let his hands drop to his sides and allowed himself to be filled to the brim by emptiness. The boy couldn't be far but he might as well have been on the moon. It seemed to take a very long time for the ferry to make its way across the bay and maneuver into the pier, like a foot slipping into a shoe. Tom stood by the entrance to the gangway with the other passengers and waited there while they embarked, and he watched one last passenger, a girl, come running down the hill in a pair of cowboy boots. And he watched, as well, the ferry pull away from the pier and make a slow, laborious turn in the bay, and the white-wash trail of it as it motored toward the strait.

Back at the house, a note from Bobbie on the kitchen table. She'd gone down to the beach via the trail at the back of her property and wanted Tom to join her. And though he thought the smartest thing to do at this point was wait at the house until the next ferry sailing, he headed out the back door to find the trail. Maybe she'd known where Curt was all along, and was now ready to reveal him, like a prize. With Bobbie, you never knew.

He found her standing at the shore, hands on her hips, looking out toward a small island. When he approached her, she jutted her chin toward the island.

"At first I couldn't see past my own goddamn nose, but now look—you see there? On the rocks towards the right side? You see someone moving there?" she said, squinting. "Mist lifted and there he was."

Tom looked and saw nothing but a rock of an island covered in short trees.

"My kayak's gone. I know it's him," she said. "Look!" She pointed excitedly.

Tom looked again and found that Bobbie was right. Someone was moving among the rocks.

So they'd found him. There they were on the beach, watching. At first it was just Bobbie, but then his dad came and stood next to her. And then they left, picking their way back up the beach. Probably gone off to call the police. Curtis thought about getting in and swimming for it, but he was still so cold and there was no sign of the sun, and he felt weak as a baby.

A little later, the buzz of a motorboat woke him from a half sleep. He had been dreaming of drinking cold water straight from the tap. He opened his eyes to see that his dad was alone in an aluminum dinghy, strong-arming the tiller at the back, wind in his face. He coasted up to the rock where Curtis sat and cut the engine, moved to the front of the boat, and tossed up a line.

"Tie this to a tree or something," he said.

Getting up, Curtis felt light-headed and had to sit again. He retrieved the rope with his foot and dragged it until he could reach it with his hand, and wrapped it a few times around the nearest trunk.

"Now give me a hand," his dad said. He balanced on the seat at the front of the boat and offered his hand up to Curtis. He carried Bobbie's duffel bag over his shoulder.

Curtis took his dad's hand and pulled weakly. His dad looked at him angrily and yanked his own hand away, and scrambled up the rock without any help.

"Have you got any water in there?" Curtis asked, eyeing the bag. He looked even paler than before and was shivering.

His dad nodded. "And a blanket. Your grandmother isn't as hard a girl as she pretends to be. She packed some food too." He made Curtis take off his shirt, and wrapped the blanket tightly around him. Curtis drank greedily from the bottle of water he was offered, but refused the napkin full of crumbling date bread.

"Why are your clothes damp?" his dad asked.

"Fucken kayak sank."

"Shit. Where?"

"Other side of the island. I had to swim for it."

"You jackass," his dad said, laughing. He rubbed Curtis's

back roughly, trying to warm him. He took off his own boots and socks, and pulled the socks over Curtis's blue-veined feet. "What was your plan?"

"To get away from you."

His dad continued to rub Curtis's back, his arms. Curtis looked down through the clear green water where it pulsed against this small island, pulling at the locks of black weed that clung to the rocks.

"I thought your mom was going to hurt you, when she took off with you. The stuff that went through her head— it was pretty grim. The things she said scared me sometimes. That's why I couldn't let you guys stay here. It wasn't her fault, though, Curt. She was sick."

"So why didn't you do something about it?" He pushed his dad's hand away with a shrug.

"I did what I could." He picked at the moss on the rock.

"You could have put her in a hospital or something."

"I wasn't much older than you are now. I did my best."

"Made the most of a bad situation, eh?"

His dad waited a moment before he spoke. "You've got this idea about me."

"I think it's pretty accurate," Curtis said, cutting him off. His stomach tumbled again and he dropped his head between his legs and swayed.

"You all right?"

"Nauseous."

His dad put a hand on Curtis's knee and waited for him to look up before he spoke again. "What I was going to say is, you're right. I didn't want you, not even when I first held you, or even after that. But that day your mom took you away from me, the thoughts that were coming to me on the drive down here to get you? It woke me the fuck up. I knew if things got really bad, you could have ended up dead. She wouldn't have meant to do it, but it could have happened. Everything shifted for me then—my life, it belonged to you. I didn't want it anymore for myself. It was the most incredible feeling."

"Why are you telling me this now?"

"I want you to understand. I can't leave this island without you. Never could. What kind of life do you think it's going to be, running from the police? You'll be alone, all the time."

"Sounds like what you've always wanted for yourself."

"I know you think that. A lot of people think that."

"Isn't it true?"

"What's true is, I've never been any good at giving people what they need. I know that. I don't see a way out of it."

"You never acted like you cared," Curtis said, and put his head back between his knees.

Bobbie was furious about the loss of the kayak, and in spite of Tom's promises to replace it, she slammed the kitchen door and shut herself into the hut where she cooked up her potions. Curtis was in the bathroom suffering with some kind of stomach thing, so Tom went out to the front porch and sat on the top step. After some time, the screen door creaked open and he felt the porch boards move, and Curtis sat next to him, still wrapped in the blanket. He drank water from a mason jar.

"I can see what it's doing to you, Curt. The guilt."

"What?"

"Don't you feel guilty?"

"Of course I do."

Tom's sockless feet sweat and stuck to the insides of his boots. "If you turn around, right now, and tell them what you did, show them you're sorry, it'll all come out better. Better than this, at least."

"But I'll have to go to jail."

"You might."

"And I'll have a record."

"And you'll have a record? Curt, that girl is fucken dead."

Curtis retreated into his blanket, and when he looked at Tom, his eyes were wet. "It wasn't ever going to be any different than this. The first few days after it happened, I kept thinking about all these minor details. Like, what if I left the party a couple seconds later than I did? Or a couple seconds earlier? Or what if my bike pump was where it was meant to be? Even if my truck was parked at the other end of the road. But none of those things happened, and when I hit her, I was in the only place I was meant to be at that second, and so was she."

"Well that's a mighty fine way of looking at it. Pretty much absolves you of any responsibility at all."

"It doesn't mean I'm not sorry."

Tom pulled off his boots and tossed them onto the lawn, pressed his hot feet into the warped, rough boards of the steps. "You think this was fate, like the universe designed some kind of role for you to play? You're wrong. There's no script. Universe doesn't give a rat's ass what you do. But it hands you this one chance to be here and you do what you can with the time you've got. You better make it good. For yourself. For no one else."

They sat together, not talking, long enough to witness several breaks in the clouds, when color bloomed and short afternoon shadows stepped across the lawn for seconds before they all softened and dissolved again into the gray. Not daring to move, Tom watched the clouds flowing east past this small island to the mainland, where they'd collect in the updraft from the mountains. The rain here seemed constant, so abundant that the plants appeared to rise up to meet it and suck it greedily out of the sky, as if to say, *stay, stay*. He had to hand it to Curtis: this was the perfect place to dig in and hide from the world.

"I keep seeing her," Curtis said. "Sometimes she's alive; she's laughing at me. Or there's bugs all over her, and she's all cut and bruised and bloody. I'm pretty sure I spoke to her, at the party. We were in the kitchen. A couple of weeks ago she was nothing to me, you know? You speak to some girl at a party and then you forget about it. But now, she's everywhere."

"Were you drunk?"

"A bit. I was pretty high. It was that whole thing with Tonya. I wanted to drive somewhere and watch the sunrise."

"Any drugs in the truck now?"

"Don't know. Probably." Curtis looked out across the yard. "Tell me what to do."

"Come home."

# 27

**They left** the island on the first ferry in the morning, and checked into a motel in Nanaimo. Curtis got into the bath and Tom drove to a drugstore and bought scissors and a pack of disposable razors. Next he went to a strip mall and bought a dark-blue polo shirt, a pair of khaki pants, socks, and underwear. He stopped at a drive-through for two breakfasts of egg and sausage burgers, black coffees. Curtis sat in his towel in a straight-backed chair in front of the bureau mirror while Tom cut his hair. They didn't speak much.

Bobbie had been hopping mad when they left, partly because of the kayak, but mainly, it seemed, because who in the hell was going to do the shingling on the neighbor's shed? With his hand on his heart, Tom promised that as soon as he could, he would come back and honor her end of the bargain. He had, after all, eaten half the fish.

Curtis drank the coffee but left the food. As he sat there in his towel, the extent of his bad health was a hard thing to look at. His skin was pale, the freckles stark. The muscles in his back seemed to sag; the knobs of his spine poked angrily against the skin. Every now and again he began to shake, and

Tom would put his hands on Curtis's neck or shoulders until the shaking stopped.

Carolina would have something to say about all of this. She would be able to put into words what Tom couldn't. There was some kind of exchange happening here. Petals of Curtis's wet hair fell onto his shoulders and onto the floor, where they dried to fluff and would be left. Tom felt a lightness from being close to this boy, to his pale skin with the last drops of water slowly drying on his neck.

When Curtis was dressed in his new clothes, his hair clean and cut, his face shaved, Tom sat with him on the edge of the bed until the boy stood and went for the door.

They passed a baseball diamond, a liquor store and a pub, two boys on bikes in a scrubby, empty lot, and pulled into the parking lot of the RCMP office. A two-story, pale-blue and white clapboard building, it looked more like a travel agency or a dentist's office than a police station.

A small, clean room with a breeze coming through an open window that caught the edges of a weighted stack of paper. Blue carpet, the hum of fluorescent lighting, a row of metal chairs by the wall. Tom's arm protective around Curtis's shoulders.

The officer behind the desk, a woman with tight silver curls, wearing a white button-down shirt and a blue tie, smiled at them warmly. Curtis told her why they were there.

She knew who they were—everyone up the shore did, she said—and she advised Curtis to remain silent until he could be transferred to the investigating officer from Whistler, and that he ought to call an attorney. Evidently unsure of what to do, she first locked Curtis in a back room alone but then invited Tom to sit with him. Curtis fidgeted and bounced his knee and started to shake so Tom knocked on the door and asked for a blanket. The woman came in with two coffees and a rough wool blanket and told them that the officer would be with them in a few hours.

"Is that Brendon?" Tom asked.

"I wouldn't know his first name."

"What about that attorney? I don't know who to call."

"I'll get you a number," she said.

"I'd like it to be someone who's been referred by somebody I know."

"It doesn't matter too much for the interview," she said. "As long as you've got someone present." She glanced at Curtis and asked him if he needed anything else.

He shook his head.

Through the heavy door came the muffled sounds of an office waking up, phones and footsteps and doors opening and closing.

"I think we've made her day," Tom said.

"Who's Brendon?"

"He's the guy who's been looking for you. He came to see me."

Curtis licked his lips. "I'm so sorry, Dad."

"No, I'm sorry. I messed up. I should have thought of the lawyer."

"It's okay."

"It's not okay. We've got to keep our heads screwed on right."

Brendon arrived in the late afternoon, apologizing. He'd been in the city. The signs of haste were on him, blown hair and a trickle of sweat at his temple. He propped open the door with a small end table and sat in a chair opposite Curtis and introduced himself.

"You don't need to be scared," he began. "I'm going to read you your charter rights, and your only job then is to keep quiet. In fact, you try to say anything to me without an attorney present and I'm gonna plug my ears. You got it?"

When a lawyer eventually arrived from a local firm, she and Curtis went into a room with Brendon and another officer and closed the door. An hour later Brendon came out and filled three cups with water from a cooler, and went back in and closed the door. Tom went outside and sat on the steps. Dusky-blue sky, cloudless, the air still as a pause. A cicada buzzed in the cedars on the far side of the road. From the other side of the parking lot came the hollow crack of an aluminum bat hitting a leather ball. Cars passed and all the drivers seemed to glance at the man sitting alone on the police station steps.

He traced his fingers along a knife scar at the base of his palm and tried to remember other times in his life when his world had changed so entirely. Always had to do with these kids: when he first heard about them, when they were born. When, one morning, he went into the bathroom for a piss and found a note propped up against the mirror.

He never, never wished death on her. And the thought of her curled up in a snowbank, eyes half shut to the world— that still hurt. He supposed she was the love of his life, if you bought into that kind of thing: first, euphoric, tortured. But now, after a lifetime without her, he could only thank her for leaving, for the hurt of that abandonment was worlds less than what she would have caused if she'd stayed.

When the interview finished, Tom was invited back into the room with Curtis and the lawyer. Curtis had stopped shaking, but his eyes were sunk in, as if the story inside him was like air in a balloon and now that it was told, here was the wilted rubber left over.

"He did really well," said the lawyer, smiling at Curtis. Her hand was on his shoulder.

"What happens now?" Tom asked.

She took a deep breath and sat up straight in her chair. "In light of the time that's passed since the accident—we're going on three weeks now—and the amount of forensic evidence the police have collected from the scene and from the vehicle, along with Curtis's confession, they'll be processing him into the system and lodging him at the police station in Whistler, where the offense occurred. They'll keep him there while they file their charge to the Crown counsel. You can apply for bail, but I think, once he's charged, they'll release him home to you on his own recognizance."

"What exactly is he being charged with?"

"We don't know yet. The thing that's going to harm you the most, Curtis, is that you failed to offer assistance to the injured girl and left the scene and, on your own admission, went into hiding. That carries the heaviest penalty."

"I thought she was already dead," he said.

"Legally, I'm afraid, that doesn't matter. The point is, you left."

**28**

**In the** autumn of the following year, Erin started at the university in town and decided that she wanted a new dog. A big dog, one that would knock over lamps with its tail and shed hair all over the house. One that could take you out at the knees, leave muddy prints on your thighs, hot breath and warm tongue. Tom found out about a guy who bred German shepherds up near Hook Lake, so on the first Sunday in October he let his daughter drive him up there, both of them eating burgers out of paper bags in their laps. Early snow had fallen the day before, filling in the holes and divots and cracks in the landscape, like preparing a wall for fresh paint. Tom pumped the heat and Erin kept her window open a crack because, she complained, she couldn't breathe: she was choking on the smell of the diesel.

She was excited. Wouldn't say so, but he knew. She told him stuff about people she'd met at university, and pointed to the burned-out husk of a barn—look at that! She offered him the last of her fries. In the space between them, between the lines of everything they said, there was Curtis and the girl who was dead over a year now—this thing had become a part of them.

They missed the turn to the breeder's farm and had to double back, adding ten kilometers to the trip. Erin drove faster.

"Lighten up, girl. The puppies aren't going anywhere."

"What if someone else gets there first? And they pick the one that I would've picked? I'll always know I've got the wrong dog."

"Not true."

"But you don't know."

"Whatever dog you get will be your dog."

"Is this the road we want?" She braked and swung onto a dirt road that crossed a field of tall grass and goldenrod.

"And if you're right, and someone else does get there first and pick the dog you would have picked, one day soon you'll be glad they did."

"You're talking shit."

He grabbed her knee and squeezed it and she swatted his hand away. He watched her profile racing across the blue October sky and the yellow blur of goldenrod. His kids were the best part of him.

The kennel was comprised of a pair of low, long sheds at the back edge of a plowed field. When they got out of the truck, a gang of dogs, all different breeds, bounded across the yard toward them. A man in work boots with the laces untied came around from the back of the single-story brick house and shook hands first with Erin and then with Tom. He took them to a chain-link cage at the far end of the kennel, where a tumble of shepherd puppies yelped and sprang and took one another's ears in the grips of their soft muzzles.

"You said over the phone you wanted a bitch? That black-faced one in the corner—she's the only one of the litter. You want to have a look at her?"

"What's her nature like?"

"It's early to tell but her parents are beauties. I've had the mother six years—best dog I ever had. You be firm with this one right from the start and she'll be a good dog to you."

"Same's true for most dogs," said Tom. He looked at Erin, who was on her knees in front of the cage, pulling on the jaw of one of the dogs through the links.

On the drive home, Erin sat in the backseat next to her new dog, the animal whimpering in a slatted box. She caught Tom's eye in the rearview mirror and thanked him, then they drove without speaking.

After some time, she said, "This is my dog."

"Yup."

And a little while after that, she said, "She'll be grown-up by the time Curt gets out."

"She will."

The moment Curtis saw his dad standing on Bobbie's front porch, that familiar, strong neck with the neatly clipped red hair, those shoulders, he thought he'd been saved. His dad, with deeply calloused hands and the heart of a bear, had found him and everything was going to be all right. He would fix it, because that was what he did. But as soon as his dad announced his intentions, Curtis saw the road ahead clearly, saw himself as a stone caught in the tire of some heavy-load truck.

Prison cells were pretty much as he'd expected them to be. The rivets in the slats of the bunk above, creased photos stuck to the wall with powdery gobs of toothpaste, a pair of institutional brown work shoes neatly placed under a small desk.

He could have pretended for months, for years, even. Because Aguanish Island wasn't real. He was beginning to wonder if Bobbie was even real, or if he'd been living in that little cottage with a ghost. That island was a bubble in the ocean where people hung crystals and bones from their windows and meditated to drums and bartered cedar-weave baskets for clay pots of honey. Honey so raw, it was speckled with flakes of wing and segments of leg. They would have hidden him there; they would have forgiven.

Today was day one oh seven locked up. His cell mate told him not to count, and Curtis tried, but every morning the new day's number woke him like an alarm. It was impossible to forget.

His cell mate was all right. In his fifties, skin and bones, a long face and watery blue eyes rimmed by hanging pockets of skin. He'd been in prison for most of twenty-five years and told Curtis what he could trade for x number of smokes, how to scam extra bread at lunch, how to get a hand job on a visit.

"The thing you've got to do is," he said to Curtis one night while they watched TV on their small set, "you've got to forget your life outside. Forget you're not a con like the rest of us, because no one's going to treat you special. You think you don't belong here. But you're here, so you belong. You understand what I'm telling you? Any of these boys get wind that you think you're above them, they'll knock you flat. This place doesn't pick and choose. We're all the same."

His cell mate was tidy as a pin, hung his regulation coat from the knob of his top bunk and lined up his canteen on the windowsill and desk, so the cell looked like a commissary. One perfect row of bottles of hair gel, one row of deodorant. Boxes of juice, cocoa, instant noodles, pens, matchbooks. All ordered, inventoried in his head to the last sachet of sugar. Curtis's dad would've loved him. He told good stories, and when the lights went out and the cell was black (though on some nights silver with the light of the moon), he talked about warehouses he'd robbed, telemarketing scams, mail fraud. Curtis listened and tried to hold on to the words, but when sleep took him, it took him hard, as if he'd been pushed from behind. It took him down a tunnel that spit him out onto a mountain road lined with pines, and up ahead a curve, and if he could just keep running, he'd get to the other side of it, where memories died. And no matter his speed, she was there, keeping pace, inch for inch like the mirror shadow that fell between the glass and the silver surface painted behind it. Sometimes she was on the far side of the road, her faceless face trained on his. And then within a step she'd be inches away, locked in. The curve was always just ahead, and she was always there, making sure he didn't get any closer.

His dad visited every two weeks. Drove from Prince George every other Sunday night and visited on the Monday morning. That was just like him, to come every other week just because he said he would. Sometimes Erin and Samantha came, or one or two of his friends. He and his dad didn't always talk; they just drank coffee from the tuckshop. His dad would read the paper as if they were sitting in the kitchen at home. Mostly, Tom told him stuff about what he was doing, bidding for contracts for the next season, cleaning out the garage. He wasn't going to sell the company now; he couldn't anyway—not after the thing with Sweet. He'd let the place in

Smithers go. While Curtis was in jail, his dad said, he wasn't going anywhere.

And he worried too. That was new. About the color of Curtis's skin, or his weight, or how he was being treated by other people. Curtis told him that it wasn't like on TV, with guys getting done in the showers. They showered alone, and he spent most of his day in a classroom, and the evenings playing pool, or reading. In time, he would be moved to a corrections center closer to home where they worked at fish hatcheries and fruit farms. These were the things he told his dad, and his dad would look at him, and wait for him to say more. And what he couldn't tell Tom was this: that the hardest thing about being in prison wasn't the being there at all. It was what he'd left outside.

He was on the news again the day he was sentenced. They showed a clip of his handcuff walk from the courthouse to the transport van. And then an interview with the girl's parents, out on the street. The father, bearded and tall, stood a little behind the mother, who did most of the talking, her clear voice strong and defiant. He got a good look at her on the screen; he hadn't been able to during the time they'd shared in the courtroom. The family was satisfied, she said, that the judge had passed the maximum sentence. They appreciated Curtis Berry's admission of guilt, and that he had waived his right to appeal, but beyond that, she said, they didn't care what became of him. He was inconsequential. He broke something in their lives that would never be fixed.

Yep.

He would never talk to his dad about these things, the fact that the hard part was this revelation about who he'd become to the people he knew and also to people he'd never met.

That there was Curtis Berry who people hated so deeply they had wiped his existence from their minds. There was Curtis in sweats behind the metal door, being very careful not to take a step wrong. And he couldn't tell him, and this was the worst thing about being in jail, that there was also Curt, whose dad was serving his sentence with him, all for nothing. Because, after all this, not a single thing was better, and he was still running.

# 29

**Weeks before** opening day of the autumn hunt, Tom drove his quad bike into the bush to where the trails ended, then hiked farther into the backwoods in search of tracks. After he found them, and several days' worth of droppings, he returned to the place often until he spotted the deer, a herd of eleven. He watched the herd for a week, watched them nimbly sniff and pick their thin-legged way through the trees, and got to recognize the different does and the fawns, the bucks. The strong ones who still had years of mating ahead of them and the weaker ones that, if taken, wouldn't leave a gap in the growth of the herd. He took note of their routine. About an hour after dawn, they came from the northeast to forage in a meadow rich with witchgrass and pigweed. In the trees around the meadow, he built a hide out of underbrush and pine, and went back to it every couple of days to integrate his scent and stalk the herd. He chose his mark: an old buck with a good rump who'd seen plenty of winters.

On the first day of the season, he woke up in the dark. He dressed in thermals, ate eggs and bacon, and repacked his bag: water and sandwiches, raincoat and toque, a box of soft tips and his two field dressing knives. The buck looked to be about a 160-pounder, and Tom would need to butcher it on-site and leave the bones if he had any chance of hauling it back to his quad bike. He secured his rifle and bag to the back of his bike and, in the dark, retraced the route he'd been following over the previous weeks.

With his rifle ready by his side, he settled himself onto the dirt floor of the hide and closed his eyes and waited for dawn. What was Curtis doing right now? Tom knew that they served breakfast at 7 a.m., and that if you weren't up and dressed with your bed made and your shoes tied tight, they took away privileges. That's how it seemed to work there— every action counted, every ounce earned. He imagined his son asleep, fetal, in a cot bed, and he imagined the cell to be monotone, gray. The blanket thin. He imagined that with every night that passed, a little bit of that haunting he'd seen in Curtis's face on Aguanish was fading, like lake mist burning off in the sun, leaving behind a version of Curtis that was closer to the boy he knew. In a few days, across a long plastic table, he would tell Curtis about today, describe it with as much detail as he could. Riding ditches on the quad bike, the knife tips of the tallest pines catching the first of the yellow light, the chatter and crick of the bush. For now, he would do the living for both of them.

As the blue of dawn dissolved to a crisp white morning, Tom sensed the first crackles of hooves as the herd made its way toward the meadow. He rubbed feeling into his cold hands and clicked the safety off his rifle, waited motionless until he saw his buck. It came into the clearing side by side with a young doe, and they stood together, munching witch-grass. He shifted his knees and both deer startled, looking straight at the hide. The buck bounded out of sight while the doe continued to eat, stopping every few seconds to sniff the air. A few others ambled in the meadow, constantly on the move, alert. After a few minutes his buck returned and stood alone, stood the way only a deer could, calm as a windless lake but ready to blow. Tom raised his rifle and tucked the buttstock into the pocket of his shoulder, and silently rested the barrel in the cup of his left hand. With that same hand he pulled back on the rifle so it sat snugly against his shoulder, and he kept the pressure there. He drew the stock up to his eye and rested his cheekbone against the cool metal and watched the buck through the scope, as if he were squaring up a photograph, visualizing the placement of the shot: just above the front left leg, at a forty-five-degree angle. He pictured the round passing through the heart, stopping the flow of blood, and then passing through the lung and preventing the intake of oxygen. He would take the shot when the fog around the buck's snout showed that he was exhaling. A clean and instant death.

The buck faced him, thirty meters away, and Tom waited for him to turn away, just slightly, to get his angle. His finger stroked the trigger while the buck stood, gently shifting its weight from one front foot to the other. It dipped its head to the ground and took a step forward, a step back, raised its head again, and began to move into the right position. Tom stopped breathing.

Something crashed and echoed in the bush somewhere off to the left, and in a clap the herd scattered and was gone. Tom engaged the safety on his rifle and propped it against the wall of the hide. He would come back tomorrow; he could wait.

# Epilogue

**A girl** with one blue eye, one brown, walks toward home on an empty road that follows the lower folds of a wooded mountain. She is a little drunk, and a little high, and she finds it gratifying to crunch bits of glass and gravel beneath the rubber soles of her white high-top sneakers.

There was a full moon the night she was born, her mother often tells her. Her mother says: We were driving to the hospital and I didn't want to be in the car. You were coming so fast; I felt trapped. I looked up through the window and there was the moon, full as my own belly, and for a moment, I was completely detached. I was free. And I thought, good, one day I will be able to tell you that you were born on a full moon.

When she was six years old, she learned to ride a horse at the stables in Pemberton, learned to ride with the shadow of Mount Currie at her heels. She could take her feet out of the stirrups and rotate 360 degrees in the saddle; she could trot confidently with her small arms stretched high above her head, as if she were flying.

And when she was eleven—her father tells this story all the time; it's family legend—she knocked herself unconscious water-skiing on the lake. No life jacket, and she went under.

When he jumped in after her, he could just make out the bright-green stripes of her bathing suit, fading slowly to brown as the water took her deeper.

Tonight the moon is full but partially concealed by the heavy gray clouds that seem to sprout from the top of the mountain. Tightly packed pine trees make a tunnel of the road. White light sweeps across their branches, growing from weak to strong, and before the headlights are on her, before the truck connects with her body, crushing her pelvis, she is thinking only of the smallest detail, of the grit beneath her shoes. She is lifted off her feet and comes to rest in a ditch under the pines. And the wind blows a song through their stiff boughs as they stand witness in the dark, and they will keep this song a secret.

# ACKNOWLEDGMENTS

Thank you, James, for your endless encouragement, faith, and love, for all answers medicinal and mechanic, and for the weekends you let me go. And thank you, Eve, Ali, and Kieran, for leaving the study door closed when I asked, no matter how desperately you wanted to open it.

A boundless thank-you to Clare Alexander, for leaving legendary phone messages and loving stories with dogs, and to all the team at Aitken Alexander. To Mary-Anne Harrington at Tinder Press and Laura Tisdel at Little, Brown, thank you for your vision, your patience, and your trust. Mary-Anne, you had me at "hello," and Laura, kudos to you for working on this book on the eve of, literally, your first hour of motherhood. Thank you so much to Carina Guiterman, Nell (I shall call you Eagle Eyes) Beram, Karen Landry, Barb Jatkola, Imogen Taylor, Tom Noble, Elizabeth Masters, Kapo Ng, Patrick Insole, and all of you who make up Tinder and Little, Brown. You've all taught me that, in spite of the loneliness of writing, in the end a novel is a collaborative thing.

For sharing your wisdom and making me believe I was able, I cannot thank enough you inspiring writers who have given so much of your knowledge and precious time: Susan Elderkin, Francis Spufford, Peggy Riley, Joanna Quinn, and

Lorna Jackson. Thank you also to the tutors on the faculty of Goldsmiths MA in Creative & Life Writing.

For a big ol' desk by a window wet with Norfolk rain, a basketful of firewood, and homemade meals (even though you promised you wouldn't cook), thank you kindly, Emma Youngs. For all firearm and hunting-related clinchers, I am eternally grateful to the guys at Bar20Arms for their passionate, detailed, well-thought-out answers to my many, many questions. And to Brian Montague of the Vancouver Police Department, thank you for giving me what I needed to avoid sounding like a television show, and for not suspecting me of turning myself in for a hit-and-run. Any inaccuracies are mine alone.

To the early readers, Rose Vukovic and Zoe Bailie—you're wonderful. And finally, my love and gratitude to you precious people, for the plethora of reasons of which I can only hope you are aware: Meghan Lea, Alexandra Lamond, RV, Stephen Lindell, Colleen Hughes, Merrill Brescia, Sue and John Napier, Adele Byrne, Rosanne and Paul Marino, Jenny and Michelle Wesanko, and my dear brother, Joshua Leipciger.

# ABOUT THE AUTHOR

Sarah Leipciger was born in Peterborough, Ontario. She spent her teenage years in Toronto, later moving to Vancouver Island to study creative writing and English literature at the University of Victoria. Leipciger left Canada in 2001 for Korea and Southeast Asia, and currently lives with her husband and three children in London, where she teaches creative writing to men in prison.

# QUESTIONS AND TOPICS FOR DISCUSSION

1. What is the significance of the title *The Mountain Can Wait*?

2. Were you surprised by Tom's betrayal of Carolina? Did you consider it a betrayal?

3. Tom often does things because they are "what needed to be done." Did you always agree with his assessment of the situation? How was the behavior of various characters in the novel swayed by either obligation or personal freedom?

4. On page 285, when Tom and Curtis are discussing the car accident, Curtis says, "It wasn't ever going to be any different than this.... When I hit her, I was in the only place I was meant to be at that second, and so was she." To this, Tom responds, "Well that's a mighty fine way of looking at it. Pretty much absolves you of any responsibility at all." What do you make of both men's assessments? Do you really think Curtis believes that what happened was the result of fate?

5. What roles do nature and landscape play in *The Mountain Can Wait*? How do the different characters interact with the land, and how are they shaped by it?

6. Discuss the relationship that Tom, Curtis, and Elka had—or have—with their parents, and how that relationship influenced their behavior later in life.

7. When Curtis first tries to tell Tom about the car accident, Tom fails to hear what he is saying and instead keeps bringing up Tonya's abortion. Do you think Tom believed that this was what Curtis was trying to discuss? What does this sort of coping mechanism say about Tom's character?

8. How is Tom's relationship with his daughter, Erin, shaped by his memories of her mother? In what ways does Elka's legacy both bring the two closer and keep them apart?

9. Although Tom is clearly very connected to nature and the land, he is also a man of rules and order. How do these two facets of his personality come together? Are they ever at odds? What does it mean to you that Tom's job is, in some ways, to impose order on nature?

10. How do you picture Curtis's future? Do you think he will find redemption? Does he deserve it?